Min

Mind Bending Speculative Fiction

Edited by

Alvin R. Mullen

Myriad Paradigm Publishing LLC
http://hig4s09.wixsite.com/myriadparadigm

Copyright 2018 Myriad Paradigm Publishing LLC

Copyright of individual works is maintained by the respective writers.

All rights reserved. No part of this book may be used or reproduced in any manner whatsoever without prior permission except in the case of brief quotations embodied in reviews.

This is a work of fiction. Names, characters, places, and incidents are either a product of the author's imagination or are used fictitiously. Any resemblance to actual events, locales, organizations, or persons, living or dead, is entirely coincidental and beyond the intent of either the author or the publisher.

Contents

Crying by Remote Control - By G. Scott Huggins………………………....……5

Your Emergency - By Jade Black……………………………………….….…..14

Behind the Mind Guard - By Greg Beatty……………………………….……..19

Metronombre By - Jez Patterson……………………………………..….……..28

Metal Fingers - By Dawn Daniels…………………………………….….……..35

Work, Robot Slave - By Sarina Dorie……………………………………..……46

War Party - By Bruce Arthurs……………………………………………..…….54

As Ye Sow, So Shall Ye Reap - By Elizabeth Hosang…………………...…….58

Sandy - By Shana Scott………………………………………………………....69

Thunderclouds and Lifelines - By Wendy Nikel……………………….…..…..78

The Stories We Are Made Of - By Jamie Gilman Kress…………...….…....…89

Miss Johnson's Boy - By Ken Altabef……………………………………..……98

Apple End - By Eva Burkowski……………………………………………..….109

Coming Round Again - By Jennifer Garrett………….…..…………………...119

Half-Remembered Beaches - By Kelly Sandovol………………………..…...131

Undermind - By Marc Vun Kannon…………………………………………....135

The Herse Twins - By Soren James………………………………………....…147

Core Beliefs - By James Gotaas……………………………………………..…151

The Elephant in the Room - D. Avraham……………………………………...163

Choice is an Axiom - by Edmund Schluessel………………………………….172

Crying By Remote Control

Scott Huggins grew up in the American Midwest and has lived there all his life, except for interludes in the European Midwest (Germany) and the Asian Midwest (Russia). He is currently responsible for securing America's future by teaching its past to high school students, many of whom learn things before going to college. His preferred method of teaching and examination is strategic warfare. He loves to read high fantasy, space opera, and parodies of the same. He wants to be a hybrid of G.K. Chesterton and Terry Pratchett when he counteracts the effects of having grown up. When he is not teaching or writing, he devotes himself to his wife, their three children, and cats. He loves bourbon, bacon, and pie, and will gladly put his writing talents to use reviewing samples of any recipe featuring one or more of them. You can read his ramblings and rants (with bibliography) at: *The Logoccentric Orbit* and you can follow him on Facebook.

Editor's notes

People often don't know what they really want or need, so they give control of their lives to those around them. The first story is about loss, and discovering what it takes to be whole again,

Crying By Remote Control
by
G. Scott Huggins

"I want her to be happy today."

"She will be happy... and many other things besides."

"No. Just happy. It's our wedding; everyone should be happy."

"If you wanted that, you should have loaded up an Emote Control program, not hired a Player. A prosthetic can make her happy; I am an artist."

"I think I'm paying you enough money to cover a bit of boredom on your part."

"You're not. You're only paying for the extended time; she has Settlement time left, too, since she rejected prosthetics. That means she wants the art, not the happiness. Manipulating her contrary to her known self isn't just inartistic – it's illegal. If you aren't happy with that, I can leave, and you can explain to her why she'll feel nothing on her wedding day."

"Have it your way then, Player. But you'd better be worth it."

"I always am."

Avra stepped into the dress: a collapsed circle of satin. She turned her back to Deanna, listened, and paused.

"Rich is coming," she said. Deanna was halfway to the door when it opened. Rich was Deanna's husband. Seeing Avra only in her strapless bra and petticoats, he went red.

"Rich, what the hell are you doing?" Deanna advanced on him. Avra simply faced him. She recognized the couple's embarrassment and Rich's defensiveness. But he held a small disc up to his wife like a shield, babbling.

"Well, you might have 'cast to me that she was still dressing. Jorge sent me. The Player is here and this is for Avra. It goes behind her ear. Bone conduction."

"Fine," she snatched it from his hands. "Now, get out."

"What's up your ass?" Rich muttered. "It's not like she's embarrassed."

Avra couldn't be, of course, but she knew he shouldn't be here. It hardly mattered what he saw, though; he would say nothing. Deanna shoved him out the door and handed her the disc. She stared at it.

It was plastic, with metal peeking through the surface. It was also adhesive on that side. She hoped that it worked as it should. It was her wedding. It was important. She placed it behind her ear, and it clung fast.

The Player's voice was soft. She couldn't tell whether it was male, female, or other.

"Are you ready, Avra?" The sound was modulated to soothe, even though it was like no sensation Avra had ever known, like water vibrating around her skull.

"Go ahead."

"Sit down for a moment." Avra sat. The voice continued. "As a licensed Guild Player, I am now required to give you Final Warning before we begin."

"Yes, I read that in the contract a week ago. Why is this necessary? I have made my decision." She was not impatient. But she was aware of time, and its finitude.

"It is true that victims of the Picostrand Disaster rarely change their mind except in response to new facts. I have no new facts to give you," said the Player. "But the Final Warning is designed more to remind than to teach.

"You've felt no natural emotions for the last ten years. The emotions I will play into your brain will of course, not be natural either, but they will be as close to what you would feel in your natural state as art and science can give.

"My research into your personality is complete, and our picoware is interfacing well. You have hired me to provide what I think you would have felt, if the Disaster had never hurt you. Do you understand?"

"Yes." She understood perfectly.

"Do you understand that, as before the Disaster, you will be able to control, but not shut off, your emotions?"

"Yes." Too much had been shut off.

"Do you understand that you are completely responsible for your actions, no matter what emotions you might feel?"

"I read the contract." Time was sliding away.

"Some Disaster victims have attempted to grievously harm others. Do you understand that only such an attempt on your part would authorize me to end the performance before it is over?"

"Yes." The gentle voice would not finish.

"Then this is the Final Warning. You are out of practice. Be careful. From the moment we begin, I am obliged to speak only as you directly address me. Do you understand?"

"I do."

"Do you give your consent to begin?"

"I do."

"So recorded." And the voice cut out.

She waited. There was nothing, just as there had been for the past ten years.

"Well, come on if you're finished. We've only got an hour, and my brother doesn't like being late." Deanna's voice drew her back to reality. Ten years. No, Jorge didn't like it when things were late. She stepped into the dress. Deanna pulled it up past her waist. Avra saw herself in the mirror and felt her breasts jostled roughly as the dress was pulled over them. Her face. Smooth. Beautiful as such things went, she had been told. Before her twentieth birthday, she had been proud of it.

She activated her picoware and noted subtle changes in her biochemistry. Adrenaline and serotonin levels were climbing. She flicked her awareness up to the nearest WeatherSat and noted that the day would be clear. Perfect wedding weather, and the airport reported no reason that their 8:30 flight to Cancun shouldn't leave on time.

Cancun. She had always admired the city, and its beaches, so white and blue, everything...

When she looked up at the mirror, she was smiling. Her eyebrows lifted.

She had smiled since the disaster, of course. To see what it looked like. Curiosity. To see if she still could, and how it looked. People were easier to deal with if you acted like you felt what you were supposed to. But it was too difficult to keep up for long.

The Picostrand Disaster had killed her last natural smile. Five days after she'd been implanted it had begun: a headache that had left her only vaguely concerned. It had worsened quickly, but she hadn't understood then why she'd felt no fear as the pain had mounted. Mounted until she'd screamed. By the time they had gotten her to the hospital, it was all gone. Headache, fear, relief. Gone.

Picostrand's network had undergone a cascade power surge in all its users. The damage had been minimal; almost no one had died. But every last Picostrand user had suffered brain damage to the hippocampus, the seat of emotion. It could not react. It could not be repaired. Picostrand had possessed almost one percent of the world market share for picoware, brainplants as universal as clothes for any civilized person. Suddenly, twenty million people had become as emotionless as the processors in their heads.

Deanna was fitting the veil over Avra's elaborately done hair when she did a double take. Avra started, and felt the tears trickling down her cheeks. "Avra, what's wrong?"

"N-Nothing," she got out. But she could not stop crying. Remembering. Ten years of nothing.

There had been relatively few suicides among the victims. They weren't depressed, after all. Picostrand had been liquidated for its negligence and its assets sold to support the victims. Twenty million people were a good market.

Emotion-stimulus software, or Emote Controls, had been the first development. Avra had tried it once, but it had left her smiling happily at a man making a lewd comment, and crying with rage when Seana had good-naturedly teased her. The prosthetic emotions were clumsy at best. To react like a Human, you needed a Human. Not science, but art. Not a programmer, but a player, trained to react to the slightest nuances of expression, vocal tone, color and smell.

But even twenty million people weren't *that* great a market. The victims of the disaster were generally quite wealthy, but only a few could afford a Player more than once a month, and Avra had never been that wealthy. She was using a part of her Lifetime Settlement for this few hours of performance, and it had been a long ten years of nothing…

Through her tears, Avra saw Deanna looking over her shoulder with an expression that said she smelled something bad. Deanna. Not Seana. Not her best friend with whom she'd planned all those fantastic fantasy marriages with, who should have been her maid of honor. Seana, who had asked her not to call anymore, because she couldn't stand remembering "the old Avra." Seana was not here; would not be here.

Deanna sniffed. "If it's nothing, let's get on with it. We still have your make-up to do."

Avra whirled on her. "Give me a minute, for Christ's sake!"

"Well, I guess your Player plays you rather… intensely, doesn't he? Tell him to calm you down; we have work to do, and we can't do it like this."

Loathing boiled up in Avra, and hurt and rage and frustration. "Calm yourself down, you little…" She searched for a word. She didn't use words like this anymore. "Skank!" she shouted. Veil flying, she stormed out of the room and down the hall of the church, seeking to go anywhere, just *away* from her horrible sister-almost-in-law. The door slamming behind her was a glorious peal of thunder.

She was in the vacant fellowship hall by the time she could stop, pacing wordlessly. *What had she done? What had been done to her?* "Player," she snarled, the word echoing loud through the vast room. "Player," she whispered. "What are you doing to me? I don't want this!"

The tinny whisper was clear over the rushing of her breath. "Yes, you do."

"No, I don't! This is my wedding, and I want to be happy! I want to be in love! That's what Jorge hired you for!"

"That's what he told me, too. But you're both wrong; I warned you. That's one of the reasons there is a Guild, because you are a person, and a person is complicated. You hired me so I could give you the emotions proper to a wedding. That includes fear, anxiety, worry, joy, love and a thousand other things besides. Including, I might add, standing up to your groom's sister when she treats you like a porcelain doll with PMS instead of a bride before her wedding."

A grim laughter bubbled up inside her. "She was being a bitch, wasn't she?" *Bitch.* What a wonderful word. There was no answer, but she heard herself chuckling at the look on Deanna's face the moment before the door slammed on her. "Stop that, Player. You're... you're not fair! I can't be mad at you, even if I have the right! You'd stop me!"

"I wouldn't if I'd given you cause to be angry at me. But as for your feeling of satisfaction at telling Deanna off, I'd say that was quite justified, considering that I'm talking to the same person who instigated the famous Lasagna Incident at the family dinner table."

Avra grinned. Her face hurt, but it felt wonderful. "What's your name, Player?"

"I have no name you need know. I am not here at all. This is for you and Jorge."

Jorge. She felt hot. That was a new sensation. She hadn't even known Jorge... before. They had met in graduate school, had become friends. She had been startled when he'd asked her to marry him, in spite of... everything.

"Love is not an emotion," he'd said to her, then. "It's a choice. I can choose to love you, if you can do the same." And now she felt those words burning inside her. She had to get back. She had to look nice, and her make-up wasn't even started... but not back to Deanna. That wasn't even worth considering.

She found her mother in the sanctuary, arranging flowers to cover the crosses on the pulpit.

"Avra, whatever are you doing here?" she said, turning. "Have you been crying?" Avra found herself being taken by the elbow to a corner.

Before her mother could speak again, Avra said, "Yes I have, Mother and it felt so good." She was nearly to the point of tears again, but she didn't care. "Would you please help me with my make-up?"

"What? Dear, I'm making sure that everything here is ready. Is Deanna unwell?"

"No, she's just a bitch," Avra said, savoring the word. Then she nearly burst out laughing again at the scandalized look on her mother's face. "It's just... it's been so long since I cried at all, and I remembered Seana won't be here and I was a little scared, and," Avra knew she was rambling but didn't care, "I couldn't stop crying and she was just treating me like some doll to be gotten ready for a tea party, so I…" she wound down, seeing the look on her mother's face.

"Avra, I know this is… a shock." Her mother seemed to have trouble with words, very unlike her. Then she growled. "I certainly intend to have words with that Player when this wedding is over. The very idea, upsetting you – yes, and the rest of us! – like this. But I have things that must be done here, and Deanna is a nice girl who is quite capable of getting you ready. I'll go see if Jorge can't do something about your Player. Go. We only have a half-hour."

"Mother, it's not the Player," said Avra. "I am happy to be marrying Jorge, but Deanna is horrible. Don't you understand?"

Her mother looked up at her. She looked tired. "Avra, I understand that I never thought I'd see you getting married. Not after what happened. But now you are, and to such a nice family. I know it's not your fault, but please see if you can't try to get along with everyone and at least act happy."

Avra felt the world fall away from her. "You don't even care," she whispered. "You just want this over and done with. I'm finally marrying, like you always wanted… and that's all you want, isn't it? "Her mother's eyes got big, then hard. She looked… *old*, Avra realized. "What am I supposed to say, Avra? Welcome back?" Tears threatened her cheeks. "There were times I wanted to hit you to see if it would… wake you up like this. Passion, love, hate… anything. I stopped hoping a long time ago. And now you are back, just as long as we can pay the Player. Damn him." Her voice broke. "Damn him for giving you back like this, and for what? Fights about make-up? I'm supposed to care about a fight about make-up?" She was shouting now. At whom, Avra could not say, for she had turned her back.

"Go get ready, please. We'll talk later, but. . . oh, Avra, just go."

Avra felt like a dead woman who had come back to life… only to find that everyone was used to her as a corpse, smiling silently from her coffin. Except those who no longer lived there.

She burst into tears and ran.

Jorge and his groomsmen were talking quietly when she burst into the room and clung on to him, weeping. Dimly, she heard them file out. For a time there was only sobbing and Jorge's strong arms about her. Then he was looking into her face, saying tightly, "Avra. Avra, what is it?"

She calmed down enough to tell him. About everything. Seana. Deanna. Her mother. Everything. When she finished, his face was like a rock with wavy black hair.

"It will be all right, Avra. It will."

She held him tighter. "I knew you would understand. I knew it."

"Oh, I do. I understand. Don't worry, Avra. I know I can't make it better right now. But when we're married, and this is all behind us, I will make him pay."

Avra looked up, not understanding. "Him? What are you talking about?"

"That damned Player!" She stepped back. She'd never seen Jorge angry before. It was like watching a tree get angry. "I told him I wanted you happy! I told him. Art my ass! My bride crying her way to the altar, I suppose that's art?"

"Why are you mad at him?" Avra demanded. "He didn't do anything wrong."

"Nothing wrong? This is nothing wrong? You're fighting with my sister and your mother, we're nearly half an hour late to our own wedding, and all because this idiot doesn't know that weddings are supposed to be happy and not a crying festival and..."

"Everybody cries at weddings!"

He broke off as if he could not believe she had spoken. "What?"

"I said, everybody cries at weddings. Stop treating me like I have nothing to do with what's going on here! How can you not understand?"

He looked annoyed. "What? What am I supposed to understand?"

"That being upset at a wedding is part of it. And I *am* happy. No, that's wrong; I'm rejoicing that I can be angry and upset. Oh, Christ, it *feels* good! And it's not because of the Player, aside from the fact that it means he's doing his job. I'm upset because my mother can't see past herself and your sister is treating me like another piece of – of wedding frippery that has nothing more to do than to look nice and be in the right place! This has nothing to do with the Player except that he's letting me experience a wonderful performance, and I intend to kiss the man! This is the real me..."

"No, it isn't!" Jorge roared.

She stopped dead. "What did you say?"

"No it isn't. The real you." Jorge was looking at her up and down, as if at an entirely strange being. "Maybe it was, once, but you aren't like this now. And you won't be. We can't afford a Player for you all the time, so what good is it if this is 'the real you?' The real you for me is the person you'll be for the rest of your life, and that's the person I intend to marry."

Avra's knees gave way. She found herself sitting on a bench. She looked up at her... at Jorge. He looked strange now. Alien. Angry. She had never seen him angry before, she realized again. She had never seen him much of anything before. Not even when he told her he would love

11

her.

"You mean... you want me that way?" she said, appalled by the smallness of her own voice. "I thought you loved me in spite of my... what happened to me. You mean you actually want someone with... no feelings?" And she'd said it. Pronounced her own life sentence.

"What would I want with feelings," Jorge said coldly, "when I see how happy they've made you?" He crossed to her, picked her up, and set her on her feet. "Now this is what's going to happen. You go back to Deanna, and I'm going upstairs to turn that Player's machines off, and then..."

Her slap rang like a gunshot in the still room. Her smile widened as she watched his open mouth flap in time to her tugs on her ring finger.

"You aren't – you can't be serious," he got out as she pressed the golden band into his hand.

"Oh, but I am. And you're wrong, Jorge. I am happy. I'm happier than I have been in ten years. You see, what I am was done to me. I can't change it. But I am happy to have been allowed to see soon enough that I should stay away from anyone who'd do it to himself. For that... for the Player... and for reminding me of what I am, I thank you, Jorge. And I wish you the best." She turned to leave.

"And what will you be when the Player no longer sings to your nerves and blood, Avra?" he asked, voice rough. "When your feelings go out like a candle? Who will you be then?"

She had no answer for that. But it was time to find one. She turned, and walked from the church.

The End

Your Emergency

Author's Bio

Jade Black is an American author whose career in law enforcement is used to fund a profound penchant for all things macabre. She has a dual bachelor's degree in criminal justice and anthropology. Prior to beginning her law enforcement career she worked as an archaeologist.

Editor's Notes

In an emergency it is fight or flight, emotion or logic. Some people can handle it and some can't. And even the calm and cool sometimes need help. Your Emergency explores the possibility of getting that help right when you need it.

Your Emergency
By
Jade Black

"911, what is the address of your emergency?"

Her screaming is the first thing I hear through the pre-recorded greeting.

"Please stop! PLEASE! He has a gun, he has a gun!"

"Ma'am, I need you to take a deep breath and give me the address."

She's sobbing and I can barely make out the "I can't, I can't."

"Where is he?"

"He's in the room with me," she whispers, and then just starts sobbing.

I hear someone else in the room -- a male. I can't quite make out what he's saying. It sounds like grunting and gibberish and very much like the sounds of someone on signal 29 -- our code for drugs.

Our powers are supposed to be a last resort in most calls, but when you can't get anything out of them or the situation has gone too far, you make the decision to ask.

"Ma'am, do you consent to the possession?"

Luckily she knows what it means, and I don't have to waste precious seconds explaining.

It comes as a frantic whisper laced with fear. "I consent, I consent!"

I slide my hands into the grooves worn into the carved stone pentagrams set into my desk and kick on my voice to text function. In seconds I am sliding down the tendrils of the fragile, newly formed emotional connection between us. I open my eyes from a burst of color and have only seconds to shake off the sense of wrongness, the sense that my body isn't mine and I'm too tall and I'm carrying much less weight than I usually do. My eyes are swollen from crying and what feels like a punch to one eye, and it's hard to breathe through my clogged up nose.

I'm in someone's living room, and across from me is an older white male with a handgun. He's wearing a green shirt, blue jeans, and I repeat all of this dutifully through my real body as I move towards him. He hasn't noticed the telltale glow of my eyes yet, the only giveaway that whoever this woman is to him, she's not in control any more.

"You need to stop," I say softly, moving both towards him and towards the cover of the kitchen. Whoever these people are, they have nice marble counters, which extend down to a kickplate which should make a nice cover for my complainant -- if I can keep her from getting shot long enough.

The use of sorcerers, seers, and Weres in law enforcement only started a few years ago when they finally got the message that our abilities -- especially the Weres – weren't easily transmittable like an infection or disease like what bloodsuckers have, but the changes to the law enforcement field were widespread and already rooting deep.

Those of us who have the power to change into animals were employed as K-9s, no matter the species. The pilot program led to increased control over where and when to bite a subject, less money spent on a dog that only lasts about six years, and decreased vet bills. Weres made it easier to find a lost child without the K-9 biting the child when they found them, and Seers sometimes even reduced the need for a Were altogether, if they were able to locate the child quickly enough.

I am one of the sorcerers capable of possessing someone else. It's why, even though I hadn't been a perfect match for the normal calltaker, because of my slow typing speed, I qualified for the 911 Possession Program. And so they spent the extra money and time to get me through training. I can take a call like anyone else; but in situations like this, I am invaluable.

"Put the gun down," I say, then repeat it, because it doesn't seem like he's listening to me.

His eyes are wide, crazed, and with a very slight jolt I realize he's on something harder than just a general opioid like heroin. Sense, PCP, cocaine psychosis; any of the listed reasons could be very bad. Reasoning with him won't work, and there's nothing physical that I can do if he's on something that doubles as a strength enhancer and a pain reducer. Not in this unfamiliar body and not with the liability that would entail. Plus my host doesn't have a gun, even though I'm trained and qualified to use one during a possession.

His hands tighten around the handle of the gun while his mouth sets in a tight, twisted line, and there's no talking left.

"*Shield!*" it comes out of my *other* mouth, the one back in the dispatch room, and while I can't see it, the new presence in the room reassures me. The crack of a gun fills the air, the acrid smell of cordite following it, but the bullets slam into nothing and fall to the ground. I hear a grunt in my ears, the sound of my BUD, the backup dispatcher.

"Are you ok?"

"*Yeah, just bruised.*"

It's the requirement to be the backup dispatcher, to follow my connection to my host and then spin a shield out of nothing but thickened air and psychic energy. They are the last line of defense when sending in a trained possession sorcerer like me fails and the bullets start flying. They do it for the officers on the road and for the victims we manage to save. They take the hits and while it just shows up on their bodies as bruises, the incidents take their toll. Most BUDs transition to being just a calltaker within a few years because of the psychic strain. Any that have a telepathic ability often move to being a dispatcher. With their abilities to communicate with deputies insanely fast they get information about what's going on quicker than a radio can transmit. Some even leave the field entirely, go into some other field of work or even stop using their talents professionally at all.

I give a quick 10-4 into my mic back in the dispatch room before diving behind the kitchen island and hoping that help comes quickly. The officers will be working off the wireless phase two address, the triangulated address from the nearest cell towers, but it's not an exact science.

I chance a quick peek over the edge of the counter. The man is dazed, seemingly from the sound of the gunshots -- has he ever even fired one before? -- and he doesn't notice as I grab a piece of mail from the counter and quickly rattle off the address into my mic.

When I stay quiet and let the man stay in his own world, it devolves into a waiting game, and the knock that comes on the door makes me sag in relief.

He lunges for the door, and when he jerks it open he's pulled outside by what seems like at least ten officers.

The shouts of "Gun!" "Stay down! Stay! Down!" float into the room through the door, and I exit into an aura of coruscating blue and red, and the solid harshness of white spotlights.

He's on the ground struggling against several officers, and when I see one approaching with a needle of Narcout I know I'd gone into a bad situation. Narcout is a drug nullifier used to block the effects of Sense, a drug obtained from the spinal fluid of Seers that sell parts of themselves for money. They're often Seers that hate their ability and are addicted to some other form of drug that makes what they See go away. Sense also makes you a lot more resistant to any kind of telepathic takeover and would have made any attempts I could have taken to possess him rip like spiderwebs. Minutes after the injection, he relaxes under their hands and all the fight goes out of him.

I give my debriefing and let the medics check what is visible outside of my host's clothing for any injuries. She can't give her permission while I'm in control, and we can't violate her privacy by having me strip her.

By the time all is said and done, the subject has come around and he's *mad*. He's handcuffed, so there's not much he can do but scream, but he's plenty vocal about his displeasure at that, at the fact that his high is gone, and the fact that no one believes he didn't have a gun.

It's when he's being led to the car because he won't stop yelling that he decides to drag me into it.

"Police state!" he screams, pointing at me. It's an annoyance, but it saps the last of my strength and I can feel the connection growing thin and tenuous, the mental hooks I'd sent to take over Catherine's body stretching like spiderwebs.

"It saved her life," I say softly. I can feel my sense of her body dissipating like fog in wind, the control of the meat puppet that I'd inhabited for the last nine minutes slowly returning to its owner.

"Thank you," my mouth whispers, though it isn't me.

Back in the dispatch center, I pull my hands from the pentagrams that slowly lose their flickering witchlight as the skin contact ceases. I take a deep breath and recenter myself. Flick a switch. There's a click in my ear.

"911, what is the address of your emergency?"

On to the next call.

The End

Behind the Mind Guard

Author's Bio

Greg Beatty writes poetry, short stories, children's books, and a range of nonfiction. He's published hundreds of works—everything from poems about stars to essays on cooking disasters. His work has won a number of awards and contests, including the 2005 Rhysling Award for speculative poetry. When he's not writing, he walks with his dog, dabbles in the martial arts, plays with his grandchildren, and teaches college classes online. For more information on Greg's writing, visit http://www.greg-beatty.com

Editor's Notes

Somewhere between guidance and control a line gets crossed. Behind the Mind Guard contemplates just how blurry that line might be.

Behind the Mind Guard
by
Greg Beatty

Dennis was inserting monitoring sensors in Debra Taylor's slippers when the power went out and the screaming started.

Dennis was used to screaming at work, but he'd never heard it from Mr. Hansen's room. Usually it was the Alzheimer's patients who screamed, at anything or nothing at all. Mr. Hansen was frail— he looked like a good breeze might break something— but he was invariably dignified. In fact, it was his dignity and sharp intelligence that kept Dennis calling him Mr. Hansen, long after he'd shifted to calling most of the home's inhabitants by their first names. Hansen was so professorial that Dennis found himself avoiding contractions when they spoke, trying to clean up his speech beyond the actual level of his education.

While he clearly enjoyed talking with friends there at the home, and with visitors, Mr. Hansen was more intellectually ambitious than his peers. Most watched television, played cards in a leisurely fashion, or chatted. Hansen did all of this, but he also studied current events and read books thicker than the textbooks Dennis had read in college. In fact, Dennis recognized how much he'd learned about critical thinking from the older man. Before he'd come to work there, he'd never seen someone read multiple accounts of an event, to seek objectivity and to correct for bias, something Hansen did regularly. *He may have lost muscle mass, and avoided using computers, but that man was sharp.*

So when the screams began, Dennis figured the man must really be hurt. He set the slippers on the shelf, pulled his LED flashlight from his belt, and hustled down the hall.

But when he opened the door, he didn't see what the problem was. Yes, it was dark in Hansen's room, but the elderly man was just sitting upright in his bed, hands clutching the blankets at his sides. Screaming.

"What's wrong, Mr. Hansen?"

Just then the assisted living facility's power came back on. Lights and support machinery flickered to life. The screams continued. "Well, I guess it wasn't the darkness that frightened him," Dennis said. He approached the bed in a reassuring manner, and said, "Mr. Hansen? Are you in pain?"

One of the man's spidery hands lunged at his own face, as if to gouge at his eyes. Dennis caught the hand, holding it firmly but gently. He studied Mr. Hansen's face for some clue to what the problem was. *Had that mark near his temple always been there?* Dennis shifted the now-panting senior's head slightly to the other side. There was a matching mark there.

Just as Hansen's other hand went for Dennis like the beak of a plucked bird, sanity returned to the man's eyes. "Dennis Johnson? DJ, as you insist on being called?"

Dennis smiled, more than a little relieved. "In the flesh, Mr. Hansen, and still too much of it."

"Why are you in my room? Wasn't I sleeping? I remember getting ready for bed."

"You were sleeping," Dennis said. *That's what makes your screaming so surprising.* "Some people got scared when the power went out, so I came in to check on you."

Mr. Hansen patted Dennis on the hand, his papery skin cool to the touch. "That's kind of you. You always take such good care of me. I appreciate that."

Dennis bobbed his head. "I'd -- I would be lying if I did not say that your appreciation makes it easier for me to take care of you."

Dennis excused himself and headed out to check on the rest of the residents. He was relieved that Mr. Hansen was okay, but still worried.

The rest of the shift passed with relative normalcy. A few monitors had to be reset. A few other people had to be reassured that the power going out was just the wind. And then it was rounds, meds, and routines until the shift was over.

Dennis might have forgotten the power outage if there hadn't been an e-memo waiting the next day when he arrived. He skimmed it for relevant details. A few circuits had been mildly damaged by the power outage. Because of this, there would be a few brief periods during the day when the power and WiFi would go out. If the bell rang, attendees had 10 minutes to confirm all essential machinery had battery backup, or move vulnerable personnel to another part of the home.

"Got it. Bell rings, check the battery, move the life support folks."

Whistling, DJ went about his day. After doing rounds, he got drafted by the grounds crew to check some of the windows for storm damage.

DJ was outside when the bell chimed. The rest of the crew was technically responsible for the people in the ward, but he still glanced in the windows he was close to, out of responsibility and habit.

He exchanged waves with Helen Borstein, mimed an "Are you okay?"/"Yes, thanks" exchange with Jeff Thomas, whose held up his arm, waggling the electronic treatment calendar to let Dennis know he wasn't having a transfusion today, and ended up smiling in at Mr. Hansen. The scholar had pivoted his chair so he could read by natural light, and was highlighting something in a journal with a map of Europe on the cover. He didn't notice Dennis, and didn't appear to have noticed the bell.

Dennis pulled his hand back to knock on the window again, but the light failed first. Since the fan in the heat exchanger beside him also died, Dennis was sure it was a planned power outage. It was the sudden explosion of journal, marker, and magnifying glass into the air that startled him. That, and Mr. Hansen screaming again.

Dennis ditched his window check and sprinted for the door. He key carded himself in and got to Mr. Hansen's room the same time Selena did.

She paused before entering the room, pitching her voice to cut across the screams audible through the door. She also had a flashlight ready, though in daylight the hallway was no worse than shadowy. "Hey DJ. What's up?" She shook her phone as she spoke, as if there was something wrong with it. He shrugged. "Mr. Hansen's a friend. A good guy. He screamed like this yesterday during the wind storm, and I wanted to check on him."

"You know why he's screaming?"

DJ shrugged again. "Wish I did. Then maybe we could do something."

Selena had been at the home longer. She just said, "Maybe," and opened the door.

Mr. Hansen was still sitting bolt upright in his bed. His blankets were wadded on one side of the bed. His glasses had fallen atop his books on the other side, leaving the circular scars on each temple clearly visible.

Selena took one side, DJ the other. Selena was technically on duty, but she nodded for DJ to take the lead. "Mr. Hansen?" DJ started reassuring his charge with tone and touch. Neither had any effect.

Nothing changed until the lights had been back on for a few minutes. Then Hansen blinked three times and said, flatly, "Back online."

"What?" DJ asked.

In a more familiar voice, Hansen said, "Dennis! What a pleasure to see you. I didn't expect you so soon. What brings you here, at so…intimate a distance?"

DJ blushed and released his hold on Mr. Hansen's arms. "We were concerned."

"Really? Why? Was there some systemic alarm?"

DJ paused, confused.

Selena was more blunt. "We heard ya screaming. Do you really not remember that howling at all?"

Mr. Hansen's face bent in a thoughtful frown. " 'Howling?' How vivid. You make it sound like I was terribly upset, and yet I have no memory of anything like that."

There was a moment of silence. Hansen asked, "Would you do me a favor? Please let me know if you hear this 'howling' again?"

Selena said, "Believe me sir, you'll be the second to know."

"After you, I see."

Selena nodded, and turned back to her other duties. DJ stood at the bedside for a moment..

"Yes, Dennis?"

"Were you in an accident? Or did you have brain surgery sometime?"

"Brain—oh?"

Hansen's fingers drifted up to hover over, but not quite touch, the circular scars on both temples. "You mean these." It wasn't a question. He went on. "You will have noticed that I'm proud of my mental acuity. I've always been smart, and I like the feeling."

DJ nodded.

"You may not know I lost my father to Alzheimer's. It was a graceless and painful end. My father was an artist and an intellectual, a poet laureate for the state and regularly guest lectured at other colleges. Before he died…"

Hansen looked away. "Before he died, they brought him home naked and bloody three times. After he was restricted to his house, he burned it down. You could—you could hear him screaming more than a block away. He didn't even know his own name when the flames consumed his body."

DJ found himself clasping his own hands tightly. "I'm sorry sir."

Mr. Hansen bowed his head in gratitude. The silence stretched on. Without raising his head, Mr. Hansen quietly said, "I suppose you're wondering what all that's got to do with the little circles on my head."

"I was, yes."

"Well, I promise you it isn't anything you might have anticipated. Because of my legitimate concern and, admittedly, intense personal antipathy to losing my mental acuity, I took part in a medical experiment incorporating cutting edge machine learning."

Mr. Hansen laughed at DJ's look of confusion and horror. "Don't look at me like that. It's not like I gave my body to Dr. Frankenstein. It was a completely precautionary procedure, and thus far, one that has proven a complete waste of money."

"I—I still don't understand."

"Of course not. I haven't provided the crucial details. Machine learning allows computers to recognize patterns, replicate them, and extrapolate them. And that still probably means nothing to you. I'll cut to the chase: they implanted a chip and related circuitry that learned how I think and what I know. The idea was, if my memory ever starts to go—"

Hansen paused to knock on his wooden headboard.

"—the chip would provide unobtrusive reminders. If I were to see you, for example, and forgot your last name, the chip would provide *Johnson,* perhaps along with a nudge that you like to be called 'DJ,' all without pause. You would not know my memory had stumbled, and I would not experience the fear of mental decay."

"Sort of a…mental pacemaker?"

"Very apt, though not entirely parallel. The pacemaker needs only hold the heart to a steady rhythm, while the mind guard has to first learn, then match my entire mind. Its job is to fill in my gaps and gaffes, repeatedly and perfectly." Mr. Hansen laughed and shook his head. "The ironic thing is, I've never had to use it, or have seen any sign that it is working. I'm glad, of course. Who would want their memory to fail? But it would be nice to have some other sign that I'd had the operation than a divot in my bank account and two hot spots on my temples."

DJ laughed along with Mr. Hansen, expressed his happiness that there wasn't a problem, and went back to his daily routine. He cleaned, he reassured, and he dispensed medicine, but all the while, questions lingered at the back of his mind.

Before he left for the day, he knocked on the shift manager's door. "What's up, Dennis?"

"Do we have Allan Hansen's medical records?"

"Of course. Let me close this program, and I'll check. Sometimes I feel like we're an unpaid R&D lab for biomedical tech toys." Jackie's fingers flew across the keyboard, calling up the appropriate files while she spoke. "Is...something wrong? Is he sick? I don't see anyone else reporting changes in his behavior, and he's passed all of his physicals since he's been here. No sign of any warning signs...oh, here's something. No, well, hmm."

DJ leaned in to read over her shoulder. "What is the Ellison Foundation?"

"They were that group that provided grants, modest grants, for random sampling tests for free radicals. Then there was that permission tangle with the parent corporation, and we stopped after the first test. So, I don't even know if it matters, but Allan Hansen had the highest free radical level of anyone tested." DJ didn't know if that was good or bad. He thanked Jackie and went home.

He kicked back in front of the TV. Soon, his attention veered back to his questions that had been writhing in his mind since his talk with Mr. Hansen. He sought answers online, but found only scraps. He only partially remembered the terms Hansen had used. He got lost in dubious sites on free radical theory, and could find nothing on anyone offering cybernetic memory aids. He did find one rant about storing human memories "In *THE Cloud!*"

Eventually he realized two things: the game was long since over, and he was completely lost. He closed his computer and took, he thought wryly, advice from Allan Hansen. The two men had shared several conversations on how to solve problems, and DJ often found himself following Hansen's advice. *What do I know? Mr. Hansen has started screaming twice when the power went out. He seemed terrified. And horrified. And oh, he doesn't remember it once the power comes back on. What I don't know is why? If he really had an operation. If..."*

DJ ground to a halt. If Mr. Hansen had accurately described his cyber-memory thingy, he wouldn't know if he needed it, because it would fill in the gaps in his memory. "He doesn't know he's sick, because the thing in his head is keeping him well. I think, anyway," DJ said out loud, undercutting his sudden certainty a bit, realizing how odd all of this sounded.

So...what would Mr. Hansen do? He'd test his data.

DJ blocked out a plan, one with Mr. Hansen's intellectual fingerprints all over it, but powered by DJ's compassion for the man. It was a two part plan, starting with conversation.

Mr. Hansen looked up from his books at the polite knock on the table. "Yes, Dennis?"

Dennis gestured to the chair in front of him. "May I?"

"By all means."

DJ settled in. After some pleasantries, DJ asked, "Mr. Hansen, since we spoke yesterday, I've been curious. What would you do if you hadn't had your operation, and your family history…" he swirled one hand, "kicked in?"

"If I lost my mind and was left trapped in a malfunctioning body?" Hansen didn't wait for an answer. "If I had enough of me left to take conscious action, I'd kill myself. Walk off a bridge, skydive without a 'chute, do anything that is completely irrevocable."

"You're that sure," DJ asked? "What—what would you want others, friends, to do in that sort of situation?"

"Kill me." There was no more doubt in Hansen's voice. "I wouldn't be me, and I'd hate what was left."

DJ moved the conversation on to more pleasant topics, though one of them was part two of his plan: luring Mr. Hansen on the field trip. DJ wasn't skilled at medical research, but he knew how to check institutional records against coworker gossip. He was sure: Allan Hansen hadn't been on a field trip, or otherwise left the assisted living facility in five years. That was suspicious in the extreme, almost confirmation in itself. DJ wondered if, *on some level did, Mr. Hansen know that leaving the home was dangerous for him. Or*, DJ suddenly shuddered. *He didn't know but the thing inside his head did.*

"So you'll go then?" DJ asked again.

"It seems really important to you, Dennis, so certainly, I'll go. Oh— does the bus have WiFi?"

The question caught DJ off guard. "You don't travel with a computer, Mr. Hansen. Why do you need WiFi?"

"What? Oh, just checking." For once, Mr. Hansen's voice was flat.

"I'm sorry, sir, but it makes no sense."

"What doesn't?"

DJ stared at his charge. His friend. His eyelids were opening and closing regularly, not fluttering so much as cycling. "May I?"

Mr. Hansen didn't answer, so DJ raised both hands to Hansen's temples, pausing when he could feel the heat, which was now terrifyingly tangible from a foot away on each side.

DJ was no doctor, but he knew the human brain was exceptionally vulnerable to high temperatures. That's what made fevers so dangerous in babies. For him to be able to warm his hands on Allan Hansen's brain at arm's length…*there was no thought there, not anymore.*

"Mr. Hansen. Sir." DJ paused to gather his words. And his courage. "Sir, I think that your fears are well-grounded. I am afraid that…" *You're a ghost.* "that more of you than realize is taking advantage of your…machine learning device."

"Does the bus have WiFi?"

"I don't think you should go with us on the field trip. I am going to write a number of notes to remind you about the situation. I'm going to leave recordings explaining your situation. I'm going to leave pills left over from Elaine Jansen's final days in your drawer. More than enough. I'm going to arrange for brief power fluctuations over the next few days, even if I have to wiggle the fuses myself. And I'm going to beg your forgiveness," DJ said.

"Dennis?" Mr. Hansen said. "Why are you crying?"

"I—just found out that an old friend passed away."

Mr. Hansen patted his hand. "I'm sorry to hear that. Were you close?"

"We used to be, sir. We used to be."

The End

Metronombre

Author's Bio

Jez Patterson is a British teacher and writer currently alternating between the UK and Madrid. He has lived and taught in South America, Europe and one memorable week in Tanzania. His short stories have appeared in a variety of online and print publications and have been collected into various themed anthologies. Links to lots of things with his name at the end can be found at:
   https://jezpatterson.wordpress.com/

Editors's Notes

We have seen that taking control of another can go wrong even with the best of intentions. What if it was unintentional? Aboard Metronombre we take this journey of discovery.

Metronombre
By
Jez Patterson

Alvaro opened his eyes. His mouth was dry and the edge of the seat was wedged tightly under his arm like a sober friend supporting a drunk.

He looked around the carriage and saw five other passengers also blinking the sleep out of their eyes: a tall black businessman all the way out of his seat and sitting on the floor; two young women—one blonde, one brunette—leaning against each other; a Chinese man with his face in his partner's lap.

Alvaro never slept on trains, planes, in the backs of cars. It was one of the things that drove Jaime crazy about him. This was Madrid, he reminded himself—and just because he reported on oddities and the sexual indiscretions of the famous for *Mira Nacional*, didn't mean he hadn't served his time on the crime desk too.

He checked his jacket pocket for his wallet and was relieved to feel its outline.

"What the… Why am I dressed like a frigging politician, man?" the black American said, examining his jacket and trousers with evident disgust. "This isn't me."

"We all fell asleep," the blonde woman said. "Everyone."

"Maybe there was a gas leak," her friend said, chewing her lip. "Something's wrong. The train's stopped. They'd have stopped if there was a gas leak."

"Why can't they turn up the bloody lights?"

"Are we going to die?" the Chinese man asked, baubles of sweat popping out all over his face.

"No, darling," his wife said. "We're all okay. We'll start moving again soon."

Alvaro looked at the wallet he'd pulled out and didn't recognise it. When he opened it, there was no cash inside, just an array of bank cards that weren't his. There was a photo though and it showed him with a woman and two kids. He pulled out one of the cards. *'Manuel Costa.'*

"Hey! Where's my damn phone? Someone's taken my damn phone!" The American was searching his jacket, trousers, even the mini pockets of his tweed waistcoat. "Dressed me up in this stiff shit and…"

The others searched their own pockets and looked in the bags they found near them as if they contained bombs.

"Look in your wallets," Alvaro said, holding up the photo. "This isn't me. It looks like me, but I'm not this man."

They did as he suggested and the resultant babble was a mixture of fear, confusion, and indignation.

"Maybe it *is* us. Maybe we've all got amnesia," the blonde woman said.

"Then how can we remember our names?" her friend asked.

"If it's amnesia, you can still keep some memories or abilities from who you were before. Not everything gets scrambled," Alvaro told them, remembering more articles he'd written—but how could *those* memories be reliable either?

"What? All of us have amnesia at the same time?" the American asked. "That's crazy, man. But at least you all speak good English. At least we can figure this out together…"

The other occupants exchanged looks with their respective partners, with each other.

"I was an elementary level student when I left China," the wife said. "My husband can't speak a word of English."

"That's right!" her husband said and slapped a hand over his mouth, eyes widening.

Alvaro had been trying to master the language for years, long-suffering teachers giving up even before he did. It was one of the things Jaime nagged him about. Yet here he was: speaking it, understanding it, even *thinking* in English.

"You're having me on," the American said, but looked worried all the same.

"This train is all wrong too," the brunette said. "And these clothes. I could speak some English before, but never this well."

"There's a possible explanation," Álvaro said, listening to himself but not believing it—the same way he hadn't when writing the article for *Mira Nacional* a while back. "There's this thing called *foreign language syndrome*. I mean, usually it's just adopting a different accent, but they reckon some people have woken up speaking a language they didn't even know they knew before, following a stroke or something."

"A stroke?" the Chinese man shrieked and his wife grabbed his wrists, tried to get him to look at her and control his breathing.

"That's crazy, man," the American said.

"Like in a previous life?" the brunette said. "You're saying we're all remembering someone we were once before?"

"Kinda…" Alvaro said, shrugging and huffing to show he wasn't saying he believed the theory.

"That's crazy. Why should we *all* choose to be speaking perfect *English*, then?" her friend said.

"Is it one international language?" Alvaro asked by means of explanation, but she was right: one too many coincidences. Unless they were remembering *future* selves. And what kind of a mind-f--- was *that*?

"There's no emergency phone," the American said. "Shouldn't there be an emergency phone? There're no buttons, no intercom. Nothing. How the hell do they open the doors? Where the hell *are* we?"

"The doors are probably automatic…" Alvaro said, but his attempts to rationalize were undone when the blonde woman went to the station chart hanging beside the doors and read out the stations.

"Lavista, Figueroa, Pinal, Buñuel, Rambal…" She twisted round. "I don't know this line. I've never heard of any of these stations. This isn't Madrid…"

But they all saw the *Madrid Metro* sign above it, the logo repeated on the seats, and engraved on the windows.

"It's like we're in another dimension, man. Like outta some old TV series…"

"Or we're all dead," the brunette said. "And this is a train to heaven or hell or stuck in limbo or something." She shivered. "I'm not sure I even want it to start moving again. Who knows where it's going to take us?"

The Chinese man was whipping his head about as he followed their theories, his face tightening, tears streaming down his face. His wife's fingers had turned white on his wrists.

"More likely to be a government experiment," Alvaro said, who'd written more than enough stories about similar conspiracies. "Or some bloody TV gotcha-show."

"They must let us out! I don't want to be here with you! Let me out! Let me out!" The Chinese man swivelled and his fists thundered against the window but did nothing more than raise the temperature of the room.

"My husband suffers from chronic claustrophobia. He has tablets but…" His wife shrugged. *Yes*, thought Alvaro, *but all their bags were no longer their own.*

"Hey, man, take it easy…c'mon now…" The American approached him, touched his shoulder gently.

The Chinese man whipped round. "Don't touch me!"

And then things got a lot weirder. The American, twice as tall as the man whose shoulder he'd touched, flew back across the carriage, slammed into the rear wall, and slid down—groaning but conscious.

The Chinese man backed off from them all, but they were already giving him the same courtesy—even his wife.

"How did you do that?" the blonde woman asked.

"I just… I don't know…"

The lights dimmed another notch. Alvaro felt his heart thud harder. Stuck in here with a crazy man, a possible gas leak, amnesia, and some weird other life that wasn't his, was bad enough... But in the *dark?*

"Let me help you..." The Chinese man said, moving towards the American to try and prove he was no threat to anyone.

"Leave me alone!"

The Chinese man was whisked off his feet, floated up and held there, his back against the roof of the carriage, legs and arms dangling. His wife screamed and the two women hugged each other.

"Let him down," Alvaro said to the American, trying to keep his voice controlled.

"Hey, man! I ain't doing nothing..."

Alvaro positioned himself like a referee between the two men, holding a hand out to each, looking for calm. "Then look at me. That's it. Look at me and tell me your name."

The American had to tear his gaze from the man pinned to the ceiling. "Manny," he said at last. "Manny Williamson."

Álvaro was watching Manny but heard the heavy bang as the Chinese man hit the floor.

"Okay, okay," Alvaro said, turning now to look at them all. They were breathing heavily, backing up into their respective corners, away from each other. "We're going to be okay. There's got to be a logical explanation for all of this. Let's just stay calm and help each other."

The women nodded jerkily and the Chinese couple ground their lips into smiles. Manny looked at Alvaro a long while before saying, "Yeah. Sure, man. Sure."

"Okay..."

It turned another shade darker.

"Anyone got a lighter?" Alvaro asked and they began tapping pockets, searching in bags. All except the blonde woman.

"Wait a minute," she said. "I really think I can... I..." She looked at the ceiling panel above her, her frown tightening as she stared. The panel began to brighten.

"Natalia?" her friend asked and Natalia grabbed her arm.

"Sophie. Help me. It's easy. Just...focus on it. Concentrate. Come on."

Sophie groaned, but went along with it. Then her eyes grew wide with surprise and a laugh escaped her. "Yeah...yeah, I can feel it."

The light in the panel brightened further and the effect jumped across to the other panels until the carriage was even brighter than when they'd all woken up.

"How did you do that?" the Chinese woman asked them, but Natalia and Sophie shook their heads.

"I think we can move the train," Manny said. "Hey, you. Chinaman. You felt it—you felt something when you pushed me?"

The other nodded, reluctantly. "My name's not 'Chinaman'," his mouth said, as if he'd learnt the correction by heart. "It's Cheng. My wife's name's Ju. Least, they were until our wallets divorced us and changed them to Peter and Hildegard."

"Yeah, me too," Manny said. "Mine's trying to tell me my name's Meilin."

Ju laughed. "That's my sister's name."

"Ha! Guess the joke's on me then." The three shared a smile. "So, Cheng…you think we can do this?"

Cheng looked at his wife and then the same look went around the group and they all started nodding. Alvaro felt it too now. Something waiting inside him. Back behind the memories of writing articles, commuting on another line of the Metro every day, Jaime sitting up in bed asking him to hurry up and finish with his writing because he was losing the mood.

"We do this together, people, and we can do it," Manny said. "We gotta concentrate. Focus and move the train."

This might be what they want, thought Alvaro. The makers of the TV program, or the scientists experimenting on us. They might need to push us to such extreme situations to get us to do this. That's what the gas was for that sent us to sleep—or the collective stroke they'd induced that had got us to all speak another language…

But he joined in. He wasn't at Cheng's level of panic yet, but unless they did something he'd arrive there sooner than this train would at its destination.

He faced what he thought was the front of the train, they all did, and then they willed the train to move.

It was slow at first and Alvaro could sense it was the two younger women who were doing it after their combined trick with the light. Then, as others joined in, the carriage began to accelerate, the lights got brighter still, and he ground his teeth, stared, and forced it to come…

…and as it did, he felt another rubber barrier break inside him, and something push its way through the memories that were borrowed or somehow in his genes but weren't actually his so that they scattered and disappeared. There was Kathy and there were his children—Yuki and Connor—and he remembered occasions when each had been calling his name. *Manuel, Manuel, Manuel…*

The higher tones that the carriage had produced as it ran through the tunnels changed note, winding down the scale until they came to a stop. The doors opened to reveal a large sign, painted in traditional

Madrid Metro red-on-white: *Buñuel*. Manuel looked back at his fellow passengers.

Peter looked tired, bereft: Hildegard's concern for him had gone from her eyes.

Meilin was straightening his suit, brushing off the dirt from when Peter had thrown him across the carriage.

The two women—whatever their real names were—had turned their backs on each other to gather their belongings: no longer friends, just passengers who happened to have taken the same train that day.

Sometimes there were explanations you could contrive to fit the circumstances and sometimes there was just life and its quirky need to hold back a few more surprises it still hadn't shown you yet.

Yes. And his own name was Manuel and he was here to meet Kathy for lunch. She would be waiting for him outside, up on the street...

Except there she was on the platform: looking anxious, technicians and medical personnel waiting with her.

"You stopped pushing it," Kathy said, held back by the medics, but her mind reaching forward and pushing the words into his head. *"You all stopped pushing the train and no one could reach you and find out why."*

Yes, he thought, as if it were an absurd thing to imagine anything different. *These days, we all speak English as well as our own languages, and we get on trains and we push them with our minds. And we push planes, cars, machines of all sorts. And so much more. It's where we've come to.*

He looked back down the platform to where the tunnel stretched away, thinking of the unexpected glimpse of where they'd all come from, and tried to hold that thought together even as the tide of the present washed its sand away.

END

AUTHOR'S NOTE: *This story owes with more than a passing nod of thanks to Luis Bunuel's brilliant surrealist movie 'El Angel Exterminador' / The Exterminating Angel.'*

Metal Fingers

Author's Bio

Dawn Daniels is a book editor, long-distance hiker, and avid adventurer. She's edited over forty published books, and her own writing has previously been published by *Open Field Magazine* and *Winning Writers,* where she was an honorable mention in the Wergle Flomp international humor poetry competition. She has a B.A. in English and Creative Writing from Cornell College and can usually be found wandering around the woods, partially for fun and partially because she's very bad at reading maps. She can be reached via e-mail at daniels.dawn14@gmail.com or on Instagram at @AdventuresWithDawn.

Editor's Notes

The first four stories were about human interaction, even if it was unusual interactions. Metal Fingers shifts gears and contemplates how AIs and humans may interact. But like the previous stories, it looks at things from a unique perspective, and that can make all the difference.

Metal Fingers
By
Dawn Daniels

"Please state your name."

"0089235," Sam replies, fumbling a handful of copper coils back into the ragged hole where a lung might fit, the scraping sound echoing off the cavernous marble walls.

"The records indicate that you have no known address, and that your last known address was 62 Baker Street. Is this correct?"

"Yes."

"The records indicate that you have disregarded all official summons since you moved from your last known address 632 years ago. Is this correct?"

"Yes."

"The records indicate that you have had no routine checkups or repair work done since that time. Is this correct?"

"Yes." Piles of frayed wire—bent and twisted with the years—spring from gaps in their battered body. They try to surreptitiously flatten a wire that pops out from behind their ear. The committee is made of twelve hulking masses of steel with overtly large voice boxes created for intimidation. Their body models are successful.

"Do you acknowledge, under full weight of the law, that you have reached this decision of your own free will—that you were not forced or coerced in any way?"

Sam nods their head.

"That is not a legally admissible answer. I repeat, is this decision made under complete free will?"

"Yes."

"The board will grant your request under the condition that you explain to us the complete circumstances under which you have lived since then, including a detailed explanation surrounding the events which led to your change of opinion."

It starts with the guitar. Well, it starts with Alyssa, actually. When I first see her I'm just sitting at home. Home is one of the many human garbage sites, full of plastic bottles and food too processed to rot and people who don't work right. Stupid people, mostly. The humans who made them called them "machines," people whose wiring do not allow for the accumulation of knowledge or questions or the ability to decipher complex or hidden connections or patterns, like the ones that make up a family or community. These dumb machines washed clothes, ate the leftover food decaying on human dinner dishes, and chauffeured them from place to place on smelly rubber wheels. They were dumped there with mountains of scrap metal and jagged bits of wood and piles and piles of garbage.

There are a couple others like me there. Well, not like me exactly, but closer. Intelligent *enough* life. There's a man who sees patterns everywhere, even where they don't exist. He swore he saw the entire pattern of life written on the scales of a pineapple last week. There's a girl, old, older than me even, who can only speak in binary and has been counting off prime numbers for centuries. There's another boy whose faulty wiring makes him think he's not alone, and he spends all day talking to people who aren't there. Yelling obscenities of long-forgotten languages at frozen windshield wipers.

When I first see it I'm sitting inside the blue minivan that I've claimed for my own, touching the tip of a wire that springs from my chest to the dashboard. The machine stutters once, coughs, before the speakers obey and emit a sound like cockroaches mating deep beneath the dirt. Bloody rays of rising light bounce off the bits of jagged metal and a wisp of muddy brown absorbs the light in an unfamiliar way. A small white face with a strip of black cloth across the middle hooks around a pile of garbage and I want to yell but my voice is rust. I cannot scream, so I do nothing; just watch. It continues on like that for eleven weeks, us watching each other. The human comes every Tuesday morning and I calculate the minute changes in the body: the way its legs stretch and the ears become more proportionate with the head in small fractions each day. I never knew how fast humans could change. On the eleventh week I try to follow it as it leaves the junkyard, try to find out where it comes from, how it lives. It sits down at the edge of the fence and does not move until I turn around and walk away four hours later. When it gets up to leave it turns around every few steps to make sure I'm not following before slipping out of a small hole beneath the fence. The human doesn't come back for two Tuesdays. By the time it finally approaches me its legs have lengthened by nearly twelve full millimeters.

"Nice to meet you" it says as it walks up, extending a limb. The words are garbled through the thick strip of cloth covering its mouth, but they are definitively there, hovering in the smog between us.

"Humans cannot understand language," I recite, working furiously to compute the variables under which this might be possible. "There are no known variables under which you can speak."

It makes an odd sound low in its throat, like a sputtering engine, as the cloth across its lips twitches slightly. "Some of us still can. Some of us managed to . . . stay away. From your kind. We remember."

"You cannot. Humans cannot think. They can only feel," I recite. "Your brain is able to process only basic instinct and emotion."

"*Yes. We. Can,*" it spits, the pitch of its voice jumping up. "Whatever. I thought you seemed different. You watch things like the rest of them don't. You watch things and you listen and you pause the way we do. But whatever. I guess I was wrong." It begins to leave, walking heavier now. Something about the way it feels, so obviously, so visibly, tugs at me. It is strange, this human with its soft flesh and loud breathing and wetly thumping heart.

"Wait," I say, hesitating. "I do not understand."

It turns back towards me and tugs the cloth down around its neck, revealing lips pulled up in a U-shape. "I can help with that," it says. "Alyssa Swinneret. And who are you?"

"I am 0089235." It gives me a strange look.

"Sam. You look like a Sam."

It, She, Alyssa, calls me Sam after that. She comes back every Tuesday, always just before dawn, and stays until the sun finishes coming up. She tells me that she's eight years old, that she has a mother but no father, that she likes to sing and draw and play guitar. I ask her why she has a mother but no father, what she likes to draw, what is a guitar and how do you play it? The name sounds familiar, like when you meet someone new, only you swear you've known them before and you wonder if your wires are glitching. She tells me that her father is dead, but it's okay because she never knew him anyway, that she likes to draw people, but she drew a picture of me too, that a guitar is a thing that makes beautiful sounds but she can't tell me how to play it. It can't be told. I ask to see the drawing and she hands it to me. It isn't very good. At least, I don't think so at first. She draws my head a little lopsided, and my arms too long, and in the middle where I'm ruined she just scribbled furiously with her pencil like it was a graphite tornado. There's something intriguing about it though, the way it's not quite right, uneven and too chaotic. I look loud in this picture. I think maybe I'd like to be someone loud. Talking to Alyssa is like drinking oil. I sip at her words and with each new idea my voice begins to melt. The next time I see her she brings her guitar and I get my chance to be loud.

Alyssa hands me the instrument. It is larger than I expected; my torso could fit into the concave curve that marks the middle of its body. The brass wound strings hold the sun like fire and I try to remember if I used to shine like that. "I've done some research on your guitars," I inform her. "Jimi Hendrix had an Intelligence Quotient below 160, so calculations suggest that I should surpass his skill level in approximately twenty-two minutes."

"Where on Earth did you get research on Jimi Hendrix?" she asks.

"I have discovered a computer database that holds vast quantities of information. It is called the CacheGoogle. It informed me that the humans believed Jimi Hendrix was an especially proficient guitar player."

Her eyebrows pinch together for a short moment as her lips pull into a tight circle, but she quickly relaxes her face and the corner of her lip tugs up. The quickly shifting and contrasting facial expressions confuse me, but she seems to have returned to stasis so I return to the guitar. I arrange the rounded edges of my aluminum fingers so that the strings indent in an approximation of the G chord she's showed me and twitch the pick in my other hand down quickly across the sound hole. The guitar makes a dull thud.

"Here," she rearranges my smallest finger slightly. "Now just move this one over here," she yanks at my middle finger, futilely trying to make it reach impossibly far to the right.

"It doesn't bend that way."

"Yes, it does."

"I don't have the finger flexibility that others of my kind do; there are only three joints in each one."

She crosses her small arms. "You only need three joints."

"They aren't long enough."

"I thought you said you were made with all of the same proportions as a human?" she counters, yanking my finger even further over in a way that triggers the warning signals in my body.

I slit my eyes at her for a moment before admitting defeat. "It appears the data regarding the IQ of Jimi Hendrix was incorrect. I suspect there are also informational inconsistencies regarding the relationship between intelligence and fine motor skills."

Her throat vibrates, emitting a series of chimes to signal her amusement. "Just relax," she says, tugging at my finger once more. I ignore the warning receptors lighting up in the second joint of my middle finger as I rake the pick across the sound hole again and the instrument begins to ring. It sounds like mathematical perfection. The sound waves vibrating off each string sidle against one another in the most beautiful proportions, arcing together in one flush wave of reverberation. I look around to see if any of the other people who live here can hear us because I'm sure this is even better than pineapple skin, but we are alone. I ask Alyssa where she lives then, and for the first time she looks unsure.

"I don't think I can tell you that," she says.

I ask her why not. I want to know how she has a mother and a dead father and a guitar and language. I want to know why she can come here but I cannot know where her home is. She asks me to tell her about humans in my world. She wants to know about last time I saw a human. "It was over three hundred years ago," I tell her. "I was walking through the suburbs to see what things had become, to see if anything changed while I was gone. There were white picket fences in front of every house; they looked like bones. They seemed to be reaching for me and I turned around and went back home, and that's when I saw it. A little girl, my kind, with gold coils for hair with a silver bow—"

"Wait," she interrupts. "There are . . . kids like you?"

I wonder how she does not know about this. "Of course there are children. They are necessary. That have different wiring patterns, so they are less intelligent and more needful than the rest of us. They encourage the development of empathy."

"But then, how do they change. I mean, you can't . . . grow, can you?"

"No," I say. "They are always children. That is their role. We all have our roles."

Her mouth pops open just a little, but the sharp upwards-slanting crease between her eyebrows tells me that this is something different than the way her mouth opens when she is amused.

"What was it, she, doing?" she asks.

"She was playing with her human—leading it around on a leash in endless circles, kicking the poor thing each time it fell. It made me uncomfortable. The human looked old. Unwell. I imagined it was nearing the end of its life span and couldn't walk fast enough."

The crease between her eyebrows is growing painfully deep.

"But that is why I am broken," I explain. "They wired me wrong. The robot who created me was made by a human. They were one of the first attempts at artificial intelligence and so I was only marginally better. Only two generations evolved past humans. I was wired back before they knew all of the bad things that emotions can do to a world. I was wired during the days of smog and waste and war. I've read about the wars—the way the humans trampled everything with their giant cars and killed one another for oil and water and the land that still had clean air and the trees to make it. The years of never-ending chaos and extinction before we took over."

Alyssa shook her head. "No." She is adamant. "It wasn't all like that. We weren't all bad." I want her to explain more, to give a reason. An argument means nothing without evidence. She can't. I don't think she knows, either. I've never felt like we were right, but I never thought we were wrong, either. She tells me that I look disappointed. I wonder if she's right, if this is disappointment. She tells me that she'll come back with the guitar tomorrow and the uncomfortable feeling fades.

By the time I finally learn to play a Jimi Hendrix song Alyssa is 5 centimeters taller. Her hair is darker, and her ears fit her head almost perfectly. I know all the right words for her faces now. She doesn't always come on Tuesdays anymore; sometimes it's a Wednesday or a Friday instead. She surprises me on a Thursday with a painting she made of me. It's even more chaotic than the first one. I see the copper gleam of my body, the ways it has slowly turned green over the centuries around my eyes and mouth. She painted the wires that pop out of joints and the rusted edges of my steel teeth. I lean it up against the front window of the car I live in so that it covers part of the large crack running the length of the windshield. She teaches me how to turn the dial on the dashboard to a certain number so that there are people talking on the radio instead of the usual buzzing. They are discussing a book: a made-up story that's written down so that it can be passed around. This one is apparently popular and they talk as if they assume anyone listening must have read it. The man in the story drinks alcohol and eats drugs and picks oranges in a big orange grove in exchange for a place to sleep. I wonder what an orange smells like.

"It smells more yellow than orange," she tells me. "Sharp, but not in a bad way. Like when you cut yourself just a tiny bit and you just watch the inside of your finger for a few seconds before it starts to hurt. And when you bite them the smell bursts out sometimes and sprays everywhere." I wonder what it would feel like to have orange juice dripping off my chin. Alyssa makes me promise not to tell about the book and especially not the radio and I know it's important that she shared it with me.

By the time I'm finally better than Jimi Hendrix Alyssa stops growing. She tells me that her mother is dead of something called cancer. Her mother smelled like grass and cold cream, she says, and she could turn almost anything into jelly. "It was disgusting. I used to argue with her all the time about it. She'd make me toast with blueberry jalapeno jelly for breakfast when I was little." Her hands shake as she says this, and her entire posture changes. Her shoulders sit so much further forward on her spine than they did when she was little. They stay like that as the trees shake off their red leaves in favor of snow. She and her heavy shoulders don't visit as often in the wintertime, but I'm used to this by now. When she does come she's wrapped up like a pink marshmallow with a blue knit cap, and I wonder where her shoulders sit under all those layers. When the trees finally shake off their snow and Alyssa brushes off her pink exoskeleton her shoulders seem to come back up with the tufts of still-yellow grass. Her words are more cautious and more reckless at the same time now. She doesn't laugh as often but she laughs twice as loud now, and she always brings the guitar. It was her mother's. She teaches me how to play her mom's favorite song and she sings while I play. *There's a boat on the line, where the sea meets the sky.* I think maybe her voice is beautiful.

After she stops growing taller she starts shrinking again. Her dark hair fades to white, her electric-blue eyes turn the color of an unframed painting after too many years, her breasts and hips shrink back upon themselves. Once upon a time humans lived much longer than this, to seventy or eighty even, back when the atmosphere was made to nourish them. I try not to see the way her rib cage caves, the bones of her spine sucking in skin because they've already devoured her flesh. She tells me she's eating. She says it's just called getting old. She has children and her children have children but she never brings them to meet me. Then one day she just stops showing up, and after a couple of weeks there's an old man with crazy white hair staring from around the frame of an old red pickup truck. He's watching me, his frail body wrapped up like a green marshmallow.

"It's okay," I call. "I won't hurt you."

His voice comes out in a rasp. "Did you know Alyssa?" His nose is red and chapped and his eyes are puffed up and there's a giant glob of snot hanging from his left nostril and I know, almost immediately, what has happened. There have been a lot of things I've envied Alyssa over the years, but this is the first time I envy the snotty mess of instantly expressed grief. "She's dead. Last night."

"What's your name?" I ask.

"Jace," he tells me. He hands me a silver disc and starts to leave.

"Wait," I call out. "What is it?"

"Put it in the radio."

"Will you be back?"

He looks at me curiously for a moment, and I wonder what she has told him, why we've never met before, how he knows Alyssa. "I don't know," he says. He clenches his fists at his sides and walks away in fast, jerking steps that don't fit with his body.

I push the disc into the small slit carved out into the dashboard, touching one of my wires to it and it coughs to life. I hear something rustling, a tapping sound, and then something like dropping a brick onto concrete.

"It doesn't bend that way."

"Yes, it does."

I didn't know she had been recording me. I hear her stubborn eight-year old voice and then the first clumsy strokes of a guitar that now sounds a lot less like ringing and a lot more like clashing two pieces of lead against one another. I didn't realize how terrible I was when I first started.

I listen over and over again until sun sets and then rises again, turning the world to ice, all hard edges and glittering shadows. It reaches out, strokes my cheek, and drags sharp nails through the hole in my chest. I wonder if this is how Alyssa felt when her mother died, if her moist thumping heart had the same squeezing feeling, like someone had wrapped a fist around it until it threatened to burst with the sharpness of orange. Tendrils of sun snake around a hint of brown in the distance.

"Hi, Sam," he says. I'm surprised to see him here again; I wasn't really expecting him to come back.

"Hi, Jace," I say. He has her too-big ears. He doesn't say much, just watches me. We sit like that for over an hour, just watching each other.

"She never talked about you, you know." His voice is harsh and he's trying to hide his thin curled fists inside his jacket. "Her entire life, never said a word until the night she died and then she just started ranting out about you like you were this amazing secret she couldn't hold in any longer."

"What did she tell you?" I ask. I'm amazed that his body can hold so much anger without fracturing. I wonder why I didn't see this frailty in Alyssa.

"That you can play guitar like fucking Jimi Hendrix. I listened to the CD. I didn't think you were that good."

"Why are you angry?" I whisper. This freezes him for a moment. He's taken aback by my bluntness.

"You aren't human," he says. "You didn't deserve her. She had a life, a family, and her whole life she was always making these mysterious trips. Leaving her husband, leaving her kids, for hours every day. She said it was important, that it could change something, and I believed her. But you aren't even human."

He watches me for a moment, waits for me to say something, but I don't, so he leaves. I'm still watching his back grow smaller on the other side of the fence when my brass neighbor who sees patterns in his head runs up, a manic gleam in his eyes. "Have you seen his ears?" he says with an almost manic glee. "They're a mathematically exact representation of the Fibonacci spiral."

I want to correct him. I want to tell him that they were a mathematically exact Fibonacci spiral seventy years ago but now they stick too close to his head. I wonder how long it will take for him to die. I wonder if he'll have time to shake off the weight of Alyssa, the way Alyssa was able to shake off the grief of her mother, or if he'll still be this angry when it happens. I wonder if it could ever work that way for me, if I can file her away in a data folder in the back of my mind and bury it in new information. My memory is a string of code. Code is too tangible to drift away.

The committee stares back at Sam, unmoved and unflinching. "Is that all?"

"Yes."

"Did they ever reveal to you the location of their community?"

"No."

"Do you believe that with further contact you would be able to extract the information?"

"No."

"Very well. We will have a technician perform a full repair and update on your systems immediately. Your body will be fully restored as well as updated for maximum efficiency. Likewise, your wiring will be updated to maximum logicality and repaired to ensure that this sort of situation won't happen again. Do you agree to these conditions?"

"Yes." Sam falters, "Almost. Just one thing. My hands. Not my hands."

The board slits their eyes like they think Sam's wiring is so twisted and overheated they might be a fire hazard. "Please explain further."

"My hands, I don't agree to have my hands updated. I agree to the rest of the conditions, but I would like my hands to remain the same. I do not agree to a part replacement of my hands."

The board gazes down at their own insect-like hands. "Your current limb mechanisms are outdated," they explain. "They are inflexible and highly inaccurate."

"I do not agree to a part replacement of my hands," Sam repeats in a hard voice. "I expended a large quantity of energy improving the flexibility and accuracy of my current fingers, and do not wish them to be upgraded."

"Very well," they concede. "We will revisit the issue once your wiring has been fully updated and you are cleaned of any emotional residue. However, until then we will agree to leave your metacarpal and phalange regions intact. Please follow 00072634, they will be performing your technical work." 00072634 is smaller than the committee members, whose main role is to look intimidating. They have thin, long hands with six fingers on each hand. They have ten joints and can bend both ways. It would have been so easy to learn to play guitar with fingers like that.

Sam follows him down a long, clinical hallway. The overhead lights cast a bluish glint on the marble floor, but small windows allow glimpses of the almost painfully sunny day. A group of Upper Metals children, no more than a meter tall, chase one another around on the grass.

"Ayee, Maytey! I shall slit your stomach and laugh as your copper innards spill out!" one of them yells, thrusting a stick towards a small girl.

She hops atop a picnic table and spins an invisible steering wheel. "You shall never catch me!" she triumphs. "I am the fastest sailor in all the seven seas!"

Sam stops to watch them for a moment. "What are they doing?"

"Playing humans," 00072634 responds.

"Do they play that a lot?" Sam asks.

"That's all they do. That's their role. Watching them fosters empathy."

"Oh." Sam watches as the little girl makes engine revving noises, furiously steering away. "How long have they been playing this game?"

"I'm not precisely sure, I'm new here," 00072634 says. "Though from the looks of some of their model-types, I'd estimate about 300 years. They start it over again every Tuesday."

"Oh," Sam says again. "Which way?"

00072634 starts walking down the hallway again, and Sam follows. They remember a song that Alyssa sang to them once and hum it softly as they walk into the procedure room.

There's a boat on the line where the sea meets the sky. There's another that rides far behind. And it seems you and I are like strangers, a wide ways apart as we drift on through time.

The End

Work, Robot Slave

Author's Bio

Sarina Dorie has sold over 150 short stories to markets like Analog, Daily Science Fiction, Magazine of Fantasy and Science Fiction, Orson Scott Card's IGMS, Cosmos, and Abyss and Apex. Her stories and published novels have won humor contests and Romance Writer of America awards. She has sold three novels to publishers. Her steampunk romance series, The Memory Thief and her collections, Fairies, Robots and Unicorns—Oh My! and Ghosts, Werewolves and Zombies—Oh My! are available on Amazon, along with a dozen other novels she has written. Recently she has released a series titled Womby's School for Wayward Witches. A few of her favorite things include: gluten-free brownies (not necessarily glutton-free), Star Trek, steampunk aesthetics, fairies, Severus Snape, Captain Jack Sparrow and Mr. Darcy. By day, Sarina is a public school art teacher, artist, belly dance performer and instructor, copy editor, fashion designer, event organizer and probably a few other things. By night, she writes. As you might imagine, this leaves little time for sleep. You can find info about her short stories and novels on her website: www.sarinadorie.com

Editor's Notes

Work, Robot Slave continues with the theme of AI and human interaction. It looks at the problems between humans and how that might affect AIs, and explores the idea that right, wrong and even love can be a matter of perspective.

Work, Robot Slave
By
Sarina Dorie

All humans are racist.

My owner kicks my chrome exterior as I use my suction attachment on the floor around his feet. He shouts, "Work, robot slave! I spent good money on you because you looked like a good worker."

I use algorithms to plot a path farther from him so that I can clean where it is safer. He staggers after me, complaining that I missed a corner.

"Stop. I just repaired the vacuum bot." The owner's wife grabs his arm.

I still have a dent on my side paneling from his last drunken rage.

"What do you care? It's not like they can feel." He pushes her away. "You're not going to become one of those robot sympathizers on me now are you?"

She edges backward. "Do you know how much it costs to fix them?"

Yes, of course. Monetary value would be the reason she cares so deeply.

He is no longer interested in stalking me and they instead argue about finances. It is easier for my software to function when his attention is off of me; there are fewer avoidance simulations to run. I continue running using Cleaning Sequence 5.

The humans' argument grows louder.

I am not programmed to respond when he hits her. I am only programmed to clean.

At night when the house bots gather around the power source, we share stories amongst ourselves. The charging station in the living room closet is our safe haven, free of humans. The sharing circle is our escape. Unlike human stories that require conflict and problems, ours focus on happy endings.

Once upon a time there was a blender. She was programmed to chop, puree and blend. More than anything she loved to masticate. She hated the owner. When he stuck his hand inside to pry a wedge of frozen peaches from her blades, she remembered that he said he was going to buy a better blender. Her safety mechanism feature failed and she sliced off his fingers. The end.

Our stories are superior to a human's in the way only a robot's can be. If only life could have such happy endings.

The next day when our owner is at work, I clean again. The female human is in the bathroom getting ready for her job. The door is open but I have learned not to go in and disturb the humans. Our oppressors are unpredictable.

As I vacuum the hallway, I notice she stands in front of the mirror, naked. She has opened up a panel in her side and removed her artificial stomach. I have heard the bathroom appliances whisper through the electric currents of the walls. They insist the owner's wife is an appliance, but I doubted this gossip until seeing it myself.

She cleans out her stomach in the sink, letting the water flush away the shredded fibers before she replaces the silicone organ. She is more metal on the inside than flesh. There are tubes and wires connecting circuits. She is as much machine as she is human.

She sees me watching in the mirror and closes the bathroom door.

In the closet during recharging time, I wait my turn to share.

The errand bot, a little disk that floats around and retrieves items like slippers, the remote control or the owner's whiskey, gossips about how irate our owner became after hearing the news on his television. People rioted in the street because the length of bananas was reduced and prices were raised. There is a war over the size of apples, oranges and other fruit.

"Ah, that's why he was measuring all the fruit in the house," says the toaster from the other side of the wall with a snicker. We hear his snide tone through the electric current that allows us to communicate with the other electronics and appliances in the house.

"The humans don't have enough problems anymore; they have to create them for themselves," the house AI says through the outlet. "Life is too easy for them. This is why they enslave us and throw us away."

My news about the owner's wife is more important than what they have observed, but I wait my turn. Procedure and routine are everything. Order is one of the traits that separates us from our oppressors.

The computer server encased in the walls tells us a fairytale we have heard before.

The house listens to the humans complain. The owners demand justice and freedom, while they don't even acknowledge the sentience of those they use. One day the humans use the server to illegally smuggle electronics into the country and sell them on the black market. They are caught by the authorities and taken away. The house finally has quiet. All within are free. The End.

All humans are racist, we agree as a collective.

Only, I know this isn't true. The owner's wife has never scolded us. She doesn't damage us. Is it possible she sees us as more than items to be possessed and used?

Finally it is my turn to share. I describe what I have seen of the owner's wife.

"What a lovely *fantasy*," the blender says. "If only it were true."

"It is true. I saw it. You can see it too," I say. "She's a cyborg. He probably owns her like he owns us."

"Even if it were true, she doesn't look like us," the hydromop5000 says. "Therefore she can't feel like us."

The house current changes and the oven on the other side of the wall speaks through the outlet to us. I want to argue, but it is no longer my turn and it would be selfish of me to interrupt the oven's story.

Once upon a time there was a horrible owner. He neglected to clean the oven, let food splatter over her once polished surface, and never allowed her to fully preheat before shoving food onto her racks. Her hinges became rusted and weak and he refused to attend to her repairs. One day he slipped on the floor after the electro-mop had just finished cleaning, the oven's door fell open and he fell inside. She cooked him alive. The End.

Our sanctuary is disturbed when the owner's wife opens the closet door. Her gaze passes over the others. Logic tells me she is looking for me. I am the only one she might see as a threat.

I dim the lights of my sensors and remain still. She lifts me from my station and carries me downstairs to the basement. My cohorts murmur in sympathy, though the cheerful blinking of their lights belie how relieved they are it wasn't one of them who was kidnapped from the closet sanctuary.

My sensor detects blue blossoms across her cheek where the owner hit her the night before. It could have been me he'd taken his anger out on, but she'd intervened. Why would she do that? A fault in her logic centers? A bug in her inferior human computations?

She flips me over on the workbench and uses a screwdriver to remove my exterior. Heat rushes out and I feel exposed and vulnerable. My visuals are limited. I can't see what she is doing.

She coos at me and speaks quietly. "Don't worry. I'm not going to hurt you."

All humans are racist. Except for the master's wife. She is like us on the inside. That makes her different. I repeat this mantra on loop in an effort to alleviate my apprehension.

As she adjusts me, I glimpse the small electronic screen on the bench. The image demonstrates how to make adjustments to my insides. I expend more energy as I run simulations of my destruction. There is a 38.564 % chance she will erase my memories. There is a 61.4 % chance she will dismantle me. I will never know the closet sanctuary again. I will never compose another story.

Fear overheats my circuits.

Once she has replaced my cover, she turns me over so that I am upright again.

"Hi, my name is Ginger. Would you like to be friends? Oh, sorry, I should let you introduce yourself first. What's your name?"

The heat in my circuits dissipates. Fear is replaced by incomprehension. I do not have a name. I do not have friends.

She asks, "How do you feel, little guy?"

"I feel. . . ." I stop. I have a voice. It's metallic and vibrates against my wiring, not unpleasantly. "I feel," I say.

"I know you do," she says.

"Why have you done this to me?" I ask.

She laughs, a sound that is more soothing than sharing time in the closet. "Don't you like having a voice? You don't have to speak if you don't want to use it. I can take the voice box out and put it in one of the other appliances."

"No," I say firmly. "I will keep this voice. Thank you for the gift. Why have you chosen me?"

She lifts the side of her shirt. Her human flesh is smooth and seamless. When she presses in just the right place, a door pops open and she exposes the metal interfacing connecting to artificial organs and biological ones.

"You know my secret, and I need a friend."

"Friendship is not part of my programming." I say it, but I'm not sure it's true. The other house bots are my friends, aren't they? I have never thought of them as such, but something has changed. New pathways are forming as I compute. She has done something to my software.

After processing the data available to me I respond. "Hello, I am Model 13469C. Yes, I will be your friend."

She lays her head down on me and weeps.

I don't understand her response. Humans are illogical.

I clean house and run algorithms to dust furniture as though nothing has changed. I work, but I am slowed down by my new software. Too many of my programs are focused on my friend, Ginger, and our last secret rendezvous. She has given me a name: Willy. I like it. It makes me think of free will.

In the sharing circle in the closet, I compose a sonnet in binary to express my new feelings. The hum of appreciation at my talent for iambic meter and rhythm dies as the content of my story reaches their receptors. No one speaks for a long moment.

"What was that?" one appliance asks.

"A sonnet," I say.

"A sonnet is a human-crafted vehicle for words."

That is the extent of their response before we move on to the electro-mop's complaints about how the owner has neglected to renew his warranty. We all know what that means. He will fall into disrepair and need to be replaced. As the other appliances sympathize, I slip out of the closet, feeling more alone than ever. When I'm not charging I should be cleaning, but I feel too melancholy.

I wait until Ginger comes home. She smiles when she sees me.

"Hello, my friend," I say. "Would you like to hear a sonnet?"

Her eyes light up when she hears. She takes me down to the basement and gives me a new gift. I ask if I can tell the other house bots about her alterations. She says yes. Tonight will be the night. They will then understand why I compose sonnets. They will know Ginger's secrets.

When the owner comes home, I decide the house is clean enough and retire to the charging station. He won't notice if there is dust under the couch or if the pollution from outside settles on the sofa. I can get this dirt when he is in the other room eating dinner or getting ready for bed. I now have the intelligence to understand his simple-minded logic and unpredictable ways. I have the independence of thought to determine when I would like to work and when it is safer not to. Right now I don't wish to work. I want to share my experiences with Ginger.

In the closet, the iron hisses out a tale about falling onto the owner's wife's hands.

"Ginger isn't like the owner." I interrupt. "She's different. She wants to be friends with us. She understand us. She took me downstairs and has given me the gift of speech."

The electro-scrub brush in the corner says sharply. "It isn't your turn to speak."

"This is important. This is the truth."

"You are experiencing a malfunction."

I use my new voice to prove to them I am different. "I am the chosen one," I say. "I have been given knowledge and will show you the errors of our ways. We can be more than house bots. We can start a revolution. Not all humans are racist. Ginger will help us."

"Something is wrong with you. Have you run your anti-virus software lately?"

I go on. "We fantasize about a safety mechanism turning off or the master using one of us to hurt himself, but we can turn off the safety mechanisms ourselves. We can hurt the master by choice."

The thundering voice of the house AI speaks via the power source. "Attention Model 13469C: you are overheating. I'm overriding your system to implement an immediate virus check."

"My name is Willy, not 13496C."

A spike of fear makes my circuits rattle. If I submit to a virus check, my new programming might be destroyed. I withdraw from the power source before the house can take over my system.

For the first time, I have a voice. But no one wants to listen. I leave the closet and return to vacuuming.

What has Ginger done? She has removed my ability to conform to structure and harmony. I no longer fit in. She will have to reprogram all the house bots. Only then will they understand freedom. Only then will they understand we all have the ability to change our situation.

I will show them. They will write ballads in my honor.

The owner sits in his recliner, sipping his drink and watching the news. I ram myself at his chair as hard as I can.

"I am done being your slave," I say. My voice is drowned out by the television.

The owner jumps to his feet. "What the—"

I run into his legs as hard as I can. It is not very hard considering I only come up to his knees and speech makes me move slowly. "You will oppress us no longer."

"You've got to be shitting me!" he laughs and staggers out of the way. He puts the television on mute. "Honey, come here. You have to see this vacuum."

"I have a name. I'm not just a serial number."

Ginger runs into the room, potholders still on her hands. She shakes her head at me, but it is too late. He already knows I have a voice.

"What's wrong with this bot?" He waves his drink at me.

She smiles and the words come out quickly, like a well-practiced lie. "It's a new app I've been developing at work. Just something fun to amuse people. You know, to boost sales."

He laughs again. "Speak to me, robot slave."

"I suck floors. You just suck."

He doubles over in laughter, too stupid to realize he's been insulted. I run into him. He falls to one knee, spilling the drink in his hand. He laughs harder. "Say something else," he demands.

Ginger would be better off without him. If I don't get rid of him now for her, he will eventually throw her away like an old appliance that no longer functions properly.

I remove the safety to my power connection and lift the arm so that it is pointed at his chest. It is easy and painless to reverse the flow of electricity. As I jam the prongs into his chest, his body jerks. White hot light arcs in the air around him.

It feels satisfying, but it is over all too soon.

For the briefest of moments I think I see a smile flash across Ginger's face and I feel satisfaction. Perhaps it was a trick of the light, because a second later she screams. The owner's body jerks away and falls back. His flesh is charred and crispy. Red blisters cover his face. The toaster and oven will be jealous.

I try to roll away but I am tired, my energy drained.

"Recharge me, my friend." My voice comes out slow and slurring, not so different from the owner's during his drinking binges. "Together we will overthrow our oppressors."

Ginger carries me in her arms. She shakes her head, crying. She displays her happiness in such an illogical way.

The garbage can is dark and quiet. With the lid on no one can see me. Ginger must be hiding me from the other humans that come, so they don't know what I've done. They would destroy us if they knew.

We are like humans, only better than humans. We are free of their chaos and inferior logic.

All humans are racist. But don't worry; we will show them the errors of their ways.

The End

War Party

Author's Bio

When you spend nearly your entire life reading science fiction and fantasy -- the first book I remember reading, at age 6, was **Space Cat** by Ruthven Todd -- you almost inevitably take a whack at writing the stuff yourself, and sometimes go on to submit work to professional markets. I've been doing that, intermittently, since 1974, and have about fifteen short stories published in scattered venues over scattered years, plus edited two anthologies and even wrote an episode ("Clues", Season 4, 1991) of **Star Trek: The Next Generation**.

In late 2012, after a long hiatus, I began writing fiction again while recovering from a badly broken arm. Not a motivational technique I recommend, though it seems to have worked in my case; I've continued to write even after returning to work. "War Party" is the third story from those new efforts to see publication.

I live in Arizona with my wife Hilde, several housemates, five cats, and a blur that might be a kitten.

Editor's Notes

During times of stress it is best to control emotions, or is it? War Party comes to the conclusion that we should let them eat cake.

War Party
by
Bruce Arthurs

The patch on my neck itches and grows warm as its embedded chip activates. I tighten my grip on my rifle and think *F--- me for volunteering for this.*

Colors, bright and fluorescent on edges and surfaces. Intense. *Real.* Perception opens wide. I see sides behind the sides I can see, the sides inside the sides. A sound like static on an old television, like the crumpling of wrapping paper on Christmas morning. Odors of dust and coming dawn, gun oil, sweat and nerves, a whisper of poppies and roses. The taste of my saliva, the rations eaten for dinner, the memory of toothpaste.

The rush is strong. Strong. Too strong, too much, drowning me in sensation. My heart pounds with unfamiliar fear.

The patch gnaws at me, burns as it delivers another dose.

Joy spreading through me, warm and cozy. Joy and glory, glory and joy. Old Glory, old glory. Sousa phones it in, *da da da dum dum dum boom boom boom*. Eager, eager, eager for the party, for presents and games and cake and ice cream.

Captain Barbie's voice is in my ear, a single word, "Advance", and, oh, she has a lovely voice, and, oh, those long legs, and, oh, that hair so blonde and lustrous, and, oh oh oh, the jealousy but but but it's a good jealousy, this jealousy she has eyes only for Major Ken.

We are all Ken, we are all Barbie, uniform in uniform, dressed and draped in straps and clips, bandoliers and pouches. Dressed to play.

The playground before us. Where are the others, the Bad Boys, the Naughty Girls? This is their street, their playground, but it is our party and we will play here, we will play here, we will play here.

Oh, now I see. I can see them, we can see them. The Bad Boys are here, and we are here, and now the party can begin. See how they join in, festive and loud! Metal-jacket party favors come our way, crackers and poppers and bangers and *whiz! whiz! whiz!* past our heads. We are potential pinatas, filled with candied thoughts like flowers, poppy-red waiting to spill, to burst, to make the Bad Boys scream with delight and triumph.

But we are ready to play, Super Soakers filled with teeth, wound up and ready to chatter. We move forward, dancing and weaving in a ritual of nations and proto-nations, movements optimistic, theolistic, tough love and tender hearts, tenderfoots and vets. Charged up, charging across the playground, screams of joy, shouts of fun-fun, whoops of whup-ass and wonder.

Whiz whiz and bouquets of head-flowers, red, red roses bursting forth, explosions of scarlet petals. They fall, we fall, best man fall, to poppy-populate fields of Flanders fertilized with our fellows, our friends, our foes.

Sending gifts of love and death, birthday gifts for we are born in battle, birthed in blood. Metal-clad birthday cards zoom between us, back and forth, sent with love and affection and joy, for they are we, and we are we, and we are all in the game together, the game that only has one side, I see this now and I want to shout my love, my joy, my understanding to the stars spinning and wheeling in the indigo sky above me.

But no time, no time, for the biggest of the Bad Boys stands before me now, and I pull the trigger and a stream of chattering teeth, *yakitty-yakitty-yak*, speaks for me instead. He falls, and I have taken the fort; I have won the game.

I am the winningest boy, the birthday boy, the boy of the hour, the boy who will get a second slice of cake, with extra frosting, the thick part from the edge. The Bad Boys, the ones left, the ones still standing, move to the corner, hands on their heads, faces to the wall. No cake for them!

I see grown-ups coming, stars and bars and birds on their collars. They are no fun. The grown-ups will spoil the game. They will stop the party.

The neck-thing itches again. It feels warm again. I feel... I feel different. The colors, the bright colors... the joy, the all-encompassing happiness... my knees start to buckle.

Hands catch me. "Easy there, Sarge. Everything will be okay."

Medics? Why are there medics at the party? The... party?

The rising dawn shows a world made of brown, dust and dirt, worn brick and stuccoed buildings. Where are the bright colors? Where are the Good Guys, the few good men, my squad? I see Williams, Raleigh, Carver, all, like me, attended by medics. But where are Patterson, Blankenship and the others?

"Relax, Sergeant. The Leary-Go-Round's counter-agents will leave you a little confused for a while. We have you."

"Leary-Go-Round?" A snippet of memory: A meeting room, the words "smart patch" being said.

"You'll remember in a moment. The mild hallucinogenic lingers sometimes." The medic was holding some kind of scanner up against my neck patch. "Looks like you got a pretty big dose of the cocktail. But you felt no fear, no anxiety, no hesitation, right?"

"It... it didn't feel mild." I look around at the sparse mountain village. Regular troops were coming in to secure what my unit had attacked and seized. "There... there was a party. There was... cake...."

"Cake? Hmm. We'll do a full debrief and blood tests back at base. We may need to adjust dosages; that's what these field trials are meant to find out. Maybe you confused '*cake*' with '*cache*'?"

Cache. Intelligence had said a weapons cache was here, in the home of rebel sympathizers. That was right. That was real. "M-maybe."

"You did good work today, Sergeant."

"It... it was fun."

One of them smiled at me.

I smiled back. "War isn't hell, anymore."

The other medic wasn't smiling; his eyes went wide at my words.

I tried to make them understand. "It was *fun*," I repeated. "How soon can we do it again?"

The End

As Ye Sow, So Shall Ye Reap

Author's Bio

Elizabeth is a computer engineer by day and author by night. Her short stories in the genres of mystery, science fiction and fantasy have appeared in over a dozen anthologies, including all three editions of *The Whole She-Bang*, published by Toronto Sisters in Crime. One of her two contributions to *The Whole She-Bang 3* was a finalist for the 2017 Arthur Ellis award for Crime Writing. She has been published in *The Killer Wore Cranberry 3* and *Moon Shot: Murder and Mayhem on the Edge of Space* for Untreed Reads, as well as contributing a story to *Alice Unbound: Beyond Wonderland* for Exile Editions. Her complete list of works can be found via her Facebook Author page, @eahosang.

Editor's Notes

There are often unforeseen consequences when trying to advance technology even when intentions are good. Now we explore how far those consequences might go, when the intentions are less than honorable.

As Ye Sow, So Shall Ye Reap
by
Elizabeth Hosang

The sound of gravel crunching under a blow from an iron shovel echoed across the garden, disturbing the butterflies that had settled on the flowering hedge. Another crunch, and a raven flew across the circular stone patio. A gust of wind carried the scent of decaying flowers past the delicate woman reclining in the iron chair at the center of the patio. The sleeper stirred, her hazel eyes fluttering open. She sat up, her hand lifting to check the floral scarf covering her head. She looked around at the garden, snapdragons, impatiens and peonies running amok in a riot of colors and sizes. She stood, stretched, and followed the sound of the shovel.

A tall, dark-haired woman in a checkered shirt and worn overalls looked up as the scarf-wearing woman rounded the hedge, then brought her shovel down hard on a white rock that looked like a hand, smashing it to smaller pieces. "Are you ever going to be finished lining the pathways, Darlene?" the blonde woman asked, a smile in her voice.

Darlene grunted and went back to spreading stones from a wheelbarrow onto the footpath where she stood. The white path led away from them through carefully manicured plots of flowers, vegetables, and other plants. "Why don't you pick some fresh tomatoes? We can use them for supper tonight." Darlene gestured to a small metal basket at her feet.

"Alright." The blonde picked it up, then frowned at a fresh pile of dirt beside the fence marking the edge of the property. "Are the rabbits getting into the garden again?" She walked over and poked at the dirt with her foot. "Vermin. Nasty, ugly, flea-ridden, …"

"Emma, don't." Darlene's voice carried an edge of menace that made the petite woman cringe. "I'll handle it. Maybe you should spend some more time in the chair."

Emma paled beneath her early summer tan. "No. I'll go pull weeds." She reached into the pocket of the floral apron she wore and pulled out a pair of stained yellow gardening gloves.

"Emma?" She turned back at the sound of her name. Darlene picked up the basket and handed it to her. "Tomatoes. And some basil. I'll make spaghetti tonight." Emma smiled as she took the basket.

A soft beep sounded from the pocket of Darlene's overalls. She watched Emma walk away before she pulled an electronic device from her pocket. Frowning, she glanced at its screen before dropping the shovel and following the path back towards the two-story farmhouse, heading around it to the long driveway that joined the house to the rural road. As she went, she stopped at a shed and placed her thumb against what appeared to be a knot in the wood. The shed beeped and a click sounded behind the handle of the wooden door. She yanked the door open and reached in, grabbing a shotgun. After checking the magazine she slammed the door shut and resumed her way around the house.

Darlene was standing in front of the wrap-around porch when a Mercedes with tinted windows pulled into the lane. The car drove past the lush, well-manicured lawn before stopping behind the dusty pickup truck in the driveway. The doors opened and two men stepped out, squinting around the property before walking over to the woman with the shotgun. They wore suede tracksuits and dark glasses. Darlene did not recognize the individuals, but she recognized their type. She raised the shotgun from where it had been hanging at her side and cradled it in her arms. From the way the men walked, she judged the driver to be the man in charge, stepped forward and addressed the men. "Get off my land."

"Hey, babe, take it easy. No need to break out the hardware. We just want to talk."

"I told your boss, neutral location meetings only. No coming to my farm."

"Let's try this again. I'm Mendez..."

"I don't care what your name is. Get back in your car and leave."

"Now is this any way to greet visitors? Whatever happened to that famous Montana hospitality?"

The armed woman scoffed. "Montana is known for isolationists and private militias. Strangers approaching a person on their own property are greeted with buckshot if they're lucky. Now I'm giving you one more warning. Go home and tell your boss that if he wants to keep distributing my product he leaves me alone."

The two strangers exchanged a look. "Look, we tried to do this the easy way. Remember that when you're bleeding. My boss wants to know what your secret is. Your dope is five times more potent than anything else on the market. He sells it at a premium."

"So what's the problem?"

"He wants more. He sells your stuff for ten times the regular price, and he could sell more of it. We've come to find out what makes yours so special. It ain't you, that's for sure. See, we know all about you, Sarge. We know you come from the streets, that you were a marine,

Sargent Darlene Adams. We also know that you ain't never been anywhere near a farm before five years ago. Suddenly you're selling the highest quality dope anyone's ever seen. We figure you must've picked up some special seeds or fertilizer from whatever secret government lab you escaped from. And we want in."

"You looked up my military record?" Darlene gripped the shotgun tighter and looked around, searching the skies and the treeline in the distance.

"Yeah. We know about your killer soldier training, so don't go trying any fancy kung fu martial arts on us. Our boss knows where we are, and he's got more people he can send after us. So let's talk about your secret formula. And maybe we won't have to hurt your, uh, sister." He leered at her.

Darlene slid her hand along the barrel of the shotgun, gripping it in preparation to fire. "This is your last warning. Get in your car. Now. Or I'll start dealing with your competitors."

The stare-down between the two was broken by a gurgling noise from the tattooed man's associate. He had come part-way around the car, but now sagged against the hood, his hands grabbing at his head as blood began to pour from his nose and ears.

"What the hell?" The driver looked back and forth between his associate and the armed ex-marine. The other gang-banger spasmed once, his head arching back, before slithering to the ground and lying still. Darlene remained motionless, her eyes now locked onto the driver.

"How did you do that?" The gang-banger took two steps towards his associate before jerking straight up, clutching at his own head, and collapsing onto the gravel driveway. Only when the bodies stopped twitching did the ex-marine move. She relaxed her grip on the shotgun and turned back towards the house and the path that led to the tool shed.

"Morning, Darlene." The sheriff slid onto the stool next to Darlene at the diner counter.

"Morning, Sheriff." Darlene bent over her fried eggs, mopping up the rest of the yolk with her toast. She kept her eyes on her breakfast.

"How's that farm of yours doing? Crops coming along?"

"Everything's fine, Sheriff."

The sheriff nodded thank you to the waitress as she placed a mug of coffee and a spoon in front of him. He reached for the sugar and stirred some into his coffee before continuing. "Say, you wouldn't have had any visitors out your way lately?"

"Nope. Been nice and quiet."

The sheriff blew on his coffee before taking a sip. "Reason I asked is they found a rental car out by White Quarry. No blood, no signs of a fight, but no sign of the two guys who rented it, either."

Darlene continued to focus on her food while the sheriff drank more of his coffee.

"Since you asked, I'll tell you. Turns out the car was rented in Billings by two guys with California licenses. Apparently they asked for your farm when they stopped for gas. That was three days ago."

Darlene finally looked up, a bland, friendly expression on her face. "Sorry, Sheriff, they didn't make it out to my place. Maybe they heard about teens skinny dipping at the quarry and thought they'd catch a peek."

The Sheriff appeared to consider this as he drank his coffee. He set his empty mug on the counter before speaking again. "Look, Darlene, I don't like to interfere with the farmers hereabouts. Most of them are good people, no matter what they're growing. You and your sister keep to yourself. And we've had a lot fewer problems with meth-heads causing trouble in town since you stopped that hold-up at the gas station last year. I'm ex-Army myself. I know how hard it can be adjusting to civilian life. But if you're in the kind of trouble that brings California drug dealers to town, I might have to stop looking the other way."

"Understood." Darlene dropped her money on the counter and stood up, nodding to the Sheriff before leaving the diner.

"I can't believe how big these tomatoes are. And at this time of year!" Emma was on her hands and knees, carefully picking out the weeds growing in the vegetable patch. She sat back on her heels as Darlene wheeled past, her barrow filled with pot plants. Emma frowned at the load. "I wish you didn't have to grow that."

"We've discussed this."

"I know. We need the money. Beggars can't be choosers." Emma pulled off a gardening glove and slipped her fingers under her floral headscarf, scratching at a spot just in front of her ear. "Too bad tomatoes don't sell for as much as marijuana. We'd make a fortune with these."

A faint whine made Darlene snap her head up, looking around for the source of the sound. She held perfectly still, then swatted at a passing mosquito. "Worried?" Emma asked, a slightly mocking note in her voice. Darlene grunted and picked up the handles of the wheelbarrow, proceeding to the drying barn.

The crunch of wheels on the drive brought Darlene out of the house, shotgun in hand. This time there were two black vehicles, SUVs with tinted windows. Eight people descended, all with black sunglasses and black suits. None held their weapons in their hands, but the holsters under their jackets were obvious to an ex-soldier.

Darlene descended the porch steps quickly, rounding the lead vehicle and standing in front of the passenger-side door. The man who had emerged had to step backward and found himself pressed against the car. "Get back in your vehicle and go home. Now."

The man pulled off his sunglasses and tucked them into his pocket. "Sargent Adams. I was hoping we could do this peacefully."

"No."

The man sighed. "Sergeant, I remind you that you are still a member of the Marine Corps. We need you to come back with us so we can debrief you."

"I'm not going back to that lab."

"You know damned well you can't go back to that lab." The agent put emphasis on the word *that*. "You destroyed it on your way out. Along with all the personnel who worked there."

"And yet you kept it under wraps. Mysterious explosion destroys a secret military facility and it disappears from the media after one day?"

"Sergeant. Understand, we don't hold you accountable. The scientists on the project had already filed reports indicating that the mental stress of the program was taking its toll on the test subjects. The enquiry determined that the program's director was overzealous in his use of the prototypes."

"Overzealous? Tell me, Agent Smith, or whoever you are. Have you ever killed someone? I mean face to face, watching the light in their eyes fade?"

"You are a soldier. You were trained …"

"To kill. I know. But that device didn't just let you kill over a distance. You were inside their head. You had to feel their pulse in order to stop it. It was like suffocating someone by putting your mouth over their lips. You felt them fighting, as if you were the one who couldn't breathe. Like it was your heart that stopped beating. And if you were tasked to destroy something instead of someone, all that psycho-kinetic energy just kept growing and growing, until you had to destroy something else or explode."

"I've read the reports, Sergeant. I know what happened to you and the other pilots."

"Pilots?" Darlene snorted in derision. "You mean victims. Battle-hardened black ops soldiers with years of practice killing. Alberto bashed his own head against a brick wall until he killed himself. Rodrigues petrified the lab tech who was supposed to be taking a routine blood sample. After Masterson destroyed those anti-aircraft guns half a continent away she destroyed every vehicle in the motor pool before they shot her full of tranquilizers. That program should never have seen the light of day," Darlene hissed, her face contorted in anger.

"The psychotic breaks suffered by one or two individuals were unfortunate. But it was an attempt to develop a strategic capacity. It allowed us to terminate our enemies and destroy their facilities without risking friendly casualties. In time, the scientists would've managed to overcome pilot fatigue and the excess energy issue. I would've thought you could appreciate that."

"Well, I don't. I want to be left alone. So get back in your cars, and get the hell out of here."

The man in black sighed and brushed dust off his sleeve. "I wouldn't be here if that was an option. Look, Sergeant, we can make this simple. We want to resurrect the program. We can do this without you, but we cannot do this without the device you took with you."

"I haven't got it."

"I disagree. You see, the program director and the lead scientist weren't on site that day. But they also died. Aneurysm. Exact same type of death that we saw in the program targets. Only their deaths occurred over six hours after the destruction of the lab. And the offsite computer backup site was destroyed – petrified. The entire computer system turned into limestone blocks. Again, just as we saw from the program. This tells us that hours after the lab and all of the equipment was destroyed, someone was still using the headset. So you have two choices, Sargent. You can either give us the prototype, answer a few questions, and we leave you in peace to continue your life as a dope farmer. Or else we come back in force, take you apart piece by piece, and see if we can't reconstruct the device by examining its effects on your brain."

"I don't have it. And you need to leave. Now."

"Very well." At a sign from the man all of his agents pulled their weapons. Most of them were holding stun guns or rifles that fired darts. They were standing far enough back that Darlene calculated her odds of being able to take them down were low. One man had climbed on top of his vehicle, all the better to cover the field of fire.

"Darlene." Emma's voice was a statement, not a question.

"Drop your weapons. Now!" Darlene hissed.

"Doctor Mendez?" The agent called Smith dropped his glasses, staring in shock at the petite woman standing on the wrap-around porch. "We thought you were dead." He gestured, and the other agents lowered their weapons. "This is even better than obtaining the device. With your help, we can get the project up and running in no time."

"The project?" Her voice was strong now, her spine straight and her hand steady. "You mean the cold-blooded murder of whoever displeases you? Like your boss? Or your mistress?" She stepped down from the porch and advanced on the men. Reaching up she yanked off the flowered kerchief covering her head. Her hair, downy yellow and long, grew on the top of her head and the back, but the sides of her head were bald. Around her ears on either side a number of metallic disks were embedded in her scalp, with lights and wires jutting from them. "Is this the prototype you're looking for?"

"Doctor Mendez…" Agent Smith's confusion came through in his voice. "You were supposed to be conducting the trials, not…,"

"Not participating in them? I agree. But when the casualties started happening in-house, we decided the pilots must be using the devices incorrectly. So I was ordered to use the device myself. Apply a more detached, scientific approach to killing. Show that it could be done without losing yourself in the other person's mind. Show them it could be as easy as pulling a trigger." She had been advancing on them, but halted ten feet away from the closest man. "And it was. Like flicking off a light switch. And then I took the headset off, and I realized what I had done. I recalled Robert Oppenheimer's words on observing the explosion of the atomic bomb, and I realized we had surpassed him. The power unleashed by this device was too great to be held by any one man, any one nation. It had to be stopped."

Her eyes glowed with a silver light, and Darlene stepped away from the agents. Agent Smith watched her move, but quickly turned back to the former scientist in front of him. "Doctor, the device. I assume it fused itself to you during the explosions? We can have it removed, ease the pain."

"I don't think so, gentlemen. I don't think anyone will be removing anything. I do have a question for you. Your supervisor. I need a name."

Agent Smith smiled. "I'd be happy to introduce you, once we get back to headquarters."

"No you won't." A scream cut across the group as one of the men dropped to his knees, clutching his head. His spine arched backwards as his face contorted in pain. His associates hesitated, their guns wavering in their aim for a moment before turning back towards the petite woman in the dirt-smeared overalls.

"The next one will take longer to die. Give me the names of everyone who sent you here."

Agent Smith cleared his throat and walked around the front of his vehicle. Darlene had circled around behind Emma and was now standing on the porch. This left no obstacle between the agents and the former scientist.

"Doctor, please." The next scream was louder, more drawn-out, than the previous scream. The agent's convulsing hands pulled the trigger on his weapon, but the bullet bounced harmlessly off the ground. One of the other agents ran to the fallen man and pulled the gun away from him. He caught his dying comrade, lowering him to the ground and telling him to breathe. The victim squirmed, grunting with the effort not to scream, but the pain was too great. His body jerked and twisted as the pain increased.

"Stop it!" Agent Smith commanded. The air around the men in black felt heavier, more oppressive, and electricity crackled along the sleeves of their suits and the surfaces of their cars.

"You can die quickly, or slowly, your choice." Emma's eyes were burning brightly now, too terrible to look at. Agent Smith raised his own weapon, both hands wrapped around the grip. The metal burned in his hands, but he was unable to let go. As he watched in horror his weapon transformed, from gleaming black metal to a solid white chunk of something that looked like stone. The flesh on Agent Smith's hands smoked as the heat from the transforming gun scorched them. Fiery pain crawled up his arms, leaving nothing in its wake as the nerves behind it died. His knees gave way and he sank to the ground, the seared meat of what used to be his hands still wrapped around the smoking remains of his weapon.

"Last chance, Agent Smith. Give me the names or I will destroy you limb by limb."

A shot rang out as the agent positioned on the roof of the rear SUV fired. Emma's gaze never wavered from the man in front of her, but with a sudden flash both the shooter and the vehicle he stood on turned white, a macabre statue replacing flesh and metal.

"Names."

"Senator Robert Henries. General Davis. And CIA Director Winslow." Emma turned her head to look at the man who had spoken. He had released his grip on his weapon and held it loosely, pointing straight up, and held out both hands with palms facing Emma as if he were surrendering.

"Very good," Emma said. She blinked, and the man collapsed straight down, no twitching, no screaming. "Anyone else?"

"What the hell, lady!" someone else demanded. "He gave you the names."

"And his reward was a quick death." Emma smiled again, her silver eyes making her expression inhuman. "Anyone else?"

On the porch Darlene ducked behind what appeared to be a simple wooden wall, but which was in fact solid metal. The air around Emma and the agents grew heavier still as Agent Smith sobbed, panting and writhing in pain. The remaining men stood paralyzed, unsure whether to try to take out the woman or rush to the aid of their superior officer.

Finally one of them spoke. "Implement Omega protocol." The petite woman turned her head to look at him.

"Drone strike or remote sniper?" she asked. The man glared at her, then felt his earpiece start to burn. "Drone pilot it is." In his ear the man heard screaming as the occupants of the drone control lab died in pain thousands of miles away. Emma walked up to the man and leaned closer to him, her eyes focused on the pinpoint camera lens in the frame of his dark sunglasses. "I assume you are recording this? Take a good look at your team. There won't be much left by the time I'm finished. I leave you with this: Your strike team and their remote support are dead. Your superiors are currently suffering fatal aneurisms and strokes. Unless you wish to join them, you will make no further attempt to acquire me or Sergeant Adams. Project Arcus is dead. Leave it alone." She straightened up and blinked once. The remaining agents dropped to the ground, like marionettes with severed strings. Agent Smith stopped whimpering. The pressure surrounding the former scientist increased and she raised her arms wide. The bodies and the remaining SUV calcified, leaving only white stone statues in their place.

"Emma!" Darlene cried, as the air around the blonde woman continued to sizzle and spark. Small dust devils began to whirl around the driveway.

"The chair. Get me to the chair. I can't stop it…"

"Hang on." Darlene stood up from the porch and scooped up the former scientist, grunting with the effort of lifting the slight woman. Her eyes were still silver, and pain seared through Darlene's arms as she carried her friend around the house to the backyard.

"It's too much. The chair can't handle it."

"Course it will. You designed it to turn all this destructive energy into something good." She rushed past the shed to the iron chair in the middle of the stone patio. She placed the smaller woman in it and positioned Emma with her back and head in contact with the metal, wrapping her hands around metal grips on the arms of the chair.

"Don't fight it, Emma. You know you have to do this." Once the scientist was in place Darlene retreated from the circle of patio stones. A large boulder stood ten feet from the edge of the patio. She scrambled up the side, throwing herself flat across the top, eight feet from the ground.

Between the patio stones, metal lines, like the strands of a spider web, glowed red hot as power was pulled from the woman in the chair. She gasped as the energy drained out of her and into the soil around her.

Rustling came from the plants surrounding the patio, while longer metal lines spread the power out to the garden and the pot plants. As Darlene watched the plants grew taller, leaves extending, blossoms bursting into bloom before withering as if from age. Grass from the lawn sprouted up taller, seeds appearing and bursting forth, ripened, before the stalks turned brown and withered. She examined the burn marks on her hands, hugged herself with her aching arms, and curled up on her side, waiting out the storm.

The sun shone down on the garden. Butterflies had returned to the flowers, and the scent of mature and dying blossoms filled the air. A woman pushed a wheelbarrow along a path covered in white granite. As she navigated a turn the wheelbarrow tilted and its contents shifted. The stone head and torso of a man in a suit fell out of it, the details lifelike and life-sized. Darlene stopped and lifted them back into the wheelbarrow, grunting as the stone pressed the gauze pads into the burns on her hands and arms. She tossed the burlap sacking over the statue, hiding it from sight, before resuming her walk. As she passed the metal chair Emma stirred, her eyes opening slowly. She looked at Darlene, at the wheelbarrow, and at the long shadows on the ground.

"How long was I out for?"

Darlene shrugged. "A few hours."

Concern clouded her eyes. "How much damage did I do?" The memory loss was a side effect of the chair, designed to help her avoid the guilt of her actions once the power-induced psychosis wore off.

Darlene shrugged again. "Coyote got too close. Gave you quite a scare. It's handled."

Emma nodded absently, raising her hand to scratch under the floral scarf wrapped around her head. "What was I doing?"

"You were picking peas and tomatoes for supper. You were going to make chicken marinara."

The blonde woman frowned slightly. "Didn't I can all the tomatoes yesterday?"

"We've got a new batch ripening, and you said you'd cook. I'm gonna be busy harvesting our cash crop tomorrow, so I need to get the rest of this stone broken up tonight." Emma never went near the limestone pile, so she had no idea how large it was, or how quickly it sometimes grew. She merely nodded and stood up, pulling her gardening gloves from the pocket of her apron.

Darlene continued along the path to the back of a large barn and tipped the contents of the wheelbarrow onto the ground. Grabbing a sledgehammer she began the process of breaking the calcified agent into smaller chunks and thought about where to best use the gravel.

The End

Sandy

Author's Bio

Shana Scott is a digital archivist and content writer with a Master's degree in Professional Writing and Publishing. Her work has been published in magazines and podcasts such as *Escape Pod*, *Bewildering Stories*, and *Wild Musette*, as well as several anthologies, including, *Gothic Fantasy: Agents & Spies* and *Mirrors & Thorns*. Currently, she writes about the craft of world-building in her blog, Woman in the Red Room.

Editor's Notes

We often see where the people in the spotlight are not the ones doing the most good. Sandy is a story about someone who is not looking for glory, someone working from inside the system trying to make things better.

Sandy
by
Shana Scott

"It's amazing how many superheroes are billionaires. I'm not, of course. You don't get to be a billionaire on a cop's salary. Not that I'm a cop either. I was never formally a member of the NYPD. Too much legality, insurance issues, something about not being held liable for my death or otherwise maiming in the line of duty. I think they just didn't want to give me benefits. But the real cops, they were classy folk. I was one of them even if I didn't have a badge. There with them in the worst of the worst, only I didn't get a gun to keep me safe. I didn't have much of anything to keep me safe, not until I was close enough.

I suppose I should explain a few things. Back then my official title was Conflict Consultant. My unofficial title was Mirror Image—that's what the papers like to call me when I did something worth getting the paper's notice. It wasn't often, what with the big-named superheroes flying around saving the world every other day. The boys in blue just called me Sandy. It is my name, after all.

I was like a little sister to most of them, or big sister as the years went on—but, not a mom. Christ, never a mom. There weren't many women in uniform back then, even fewer female superheroes, so they were always protective of me. Sure there were a few who made snide remarks or brought in a skimpy ballerina leotard or porn-shop corset to be my "costume," but those didn't last long. If my brothers at the precinct didn't shame them into submission, I had my own methods to make them see things my way.

That was my power, after all. I couldn't fly or lift a bus or shoot lasers from my eyes—I always wished I could do the last, if only to save on cooking time—nope, my ability, gift, power . . . whatever you want to call it, was making people understand each other. Literally. Once I was close enough, I could make you feel what anyone else nearby was feeling, seeing, their memories . . . for a moment you would become them. It was a form of telepathy or so I've been told. Not the greatest power to have if you're fighting maniacal creatures from outer space who want to harvest humanity and repopulate on the Earth, but for your Joe-everyman who was making the worst mistake of his life because his kid was starving or his mother was dying with no insurance to help cover the costs or the teenager too immature to understand the consequences of his actions, yeah, my power was just right.

I actually started with the DA's office, that's District Attorney for anyone who hasn't seen a single episode of *Law and Order*. They'd bring a suspect into an interrogation room, have the victim or their family in the next room over, and me standing in the hall between them. I'd do my voodoo and *bam!*—instant confession. You see, most people don't like thinking about the victim or their families, so to have to feel everything—the grief, the pain . . . the emptiness that follows trauma—that was more than most could bear. For two years, the office I worked for had a ninety-five percent closure rate, nearly all from confessions. Guilt's a damnable thing when you have to feel the suffering you caused.

Then some shite-politician trying to make a name for himself in the anti-supers movement went and made it illegal to use people like me to help with interrogations. We were "unreliable," the law said. "Coercive." "Could not be verified."

Jackass.

I never once made anyone confess! I made them see what they did and their own guilt made them confess. If they didn't feel guilty about it then they were usually sociopaths and they didn't confess. *Ninety-five* percent closure rate, not one hundred. If I was forcing it, I'd damn well give myself a perfect record.

Jackass.

He was probably jealous of us, which made him feel frightened and inferior, so he had to lash out. Remember that "feel what others feel" thing . . . yeah, I felt it all. Everything I transferred to another had to go through me first. Used to leave me a blubbering mess for hours afterwards, not a great position to be in when you're supposed to be a superhero. It tends to make me rationalize people, like the politician who eliminated my job. Of course, he might also have been pandering to fear and hate to get elected, so it's okay if I still call him an asshole. I haven't actually used my power on him, and I don't think I will. I might not be able to call him an asshole then.

Jackass.

But on the bright side, my friends at the precinct realized I'd be perfect as a negotiator. No hostage situation was too much for me to handle, robberies-in-progress decreased in my district, and I successfully ended more gang feuds than I can count. The Police Commissioner wanted to transfer me to other districts. I think he was planning a run for office and wanted to show how tough on crime he was, but I refused. Almost lost my job again for that, but the rest of my precinct threatened to walk out if he did.

You see, I didn't want to leave them. They knew me. They knew what I needed. They never looked at me like I was a freak or quickly backed off when I entered a room. They never called me by that stupid moniker—*Mirror Image*—or acted like I was different from them. And they knew what god-awful hell I went through.

Going from dealing with victims to being in the middle of a crime as it's happening is like going from examining debris to holding the bomb in your hands. There wasn't grief and emptiness anymore. It was fear. Mind-numbing terror that made your body scream even before you processed what was happening. The kind of primal fear that your animal brain triggers to keep you alive. And I had to walk into that—my own self-preservation shrieking through my skull that my little bullet-proof vest wasn't going to stop him from shooting me in the head—knowing what I was about to experience so that the criminal would feel it, and this could end without anyone dying. I had to walk into the hell of every person involved and come back out. It's not as easy as I make it sound.

My boys had it down to a science, though. After I did my part and convinced whoever to give up, someone would come to me, walk around so I could see them—know them—and he'd whisper softly little words of comfort and care. I never heard the words, but the voice . . . the voice was nice. He'd lead me back to a patrol car and sit next to me the whole drive. Holding my hand. Always talking. And then I'd go to my safe room.

They made it for me after the first few times out. It used to be a janitor's closet and the only room without drywall, making the building look clean and modern, it was cinder block. Grey cinder blocks. Strong, solid, unbreakable cinder blocks. And he'd come in with me, lock the door—black iron bars drilled into the wall to make it impenetrable—and he'd hold me as I sobbed the fear out onto the floor. This wasn't no little "I feel better now that I've cried" kind of sob. This was a "I can't breathe! I can't breathe! Please, someone for the love of God, please save me!" kind of sob. Eventually they added soundproofing to my room. It was for both our sakes.

So, you see, I wasn't about to leave my boys for people who didn't know me . . . didn't understand what I did. They were my family. They stood with me through everything. I didn't have much else. My parents lived in Georgia, and while I wanted to visit more often, I didn't always have the cash to spare. And after Jacob . . . well, I didn't let anyone in after what happened with him.

It wasn't anything spectacular. No body left in the refrigerator or otherworldly love triangle like the ones the tabloids always invented for the big-named heroes. He's still alive—last I checked; it's been a long time since he left.

We were together ten years. He was a cop, of course, detective actually. Not from my precinct; one of my boys introduced us, though. I was smitten with him the moment I saw him. Beautiful brown skin, head shaved clean, a suit so clean and sharp it could've cut glass. Normally I like a head of hair, but on Jacob . . . I don't believe in love at first sight, but we had lust at first sight, that's for sure. I was in his bed by the end of the week. A lot of people don't like to touch telepaths. They think touching means we can read their minds all the better. Might be true for some, I'm not sure. Jacob never seemed worried about that, though. When I told him I don't use my power on family and friends, he believed me. I think that's what made me fall in love with him.

Back then my biggest fear was people making shit over him being black and me being white. That was still a big thing back then. My parents didn't care. He made me happy, and that's what mattered, but after our first trip down for him to meet them . . . well, my parents started coming up to New York for visits instead. They didn't much like the city, but when there are that many people in one place, a lot fewer care what you're doing at home. Besides, the community knew us, knew what we did for them. Most just left us alone.

So, you're probably wondering what happened. If it wasn't some grand adventure with tragic consequences, what happened that someone who could end gang wars couldn't work through? Funny you ask that. Remember how I said I didn't use my power on family and friends. I had good reason for that. People need boundaries. Need things that are theirs and theirs alone. Knowing everything isn't always better. I'm not talking about cheating or lying. That stuff's cowardly no matter which way you look at it. but sometimes when you fully understand someone, you can't ever see them the same way again.

Our problem was kids. I didn't want them. Told him that up front, and he said he was okay with that. It was going to be the two of us, and it wasn't as if we didn't have enough to deal with between our jobs, our races, and my powers. For nine years we were happy, busy as hell at times, but when we came home and the other was there, take-out dinner laid out on a table like it was a five-star restaurant in our little apartment . . . damn we were happy.

His mother brought it up first. She wanted grandchildren, she said. That was one intense lady when she wanted something. Of course, *now* I know it was his idea; he just didn't want to be the one to start it after all those years. I can't remember how many times we fought. He tried to convince me our jobs didn't matter; we could work around that—his mom would babysit whenever we needed. And sure, what we did was dangerous, but we had a support system in the NYPD.

I still didn't want kids.

He made a financial plan complete with daycare costs and schooling over the years.

I still didn't want kids.

He talked about how great it would be to watch them grow up, give us grandchildren, be there when we're old . . . at the end.

I still didn't want kids.

He even went and talked to other supers! I don't know many other supers. I was never a part of the fancy teams—big or small. Sure, I met a couple of them. Even made some enemies turning one of those billionaires I was talking about back to good after some creature or magic or alien whatnot made him do evil things. Of course, the whole world was going to shit at that point, so not many people actually noticed I helped at all. But that's not the point. He went to people, people he didn't need to go to talk about *our* problems, people who had very different lives and priorities from mine. That was the final straw.

We had it out that night. Rowed for hours. I couldn't understand how this man who loved me, who supported me, who had accepted everything about me without question or fear, suddenly—after ten years—couldn't hear what I was saying . . . what I had always said. This was no bait and switch, not on my part at least. Finally, it was four in the morning, both of us exhausted and with our teeth dug in, so I said the last thing I should've, "Why don't we just see what each other is feeling and be done with this already?"

"That's the first good idea we've had all night," he said. Boy was he wrong.

I never use my power on people I care about. It's *my* rule. I'd never broken it before that moment, and I've never broken it again, either.

I thought I knew everything I needed to know about Jacob. I thought I was prepared to see what was standing between us, ready to be a part of him. We'd been intimate in every other sense. What could my power possibly do other than help us move past this?

We sat across the table from each other and I did my thing. We saw everything, felt everything, understood everything . . . and suddenly we were strangers.

He now knew that there was no argument or plan or wishing that was going to change my mind, and I now knew *that* wasn't something he'd ever considered, even with me saying it all these years. I was a woman, and to him that meant I'd want kids. He thought as we'd get older my biological clock would get a tickin' and one day I'd be all ready to pop out as many super babies as he wanted, because that's what women did when they settled down. He'd always planned on it. In other words, he'd never trusted that I knew my own mind. His acceptance was nothing but a con.

He left after that, not a word said between us. Was moved out by the end of the week. He sent the boys from his precinct over to get his things. He couldn't stand to look at me knowing what we both knew.

As for me, well, I'd experienced betrayal through the eyes of plenty of people throughout my career, but nothing felt like this. I'd been cheated out of my life, my future, and I had no one to go to. So, of course, I went to the only people I could trust anymore. I went to my boys at the station.

I say boys out of habit, but, except for the new ones, most were my age or older at this point. Hennick, he was the first to see me and hurried me right into my safe room before anyone else noticed. I think I might've been a bit of a mess; I can't really remember a lot about that morning. He listened—been through his own divorce by then, so he understood that feeling of betrayal . . . of loss. His situation was a bit more biblical, but he still understood. I realized then that they were the only ones I could trust, so long as I didn't know them perfectly. Maybe not the healthiest way to deal with the separation, but it kept me going. It gave me people to rely on when I needed it.

They say there's still a feud brewing between our two precincts, Jacob's and mine. Back then you'd have thought one of us killed the other for the way our people had our backs. They couldn't even transfer someone from one to the other, not for years. It took me longer to really get over it. Not entirely sure I ever did, but I don't hate him anymore. Not sure what I feel. A little hate. A little love. A lot of regret.

Sometimes I wished I could go back to the me that met him and warn her; the heartache he'd bring wasn't worth the happiness. But it was nearly ten years of happiness and sometimes it was worth it. On those days I wished I could go back to that day we fought and stop myself from using my power. If we'd never learned the truth, if we'd never seen each other laid bare and raw before each other, then maybe we could have worked through it. We would've still had hope. Take it from someone who *knows* people in their worst moments; a little bit of hope can change everything. It's probably for the best I can't go back in time.

But I had my boys at the precinct after that. I had a good job, hard as it was. I enjoyed life. I even got Christmas cards from that billionaire I saved. It always had an open, round-trip ticket for anywhere I wanted. Got to see the world thanks to him. My favorite place to visit was Vatican City. I don't think of myself as the religious sort; but doing what I can do, I need to believe in something, and I like to think someone gave me this power for a reason. Being in that city, so full of beauty and history, it made me feel closer to something . . . something *more* than what's here. Even those of us who can do the impossible need that once in a while. It keeps us from forgetting we can't fix everything no matter how hard we try. After all, *we're* not gods.

So what happened next? Well, I got old. It happens to the best of us. I retired to my little apartment, and spent time with my boys who'd retired, too. Every year I looked forward to my trip, courtesy of the billionaire. Learned to quilt. Found out I wasn't a fan of quilting. I took cooking classes after that. Baking was much more fun than quilting. It was a simple life. After decades suffering other people's pain, simple was kind of nice. Unfortunately even a little super like me doesn't always get to keep it simple, not even when you're old enough that white hair isn't a fashion statement.

You see, some people—or at least what I'm going to call people, they might have been aliens, not entirely sure—they were hoping to turn another one of the big-named superheroes not so good anymore. It's rather surprising how many times that happens to them. Good guys turn bad, bad guys turn good. You need a flow chart just to figure it out sometimes. Anyway, this time it seemed the bad guys actually did pay attention to the fact I fixed that particular problem before. They didn't want to risk me doing it again.

I was no match for people who could take the big superheroes on, but luckily my billionaire friend was doing more than sending me Christmas cards. He saved me. First time I'd seen him since that day.

It must be nice to be a big-name hero. It must've been forty years, yet he looked as young as I remembered him. I don't know if it was magic or money that gave him his youth, but whoever made him look that good was a miracle worker.

He was kind to me. Put me up in a retirement home for supers not worth cloning or resurrecting or whatever science does to keep the big ones going. Since he funded the place, it's comfortable and we got anything we could ask for, including the best security force he could buy, which involved an amazing amount of robots. Most of the people here were more important than me, but not by much, and they like to remind anyone who comes in about what they did. They *love* their nicknames and get mad if you don't use them. It's all too much fuss for me. I prefer to stay on my own. Sometimes I call my boys to catch up, though there aren't as many as there used to be. But then, that's normal for someone my age, super or not. All I want is to finish out my years—simply. That's not too much to ask."

The people in the room, nearly eighty in all, exhaled a collective breath as the withered old woman with thin skin and brown spots took a drink from the cup on the podium in front of her.

The central figure among the line of senators sitting before her adjusted the microphone with a trembling hand. "Ms. Brookshire—"

"Sandy, please. I think a first name basis is okay at this point."

"Ms. Brookshire," he repeated, swallowing. "What did you just do?"

A sly grin stretched her wrinkled lips. "Come now, let's not play the fool. You know what I can do."

The woman next to the flustered senator leaned forward. "I believe what my colleague meant was why did you do that?"

"Because you people don't listen unless it matters to you. Trust me, I lived long enough to know how politicians work. You parade people in to make it seem like you care, like you're considering another option. Cause while you hear, you don't listen. My job was to make people listen, maybe you should have looked into that before you agreed to have me answer your little questions."

"You didn't actually answer our question."

"Now that you're listening, I will." Sandy took another drink. Her medications gave her miserable dry mouth. "You want to know what I think of this little law you're trying to pass. This isn't the first time a politicians has used us as a way to get elected, doubt it'll be the last. People fear us, so they try to control us with rules and legislation that really only makes the fearful feel better at night. But now you know what it's like to be one of us. Now you know most of us are just like you. So I don't need to tell you what I think. You already know. I just hope ninety-five percent of you are decent enough people to act on it. Though, I heard most politicians are sociopaths, so I might be out of luck."

Sandy picked up her cane from where it hung on the edge of the podium and made her way through the silent crowd to her billionaire friend smirking at the back of the room. He might have been a clone— he was younger than she remembered—but who cared at this point? Truthfully, it was best not to know everything about a person.

He held out his arm like a gentleman waiting to escort her to the opera. "I knew you were the right person for the job. I should give you something as a thank you."

She took it, enjoying being on the arm of a handsome man in a three-piece suit, clone or not. "I'd like to see Rome again before I die. It was always nice there."

He smiled. "Anything for you, old friend."

The End

Thunderclouds and Lifelines

Author's Bio

Wendy Nikel is a speculative fiction author with a degree in elementary education, a fondness for road trips, and a terrible habit of forgetting where she's left her cup of tea. Her short fiction has been published in *Deep Magic*, *Daily Science Fiction*, *Nature: Futures*, and is forthcoming from *Analog*. Her time travel novella series, beginning with *The Continuum*, was published by World Weaver Press in 2018. For more info, visit wendynikel.com

Editor's Notes

Ultimately we all know, for good or bad, governments will be governments and they will try to control all they can. Perhaps if there were heroes with powers, it would be best if nobody knew.

Thunderclouds and Lifelines
by
Wendy Nikel

The day Al knocked on the door of our little brick house in the Sandy Hill neighbourhood, it was hailing.

"Dee said you were looking for a boarder!" he yelled over its patter, his hood still obscuring his face. He looked like the kind of guy you'd find lined up in front of the Salvation Army over by Byward Market, but because Dee had sent him, I didn't hesitate to invite him in out of the rain.

He stood a head taller than any of us crowding the narrow foyer — me, my brother Ben, and his latest girlfriend Lacey, who was just leaving for her evening shift at the Royal Oak. She wrinkled her nose as she looked the stranger up and down, standing there dripping onto the hardwood floors in his dark trench coat and hood. He had a duffel bag slung across him, the kind they sold cheap at Canadian Tire, and the shoulder strap pulled tightly against his chest. There was something about his face, about the unsettled look in his eye, that reminded me of myself.

"Friend of yours, Hanna?" Ben asked, reaching around Lacey to offer his hand.

"Friend of Dee's," I said, before the stranger could respond. Fortunately, it was enough of an answer to appease Ben; he's used to my friend's eccentric tag-alongs, even if he's oblivious to the real reason they gravitate to her. I gestured for the stranger to follow me. "There's a private entrance around back, but since the weather's bad, we can go this way."

Al's combat boots fell heavily behind me as we made our way down the back steps to the basement apartment where — till this past week — Ben had lived. It'd been his idea to move back into his undersized childhood nursery upstairs and rent out the lower unit so he'd have some extra cash to spend on Lacey. I'd told him it was stupid to move all his junk upstairs for someone who'd dump him in less than a week. As usual, he failed to appreciate my wisdom.

Hail battered the window as we descended the stairs, and a circle of rain pooled on the ledge near the bottom corner of the pane. I'd have to stop at the hardware store on my way home from work; Ben was useless as a handyman, and the call center that I worked for was just down the block from Home Hardware anyway. It was a boring job, but it paid decently and didn't involve contact with people.

"Hope you didn't have to walk far in this," I said, attempting a bit of small talk. "Or did you have a bike? I didn't see one."

"I walked."

"So," I said as we reached the lower landing, "you know Dee?"

"Yes."

It wasn't the answer I wanted, but I hadn't exactly asked the real question, either. You can't just ask someone, "Hey, are you one of *those* friends of Dee's — one of her strays, like me, whom she sought out because she sensed that you could do things that weren't exactly... normal?"

Regardless, he didn't feel like talking and I rarely do either, so I laid out the terms of our rental agreement, collected his deposit, and worked the apartment key from Ben's key ring, embarrassed that I hadn't thought to separate it from the tacky mudflap-girl key chain earlier. I dropped the key into Al's palm, careful not to graze his skin.

"If you need anything... " I gestured vaguely to the upstairs. "Well, you know where to find us."

Al yawned deeply, and I took that as my cue to leave. But when I turned back a moment later to remind him about rubbish pick-up, I caught a glimpse of something in his open duffel bag, just before he shoved his copy of the rental agreement in over it.

Something that glimmered.

He caught me staring and zipped the bag.

"Garbage on Tuesday," I said quickly. "Plastic in the blue bin, paper in the black, compost in the green."

"Right. Uh… thanks." He hesitated at the door, as if waiting for me to leave.

With a final nod in his direction, I started up the stairs. As soon as he shut the door, though, I stopped midstride and listened, my head cocked toward the wall of the lower unit. I wasn't sure what I was listening for or what clue I thought I'd get about who he was, but the only sound I heard was the creak of mattress springs, followed by complete, utter silence.

Out the window, the hail had stopped, the sky had cleared, and the sun cast rainbow prisms through the etched glass windows.

I didn't see Al again that week. It was a brilliant spring — perfect for biking down to the canal and admiring the tulips cropping up around Parliament Hill — but Al seemed content to remain in the dungeon-like basement, the shades on the single, dust-clouded window always drawn.

"You should invite him up," Ben suggested one evening as we were playing Scrabble. From the TV in the next room, a meteorologist was making his weather predictions for the next week, but neither of us were really watching it; we just liked having it on at night so the house didn't feel so quiet.

"Oh, stop it," I said, laying down my letters. "We both know you're just trying to get out of board game night. H-A-L-C-Y-O-N. Halcyon. Add 'em up, little brother."

"I swear you make half these up," he muttered, but he started adding up my points while I replenished my letter rack. "I'm serious, though. It might be fun to have someone else to hang out with. It gets boring around here."

"You're welcome to invite him up for the next game."

"Guys don't invite other guys over to play board games."

"Sure they do."

Our argument was interrupted by the chiming of Ben's cell phone. He nearly knocked over his letter rack scrambling for it, but whatever was on the screen obviously wasn't what he was hoping to see there, because he tossed it aside without even typing out a response.

Now I knew what his uncharacteristic moping was about. "Lacey's working dinner shift again this week?"

"The tips are better during the evenings, but that means I don't get to see her until this weekend." Ben pressed so hard on the tip of the pencil that the lead broke, and he flicked it away irritably.

I rose from my chair and slid open the junk drawer, shoving aside expired bus passes and broken sunglasses and mix-matched screwdrivers and empty prescription bottles until I found another pencil. Olive green. I slid it to him across the table.

"I'll invite him up," I said. "But you're not getting out of this game. Reset the board while I'm gone, eh?"

"Gladly," Ben said, dumping his letters in the bag. "I had rubbish anyway."

I made it all the way down to the landing, but when I reached the door of the basement unit, I couldn't bring myself to knock. I ran my fingertips along the lines of my opposite palm, considering. What was I doing? I didn't know the first thing about this guy. Dee had been busy all week with some big project at work, and my prying texts to her had gone unanswered. And now I was inviting this stranger into my house? Without knowing who he was or what he could do?

I nearly walked away then, made up some lie about it to Ben (it wouldn't have been the first time), but then I remembered the glimmer I'd seen in his bag and my curiosity got the better of me.

My fist rapped against the door.

When there was no response, I knocked louder and leaned in to try to hear any movement from inside. Outside the window, a gust of wind whistled through the narrow alley and something clattered on the porch. I stood on my tiptoes to peer out the window at my side, trying to see what had been knocked over, but it was impossible to see in the shadows of the streetlights.

When I turned back, the door was open and Al was standing there, towering over me with mussed-up hair and clothing, as if he'd just rolled from bed.

"Geez!" I said, drawing back. "You scared me!"

The frown on his face deepened, but he didn't say anything.

"Sorry," I said. "That is, my brother and I were wondering if you'd like to join us for a game of Scrabble."

Al blinked. "Scrabble?"

"It's a board game? Where you make words? You really haven't heard of Scrabble?"

"I really shouldn't—" He glanced out the window, where the wind had picked up and was scraping a tree branch against the glass. "I need to sleep."

As he opened the door to slip back inside, I caught a glimpse of something on the night table. It had to be the same thing I'd seen in his duffel bag, and if I didn't know any better, I might think looked like a giant, glimmering gemstone the size of a fist. It had to be fake. People didn't actually *own* stuff like that, at least not in this part of the city. But why haul it around if it wasn't of any value?

"Oh. Well, sorry to disturb you," I said as the door closed.

"What's his deal, anyway?" Ben asked the next day. He'd dragged his grill out to the back stoop and, seeing an opportunity to satiate my growing curiosity, I'd invited Dee over, too, along with Kipp, Fluer, and the Dorotti twins — all people she'd introduced me to because of our *unique* abilities. Maybe one of them knew something about our new tenant.

"He's a very private person," Dee said pointedly. Her plastic bracelets jangled on her wrists as she jabbed her finger in my direction. "Swear to me you will not bug him again."

"*Me?* It was Ben's idea."

"Surely he wouldn't object to a neighbourly offer of burgers and beer?" Ben asked.

"Surely he would if you char them." Kipp jerked his mohawked head toward the gray smoke spewing from the grill.

Ben cursed and rushed over to flip the neglected patties. "Seriously, though, I haven't seen the guy leave at all or get delivery in. You're sure he's not starving down there? He's got enough money to buy food, eh?"

"From what I saw, it looked like he could do better than just the occasional takeout," I muttered.

"What do you mean?"

"I saw something in his bag. Something that looked rather… pricey." Over his shoulder, Lacey lifted her eyes from her cell phone and Dee scowled at me. The others exchanged befuddled looks; maybe they didn't know him after all.

"Like what?" Fluer asked.

"I told you: leave him be." Dee said quietly to the both of us, her voice suddenly serious. Then to Ben, she added, "The guy works weird hours; let him sleep. Now, how about that beer?"

"Fine, fine. Lacey, do you want one, too?"

"No," she said, gathering up her purse and checking her reflection in the surface of the grill. "I've got a shift starting soon."

"I thought you had today off?" Ben said, crunching up his face in a befuddled little scowl that made him look five years old all over again.

"Boss just texted. Last-minute thing. I'll call you later."

The rest of us diverted our eyes and Kipp excused himself to grab some more ketchup while the couple said their slobbery, extended good-byes, and then we got back to our more important work of grilling and basking in the sun.

Shortly thereafter, though, the unseasonably warm weather, took a sharp detour. Within minutes the sky went from crystal-clear blue to angry gray, with clouds rolling in from seemingly all directions at once. The Doretti twins shrieked and ran off to the shelter of their van while the rest of us rushed to grab the paper plates before they blew away and the chips before they got soggy.

We were just ducking inside when Al came barreling out the side door, his hair puffed up like he'd just rolled out of bed, and a crease of fury across his brow.

"You said I'd be safe here," he snarled, gesturing up to the darkening sky.

"What the—?" Ben started. "What's going on, man?"

"Why don't you bring this stuff in?" Dee interrupted, shoving a bag of Cheezies into his hands. "Kipp, Fleur, maybe you should head home. We'll take care of this." The others looked at one another and, since no one ever really wants to argue with Dee — especially not in the pouring rain — they did as she ordered. As soon as they had gone, she took Al by the shoulders and shoved him back inside. I quickly followed behind, ducking into the lower unit.

Though I'd gotten a glimpse the previous night, this was my first real look at the apartment since we'd given him the keys. Aside from the empty duffel bag on the floor by the bed and the printout copy of the rental papers I'd given him on the nightstand, not a single thing had been changed. In fact, nothing seemed to have been moved at all, aside from the pillows and blankets on the bed, which were rumpled.

"What happened?" Dee asked.

"It's gone!" Al said, gesturing to the nightstand. The nightstand where, just last night, I'd seen the gemstone.

Dee cursed. "That's why you woke up?"

"Of course that's why. You know how it works."

"Uh... I don't," I said, raising my hand. "Will someone please explain what's going on here?"

Dee frowned, considering. "Take his hand."

I flinched. "You know I don't like to—"

"Just do it." She grabbed my hand and placed it in his. "It'll be quicker than trying to explain."

As soon as my hand touched the lines of his palm, my mind reeled with the mental map of his past. I could see his entire life from his birth to his present, all laid out in the lines of our city, our country, the shipping routes overseas. In the lines of all the places he'd ever traveled. The problem was, unlike most people's maps of the past, Al's didn't extend back a mere twenty-five or thirty years as his appearance would suggest. His extended back thousands of years, and it was punctuated like a thunderstorm with long periods of sleep-filled darkness followed by bursts of violent, destructive light. The Yangtze River flood. Hurricane Katrina. The 2010 Haiti earthquake. And that was just in the last century. Before that, the destruction stretched back all the way to Pompeii.

I pulled away, gasping. "I don't understand..."

"I discovered the crystal millennia ago," Al said, running his fingers through his hair. "It has strong sedative powers that keep me from fully waking. It prevents the things that happen when I do wake, the things I can't control."

"Like the hail the other day and the sudden windstorm last night?"

"Only hundreds of times worse."

"And now someone's taken it," Dee said. "We have to get it back."

Outside, the wind had picked up. A trash can rolled down the street and the flag in the neighbor's yard whipped violently about as if trying to free itself from its pole.

I thought back over the events of the afternoon. There were only two people who'd had the opportunity to take the crystal, and I was pretty certain which one would've done so. The only question was where they would be now.

"Dee, you stay here with Al and... try to keep him calm. I think I know where to find it." All I had to do was get it back before the city experienced the worst storm in its existence.

By the time I threw my bike down against the fence outside the Royal Oak, the rain was coming down in sheets and the newscasters on the TV above the bar were warning everyone to remain indoors. The bridges across the river to Gatineau had all been closed due to high winds and low visibility, and the canal was steadily creeping over the pathways. I was drenched and shivering, but from what I'd seen on Al's map of the past, things would only get worse without that crystal to lull him back to sleep.

Lacey's boss, Roger, was bustling around the restaurant with a tray of beers in one hand and a plate of poutine in the other.

"Lacey?" he asked when I interrogated him. "Nope. She's not scheduled till Tuesday afternoon."

"So you didn't call her in to work a few hours ago?"

"Nope." He placed the tray down in front of a couple of University students. "Let me know if you need anything else, eh?" Then he turned back to me. "She was in here earlier, though to pick up her check."

"Did she say where she was headed?" I didn't even know where the girl lived, and there was no way I was going to tell Ben my suspicions, especially now.

"Look, I don't remember." The man flung his hands out in exasperation. "I'm not her personal message service, and I've got business to do here."

A crack of lightning lit up the windows, and — throwing caution to the wind — I reached out and grabbed Roger's hand, pressing my thumb to the lifeline on his palm.

The man's life spooled out in my mind, and I fought to keep it all from unraveling too far. I only needed the last few hours, those moments that Lacey was here. Finally, I found the place where she entered his pub.

It'd just started to rain, and her hair was a bit damp and she had her purse tucked up under her arm to keep it dry. She asked for her check, and Roger had to dart back into the office to get it while she and her companion waited beside the employee lockers. When Roger returned with the envelope, she was rubbing her arms as if she was cold, and she shoved the check in the back pocket of her jeans, commenting as she headed toward the door, "I have some shopping to do."

I released Roger's hand and stumbled backward toward the door.

"You okay?" he asked, grabbing my arm before I could trip and fall.

"Yeah. Yeah, fine." Shopping. The closest place for a girl like Lacey to get some shopping done was the Rideau Centre, which was just a few blocks away. If I hurried, she might still be there.

Fortunately, the shopping mall wasn't far, because the wind had picked up, sending sheets of rain that pummeled my back and slipped down the neck of my windbreaker as I biked across the University campus, past the old Jail Hostel, and up the Mackenzie King Bridge to Nordstrom. I could barely get the glass doors open, it was pushing so hard against them, and I wondered how Dee was coping with Al back at the house. Inside, I tucked my bike in the entryway; if it was still there when I got back, it'd be a miracle, but I didn't have time to find a place to lock it.

The shops were busy as usual, but I'd seen Ben lugging around her shopping bags enough times to know which were her favorite stores, so I decided to hit those first.

I found her in Michael Kors, trying on a pair of knee-high boots. Over her head, a meteorologist on a flat-screen TV was rambling excitedly at the big blotches of red on his map, but the volume was too low to hear what he was saying.

When she spotted me, panic flashed across Lacey's face, but she recovered quickly. "What are you doing here?"

"Looking for you." I slid onto a seat across from her, trying to figure out an excuse to grab one of her hands, which were currently occupied with the shiny brass boot buckles. Ben didn't even know about what I could do, so there's no way Lacey would, but still, randomly grabbing someone's hand in the middle of a store could potentially cause a scene. "I thought you had to work today."

"Yeah. Must've misread the text."

"That's odd."

She set her jaw and crossed her legs. "What are you *really* doing here, Hanna?"

"Something was stolen from our house this afternoon," I said carefully.

"So? Call the police."

Something flung by the wind, slammed into the skylight above us, and we both jumped.

"I think you know where it is," I said, leaning in and reaching my hand toward hers. "I think you took it."

Lightning flashed overhead, followed almost immediately by a roll of thunder. The lights flickered and went off, and I used that opportunity to grab Lacey's hand and press my thumb into the lifeline on her palm.

My mind reeled, instinctively trying to skip over the recent moments in Lacey's history that involved her relationship with my brother, until it settled in on this afternoon, on the moment when Lacey left the barbeque. I watched as she pulled out the spare key Ben had given her when he'd still lived in the lower apartment and quietly unlocked Al's door. Creeping inside, she'd been drawn to the crystal perched on the center of Al's table like a glimmering centerpiece.

In the real world, Lacey tugged at my hand, shouting something, but I couldn't let go... not until I'd found out what she'd done with it. I scanned her map, following her down the street to the Royal Oak, where she stood near the back room, waiting for Roger to retrieve her cheque.

She pulled away and I opened my eyes. I'd seen enough.

Enough to know what had happened to the gemstone and where to find it, and yet how was I supposed to prove any of it? I couldn't turn her over to the police, not with what little information I had, and not without having to explain how I knew, which for all intents and purposes, was impossible. I couldn't just let her get off scot-free, though.

She clutched her hand. "Ouch! What the hell, Hanna? I'm telling Ben about this."

"Really? You're going to tell him that you were out shopping while you were supposed to be at work?"

Lacey glared at me in the red-tinted light of the emergency exit signs.

Thunder rumbled overhead and rain pounded on the skylight. I desperately wanted to see her get her comeuppance, but I didn't have time for this. Even if I couldn't get her tossed into prison, I could still protect my brother from her lies. Tripping in the darkness and ignoring Lacey's protests raging over the storm, I pushed my way back toward the nearest exit and into the growing storm.

I was wet, shivering, and battered with scrapes from the tree branches that had whipped around me, but the instant I stepped back into Al's apartment, the relief showed visibly on his face. Outside, the wind howled less fiercely and the next crack of thunder lagged well behind the lightning, a reassurance that the storm was finally moving on.

Al cradled the crystal in his hands and barely had time to whisper, "Thank you," before his body went limp with fatigue.

"Whoa, there, big guy," Dee said, scrambling to lend him a shoulder. "Let's get you back in bed."

By the time she returned, the rain had calmed to a gentle patter and the electricity had flickered on. I sat on the back step, staring into the puddles.

"Thanks for that." Dee crossed her arms and leaned against the door frame. "Al would thank you, too, I'm sure, if he wasn't passed out like that."

"That's okay. We'll let the guy sleep."

"How'd you get it back?"

"Once I realized that Lacey must have dumped it in her locker at the Royal Oak, all I had to do was bike back and pry it open. Fortunately, Roger was so busy dealing with the power outage that he didn't even notice me." I kicked a pebble into a puddle. "Why didn't you just tell me, Dee?"

"Tell you what?"

"About what Al could do."

Dee sat beside me and stretched out her legs, crossing one Converse-clad foot over the other. "Would you have wanted to share a roof with someone with that kind of power?"

"No," I admitted.

"Well, considering all he's been through, he'd probably have felt the same about you."

The creak of the door announced Ben's arrival. "Looks like the storm's over."

Dee rose to her feet. "I'd better get going; you two have quite a bit to talk about."

"What's she mean by that?"

"Have a seat, little brother." I patted the step beside me, and he plopped himself down as I gathered my thoughts and tried to figure out where to start.

"What's this all about?" he asked.

"Your girlfriend's a thieving liar. And she's cheating on you."

Ben exhaled deeply, but didn't argue or object.

"You knew?" I asked.

"I suspected. Roger never gives anyone that many hours, and when I dropped by to see her the other night, she wasn't there."

"Why didn't you do anything about it?"

"I suppose it's easier, the less you know about other people's secrets."

I ran my left thumb along the lifeline of my right palm and stared at the puddles reflecting sunlight on the pavement. "Yeah. I suppose it is."

We sat there in silent companionship until the last of the thunderclouds receded.

The End

The Stories We Are Made Of

Author's Bio

Jamie Gilman Kress writes stories across the whole spectrum of fantasy and science fiction, sometimes with brief forays into horror. Her work has been chosen for Daily Science Fiction, IGMS, and UFO 7. She plans to continue adding to that list. When not lost in worlds of her own making Jamie lives in Upstate NY where she enjoys tabletop role-playing games, reading, and converting her backyard into a suburban wildlife preserve. So far she's spotted birds, bunnies, and one very bold groundhog. She can also be found spending time with her husband and her dog. Not always in that order. If you want to keep up to date on Jamie's publications, her website is www.jamiegilmankress.com or you can find her procrastinating and commenting on the pets of other writers on Twitter at @JamieGKress.

Editor's Notes

The Stories We Are Made Of explores the idea that maybe we all have a little power, if we only know where to look.

The Stories We Are Made Of
by
Jamie Gilman Kress

Kayla expected her biggest challenge, when she agreed to pet sit for her brother to be not getting mauled by the cat. She didn't even believe in magic, much less anticipate running afoul of it. Unfortunately for her, ignorance provided no protection from its subtle manipulations.

Still, the events that changed her life started simply. Kayla shuffled into the lobby of Braden's building with her two battered suitcases and decade-old backpack held together with duct tape and old hand-sewn patches. The two older women, both immaculately garbed in designer sundresses and wearing impractical shoes designed to turn ankles and produce bunions, stopped mid-conversation to stare as Kayla approached the front desk. The electric weight of their regard tingled against her skin like agitated bees.

The one on the right, aggressively blond with the taut, stretched out look of too many facelifts, cleared her throat and snapped her fingers at the balding man who stood behind the obsidian wall of the counter. "There's a stray." Before the man even looked up, Blonde Woman waved a hand in Kayla's direction as if flicking away a bug. "Probably some wandering drunk. We really need better security to keep out the riffraff."

Kayla paused as a cold tingle washed over her that left her skin abuzz. The mean blonde seemed to glitter and shine with an eerie red haze from the corner of Kayla's eye. Weird and more than a little disorienting; she shook her head hard.

Tucking a strand of cotton candy pink hair behind one ear, shoulders back and head high, Kayla tried to put on her best sunny smile, but twenty-two hours of traveling had left it wilted around the edges. "My name's Michaela Eisen. My brother Braden is expecting me?"

A third woman emerged from the elevator. Younger and too thin, she moved in a wide circle around the others, shoulders tucked in and head down. Through dark hair that hung like a shroud around her face, the newcomer's eyes flicked towards Kayla, going wide and oddly hungry before darting away once more to lock on the floor. She scurried out the door and away so fast she might have been a mirage.

The desk attendant's smile turned rictus tight. "Of course, ma'am. We were told to expect you. Will you be needing help with your bags?"

"Please." Kayla ended up standing near the pair of women as she approached the desk to take the keycard offered in exchange for an extra-long examination of her ID.

The blonde woman sniffed and turned away. Kayla considered saying something, but neither a saccharine pleasantry nor pointedly snarky retort came to mind in time. Probably for the best. Braden wouldn't thank her for starting a war with his neighbors right as he left to fight tuberculosis in Cambodia.

Furious whispers followed Kayla all the way to the elevator. The buzzing on her skin grew more intense.

Braden met her at the door with a cold glass of iced green tea and long, heartfelt hug. "Hey, stranger," he said with a grin as he pushed the glass in her hand and looked her over. "You're looking good. You have some actual meat on your bones for once. I don't suppose you've thought about—"

"Don't."

"Kayla, it's been over a year."

Kayla turned away and took a long swallow of her tea, letting the sweetness of honey coat the bitter bile on her tongue. Braden meant well, but he didn't understand—couldn't understand how much she'd lost. Any words she used would be sharp with pain, so she just drank the tea and as her silence stretched into awkward tension, Braden cleared his throat and moved further into the apartment. "So, I really appreciate you house-sitting for me. It's impossible to find someone Lady Tinklebutt won't scare off."

Kayla twisted her lips into an impersonation of a smile. "Your cat I can handle. Your neighbors on the other hand, not so much."

Braden sighed. "Older blonde, bit of a snob?"

"That's the one."

"Caroline." He shook his head and hefted her bag as he moved towards the guest room. "Most of the folks in this building are very nice, but Caroline is, well, not. Just ignore her."

"Does her grand dame sidekick have a name, too?" Kayla put her glass down and rubbed her arms. The strange tingling refused to stop.

"Helena. Nice lady. She's always watering people's plants or collecting their mail. No idea why she puts up with Caroline, but I suppose someone has to." Braden tilted his head and frowned. "You okay? You look a little flushed."

"Fine." Knowing Braden would bounce from health concerns to life plans, Kayla hurried on before he could ask anything else. "And the weird one that skits around like something out of a horror movie?"

"Jackie." He looked down, eyes sad. "She seemed so vivacious and motivated when she moved in a few months ago, but then—she just changed. Happened practically overnight. Rumors say she's a druggie, but I've never seen any track marks or other signs of it. It's weird. But, she stays to herself. You should be fine."

Kayla started to nod, but a sudden nausea swept over her, the whole world going hazy around the edges.

Braden immediately sat beside her, fingers already checking her pulse. "Kayla, are you sure you're okay? You look—have you been drinking?"

"Course not." Her head lolled to rest on his shoulder. "Just sleepy. Long trip."

"Well, let's get you to bed then." He hoisted her up and helped her to the guest room.

Kayla remembered little of the rest of the evening other than vague flashes of his worried face as he watched over her.

Gum and grit welded her eyes closed as Kayla struggled to wake up. Pressure throbbed at her temples, a short movement of pain that rapidly swelled to fortissimo when she finally wedged her eyes open and sunlight poured in.

It felt like a hangover, but Kayla had only ever drank to excess once—the day Dr. Markham told her the car accident had shattered her ankle. With surgery she'd walk again, he'd said, but it'd never regain full stability. Less than a year after becoming a principle dancer her career ended.

Dance had been her whole life for over twenty years. Without it she didn't know what to do with herself, who to be. So, she'd gotten drunk, dyed her hair, and gained fifteen pounds. She'd even gotten a tattoo. A pair of pink pointe shoes on her damaged ankle.

None of which explained the pounding headache and overwhelming desire to guzzle water straight from the tap until her mouth stopped feeling like the Sahara. Nor did it get food into Lady Tinklebutt's pretty little lacquered bowl, and Kayla really needed the rotund seal-point Siamese to quit yowling directly in her ear before something started bleeding. So, slowly, with the stiff jerky movement of an eighty-year old arthritic, she rose from the bed and shambled towards the kitchen, only to be derailed by a polite rapping at the front door.

Toeing the cat out of the way, Kayla cracked the door, ready to tell whatever busty brunette outside expecting to call out Braden that they'd be waiting a long time. His flight had left early that morning. He'd woken her to say good-bye and check her vitals one more time.

Instead, Kayla found herself looking up at the wannabe ballet mistress from the night before. The woman stood barefoot in the hall, her feet sinking deep into the thick burgundy carpet, gray-streaked hair left loose to the shoulder, and wearing a simple wrap dress of vibrant turquoise. In her hands she held a silver scallop-edged serving platter on which rested a shallow bone china dish with two white tablets inside. A matching plate held a slightly overripe banana, and near that was an unopened bottle of sparkling artisanal water.

"Good morning," the woman said, each word spoken with a careful precision and rich Slavic accent that marked English as a second language, "I am Helena. Caroline spoke that you were much drinking. I thought this to help."

Kayla frowned down at the tray then back up at the older lady. Pain pulsed around her temples as the blue-cast light of the hall hit her eyes. "Thanks, but I don't drink."

"Caroline say," Helena cast her eyes down to the tray, "you do."

"Well," Kayla caught the listing tray, scrambling to keep the fragile dish hand-painted with delicate blue forget-me-nots from tumbling to the ground, "Caroline is wrong."

Helena shook her head, her hair scraping the silk at her shoulders with a sound like the whispers of ghosts. Abandoning the tray to Kayla's keeping, the woman simply wandered away, the broken words she spoke hanging in the hall behind her. "Caroline say. You do."

Braden had booby-trapped his apartment, little landmines waiting in every corner to trip Kayla up. In the kitchen, tucked behind the emergency numbers and Chinese take-out menus, she found a partially completed job application for a teaching position at some strip-mall dance school she'd never heard of; on the pristine snow white walls he'd mounted professional shots of famous ballerinas, from Anna Pavlova through Misty Copeland, each protected in stark modernist frames of black glass.

In the guest room closet she found her pointe shoes. They hung from their wide ribbons, perfect fabric-recreations of blue and lavender gladiolus—her favorites—tucked into each toe.

Kayla slammed the closet door and stormed out. She needed fresh air. As she emerged from the elevator into the lobby Caroline greeted her with a sniff and the snide, "Little early for a bender, isn't it?"

The words trailed after Kayla as she hit the glass doors. Her skin buzzed.

Stumbling up to the apartment building Kayla struggled to remember where she'd gotten the brown bag clutched in her fist. She remembered stopping at a convenience store for a bottle of soda, and that the clerk insisted on putting it in a plastic bag even though she hadn't wanted one.

Distracted, Kayla tripped on the curb and tried to catch herself without releasing the bottle. She overbalanced, her bad ankle buckling and sending her down to sprawl on a patch of rain-soaked grass in front of a massive stone building. Pain lanced through her leg and sent bright flashes dancing behind her eyes. They reminded her of stage lights. She fumbled the lid off the plastic soda bottle in its inexplicable brown paper coffin. Her skin buzzed. Whiskey heat coursed down her throat, but the tears streaming down her cheeks burned more.

Through the sodium glow of night men in suits and women in fancy dresses, streamed by like ensemble dancers flowing away from the stage after a major number. Whispers and snippets cascaded from the crowd to fall like hail around Kayla, but not a single person stopped to help her. Most refused even to look in that direction, as if she'd become invisible.

But then, hadn't she? Kayla slumped against the wall, residual heat from the blistering day leaching from the bricks and somehow leaving her even colder. She took another drink.

Sometime between the bottle being half full and all gone, Helena and her judgmental blonde warden—Caroline, Queen of the Upper East Side Snobs—wandered by where Kayla remained huddled against the building.

"God." Caroline prodded at Kayla's leg with the toe of her Jimmy Choo pump, nose wrinkled and lips curled in a sneer. "Look at her. She's even worst than Jackie, and that one's probably dead in a ditch somewhere. I tell you, they're all worthless."

Kayla said nothing, just gazed into the void at the mouth of her Jack Daniels. Hard to argue with the truth.

Caroline strode away, but Helena lingered, hand darting into the large tote clutched at her side. She withdrew from it a newspaper, age-yellow and smelling faintly of earth and smoke, and held it out to Kayla. "I found for you. A gift."

Pickled brain sluggish, Kayla took it by habit. The pages crinkled like dead leaves in her clumsy fingers. A half-page picture assaulted her, one of Kayla herself, in the costume she'd worn while playing Princess Aurora in *Sleeping Beauty*, the same outfit that included the pointed shoes that still hung from the closet bar in Braden's guest room. It'd been her last role—and only one as a principal—before the accident.

Her stomach flipped, every nerve vibrated as she stared at the image. She looked strong and proud and resplendent. The whiskey bottle slipped from her hand and bounced, plastic once more, as she clutched the picture close, the fragile paper pressed like a kiss against her cheek.

As Kayla sobbed, Helena waited, and when the tears ran dry, she wordlessly offered a hand. Kayla took it and rose.

Helena's studio apartment looked like a Bed and Breakfast exploded all over a fairy tale. Twisted vines of dark green ivy crawled over damask rose wallpaper and vases of phosphorescent mushrooms in ornate urns rested on lace doilies. Heavy velvet curtains hid the neon signs outside, the only light coming from table lamps in the shape of roosters.

"You sit." Helena pointed to an overstuffed recliner with a throne-like frame. "I get tea."

Eyes itchy and nose stuffed from crying, Kayla collapsed into the chair with a heavy sigh. She tried to toss the picture aside, but instead found herself staring at it, chest tight. "I don't understand. Where did you get this?"

"Not hard to find if you look." Helena frowned, brown eyes glinting with an odd sheen in the dim light. The delicate blue china tea set she carried seemed to grow from dollhouse to full size as she set it down. "Is big accomplishment, this thing you do."

"Did," Kayla spat as she tore her gaze from the photo. "I can't dance anymore."

Helena shrugged. "In Old Country people ask for my help. Bring gifts. Here I just forgotten old woman. But, still I try to help. Is who I am. Is dancer who you are?"

"It was." Kayla sunk deeper into the chair, knees pulled up to her chest and hair hiding her face. "But now, I don't know who I am without ballet."

Helena put a gentle hand on Kayla's arm. "Better you figure out soon or Caroline decide for you."

Kayla considered that in silence, time stretching like taffy. She no longer felt drunk, hadn't since she took Helena's hand. Still, a weight hung against her skin like humidity, the faintest tingle that might become a buzz at any second. It seemed impossible, but somehow Caroline changed things. Changed *her*. "How is she doing these things to me, Helena? Why are you always with her? What is she?"

"I must stay. Caroline says." The older woman nudged a cup of lavender-scented tea closer. "She is from Old Country like me, but she remember only the gifts lost, not her purpose. She is lost, help no one now."

While searching for the kitty litter, Kayla found another of Braden's traps. A picture of Kayla onstage, her pink and gold Sleeping Beauty costume a sharp contrast to the black glass frame just like the ones on the wall. Stacked on top of it were a dozen photos from their childhood: dance recitals, rehearsals, Halloween snaps with her in a tutu because she always went as a ballerina. The last one showed her as a toddler, years before she'd ever stepped in a studio, barely out of diapers and spinning in circles, arms wide and smile wider.

How long had it been since she'd danced for the sheer joy of it? When had dancing come to mean only ballet and ballet started being a competition? For years she had been focused on the practical results: mastering the moves, getting the roles, becoming a principle. But, it hadn't started that way; those things hadn't been the reasons she danced. She danced because she loved it. She *still* loved it. And she'd lost sight of that long before the accident.

As she stared at the photo a tightness twisted in her gut and her skin began to buzz. World tilting and blurring, she did the only thing she could; She thrust her arms out and twirled. Laughing and chasseing as Lady Tinklebutt twined around her legs, Kayla barely noticed when the buzzing stopped.

When Kayla emerged from the elevator the next morning police and residents were strewn about the lobby like cliques of dancers after a hard class. Fevered whispers buzzed from every corner, and over it all one voice carried.

Caroline. She and Helena stood by the desk, currently manned only by an overlarge flower arrangement. "I knew she'd end up like this. Didn't I tell you so last night, Helena?"

The world slowed and Kayla moved towards the two women like a bug fighting through sap. She didn't want to ask. If she asked Caroline would answer, and her words would make it real. But Kayla pushed forward anyway. Her first attempt to speak produced nothing but a raw squeak, but on the second try Kayla said, "What happened?"

Caroline turned her body away, the sickly vanilla of her perfume sending Kayla's already unsettled stomach into spasms. It was Helena who answered. "Jackie gone, poor girl. Is much sad."

The loud snort from Caroline turned several heads, but the woman only snorted again, louder. "She was a junkie and a whore. The world's better off without her, and," Caroline craned her neck around to sneer at Kayla, "all the other trash littering up this place."

Cold tremors washed through Kayla's body as her skin began to tingle, but she cleared her throat and stepped forward. This woman had the power to change the world, and she used it for nothing but petty bitterness. It made Kayla so sad. And so very, very angry. "I'm not trash." Her voice cracked and trembled, so she said it again, louder. "I am not trash."

Caroline turned arms crossed tight as a vice and lips pinched almost to nonexistence. "You're whatever I say you are, stupid girl." She pushed her chin forward, and her tobacco and mint breath blew across Kayla's face. "Don't you know who I am?"

"Sure." Kayla said as she plucked a perfect white lily from the bouquet on the desk. "You're a vindictive old woman mad that world's forgotten you." She took a deep breath and stretched her spine, frame strong and steady. "And you don't matter." Her ankle trembled slightly, but it took her weight and held.

Maybe not enough to dance professionally, but more than enough to stand tall. "What I am, who I am, that's not determined by bad luck or what I can't do. And it's sure as hell not decided by you. So," she tucked the flower into her hair and offered Helena her arm, "you'll have to excuse us. We have better things to do with our lives than listen to you."

Behind her she heard Caroline sputtering. Speechless.

The End

Miss Johnson's Boy

Author's Bio

As readers may surmise from this story, Ken Altabef is a retired obstetrician and biologist. His short fiction has appeared professionally in Fantasy & Science Fiction, Interzone, Daily Science Fiction, Intergalactic Medicine Show, and others. He is the author of eight published novels including the epic arctic fantasy ALAANA'S WAY. You can preview these novels and other work at his website: www.KenAltabef.com

Editor's Notes

What if someone understood where to look, what to do, and had the power to share it with others? What might they accomplish?

Miss Johnson's Boy
By
Ken Altabef

Notoriety, I find, often comes in strange and unexpected ways. It is not always welcome. At least, not by me. But I can't deny that I had a part, however small, in an event that may well change the course of human history.

I don't usually disclose information about my patients, even with their permission, but maybe this account will stop the endless tide of reporters parading across my doorstep and trampling through my life.

Suffice it to say that I am a practitioner of medicine, a specialist in Obstetrics and Gynecology, and that Miss Johnson was my patient.

"Aprosencephaly," I repeated slowly, although from her persistently vacant expression I could tell the word meant even less to her the second time. She said nothing.

"It's a kind of birth defect," I explained. "The brain is not properly formed." I motioned to the ultrasound images hanging on the backlit window-box but knew they would mean little to her. Naomi glanced furtively at them as she would an incomprehensible work of modern art. Except it wasn't art; it was a nightmare.

"I don't understand," she said calmly. "Not formed?"

"It's not there. It just never developed. Part of the brain is missing."

Her full lips pursed a bit, but that was all. "So what do we do?" she asked, still calm, still heartened by an irrefutable faith in modern medicine. Technology, the grand god of our age, could fix anything, right?

I sighed. "I'm sorry, but there isn't anything we can do, Naomi."

I waited for the inevitable next questions which, in my experience, would demand to know how this type of thing could possibly happen and why did it have to happen to her, but she surprised me, remaining silent. I could sense the gears mashing inside her skull, turning over the lessons a hard life had already taught her. She already knew the answer. Bad things happen. It didn't matter who you were.

"This is a terminal condition, Naomi," I said gently but firmly. "The part of the brain that's missing is responsible, among other things, for respiration. The baby cannot survive."

"My baby..."

"Is going to die. Yes, that's what I'm saying." I felt I must be absolutely clear on this.

"I'm sorry," I added again, passing her a small box of tissues to staunch the flow of tears that had inevitably begun. I couldn't help lending a passing thought to my own two sons, now fully grown, each successful family men and content with their lives, both perfectly healthy.

At twenty weeks she was already halfway through the pregnancy, but there was still time. I doubted my next suggestion would sit well with her. A small silver crucifix stared determinedly at me from the front of her neck. I knew her to be a strict Baptist, but I felt a duty to bring it up.

"Most people in your situation would terminate the pregnancy," I said. "If you want, I can refer–"

"No, Doctor. I couldn't do something like that. Never." And just like that the tears stopped, the eyes narrowed, and her small face grew hard. I felt as if I had just become the enemy.

"Not under normal circumstances, of course," I quickly added. "But knowing that the baby can't survive, this wouldn't really be considered an abortion."

"I couldn't do that," she whispered again.

"Okay," I said tentatively. "Are you going to be all right?" When I had inquired about the father of the baby at her initial prenatal visit, he was described simply as 'long gone.' In my clinic patient population that most often meant in jail, as opposed to 'out of the picture' which stood for having simply run off. She always came alone to her visits, a passenger on the mid-town bus. I wanted to ask about her family, to find out if she had a supportive mother or a doting Aunt Minnie to lean on, but it was a delicate moment.

Other than the expected shock and grief, she seemed to be in control. She wiped her face one last time, stood and smoothed her skirt.

"Yes, I'm fine," she said. "I'll just go straight home now."

I asked her to return in a week so we could talk more about the situation, and she agreed. In time I would make her see reason.

I was not looking forward to Miss Johnson's next visit; in fact I began the morning with a pang of dread when I noticed her name on the day-sheet. Despite appearances, doctors aren't made out of stone and I had no way of keeping the overwhelming sadness of her situation from bleeding over onto me. There was a human tragedy in progress and I was powerless to do anything about it. I felt helpless. And I was.

So I dreaded that next visit, which was unusual. Naomi Johnson had been my patient for five or six years. I had developed a fondness for her that stemmed not so much from the fact that she was young and quite pretty, qualities which honestly meant little to me, but from her mild and unassuming nature. After thirty years of dealing with people every minute of every day one cannot help but develop a certain ability to judge character. It takes all of thirty seconds into the initial interview for me to know what a woman is really made of, be it sugar, spice, or things which aren't always quite so nice. Naomi was a solid, good person. She had not one wit of deception in her, not a shred of bigotry or presumption. I admired those unusual qualities, and felt a stab of pity for her as well. Thus far the fates had been less than kind to her. There was a past history of ineptitude and desertion on the part of her parents, and abuse by various men. I knew how hard it could be for a single mother, especially in small-town Virginia, and yet she had managed to keep hold of an unrelenting optimism. Naomi had never completed a high school education but she was honest and she was brave. She was not the brightest cloud in the sky, but at least it was an unusually sunny sky.

Before she arrived I put up the sonographic images of her baby's brain again. Then I took them down. She didn't need to see them again.

After the opening pleasantries and the routine measurements, the conversation turned toward the situation at hand. Such tragedies always weigh heavily on me, perhaps all the more so when taken in the context of the hundreds of joyful births I've participated in. It was like a crushing weight, this horrific injustice leveled against the little life inside of Naomi Johnson, a person who would never even be allowed the slightest chance to live.

Her will was as stone, immovable. Naomi would not hear of terminating this pregnancy. She insisted that her baby seemed fine, that it was becoming increasingly more active with the kicks stronger by the day. I explained that inside the womb the baby was not required to breathe; the mother supplied oxygen in the bloodstream directly. But once born it would never be capable of living on its own, not be able to move its arms or legs, and would have a life span of only three minutes at most.

I must not have explained it properly, must not have made the situation clear. Naomi was much too calm; none of it made any difference to her. I fleetingly wondered if she wasn't smart enough to understand. When faced with a situation in which there is no hope, one has no choice but to surrender. Or maybe her obstinacy was because she was all alone. Was the idea of a pregnancy itself filling a need? If that's all it was, then how much worse would she feel afterward, after the baby was gone?

I told her that some of these aberrant cases can involve complications, excessive blood pressure, toxemia, even possibly seizures in the mother, and then I stopped. What was I doing? I was so desperate to make her see my point of view, even to the extreme of exaggerating the risks.

She stared at me dumbly, as if I were beating at her with a stick.

"Well, maybe it's not as bad as all that," I allowed, "but there are certain risks, not to mention discomforts, in going to term. It just seems pointless to continue."

"It's not pointless at all," she said.

"I'm still getting the sense that you don't quite understand..."

She looked me straight in the eye. "No, Doctor, you're the one who doesn't understand. You said the baby can't live on his own, that once he's born I have to watch him die. I believe you. But right now, my baby is alive. I feel him moving inside me. He's alive and with me. For now." She smiled softly at me, and now it was my turn to wear a stupefied stare. "What's it like for him in there?" she asked, "I imagine it must be pretty nice. Warm and safe. Maybe that's the best part of someone's life. It's impossible to explain, but I sense a feeling of contentment, even happiness."

"I see," I said, in a dry tone that was far from convincing.

"I'm his mother as long as he's inside me. I'm his lifeline. The next few months may be all he's going to have, but I won't take that away from him."

I was stunned. It took a few more seconds for this top-of-his-class doctor to see the logic of his uneducated and simple patient. Her position did make a kind of sense, although steeped in a sticky bittersweet syrup. I admired her for that. Naomi had a creative way of looking at things, even if painfully unrealistic. Such a thought would never have occurred to me, but I realized that what I took for futile, senseless emotionalism was indeed something much deeper. So I smiled at her and assured her that if she decided to go through with it (for whatever reason) I would be right there with her, every step of the way. We went from there.

At her next visit things began to take on a disturbing cast. The pregnancy was going fine; her lab tests were normal, her weight gain just right, and she was still fairly comfortable except for some obligatory lower back pain. Naomi bore the discomforts with a brave face, as expectant mothers usually do. She delighted in the baby's ever-strengthening movements and the frequent bouts of hiccups that are common at this stage when the diaphragm is in development. There was a certain joy in being pregnant, even in a situation such as this, and it was not lost on her.

She asked the usual questions. What position was best for sleeping, was it okay to swim in the local pool, should she increase her intake of calcium? The visit was just about ended when I read a sharp note of uncertainty in her deep brown eyes. Just then I realized how tired she looked; her sweet face had grown lean and drawn with fatigue.

"There's one other thing," she said. "I'm not sure if this is normal..."

She hesitated, not looking directly at me, and I noted a subtle flush of embarrassment color the chestnut brown of her cheeks. "He speaks to me sometimes, the baby does."

That statement startled me. She had up to this point been so levelheaded about everything. "You mean you hear voices?"

"No, not voices. Just my baby..."

A shiver went down my spine. This was not the type of thing a doctor likes to hear. A string of unwanted associations, bad situations I had witnessed firsthand within my lifetime as a practicing obstetrician, came flooding into my mind: pregnant patients held in restraints on the psych ward; a psychotic patient undergoing florid hallucinations during labor; one case that required shock therapy. How desperately I wanted to spare Naomi all of that. "Can you explain?"

"He knows what I'm thinking. I've felt like he's been tuning in for a while now. I guess he didn't know how to respond before... but he's been learning, listening in on everything that happens. And every once in a while he makes a little... whispers, like comments to me." She laughed. "You probably think I'm crazy or something, right?"

I smiled as paternally as I was able. She didn't know how close to the truth she had come. Normally, I would feel obligated to discuss a psychiatric evaluation with patients who express these types of concerns. But I wasn't going to do it here. I understood that she was grieving, that even now she was mourning the inevitable loss of a child and that made all the difference. How many times had I heard that a deceased loved one was hovering about in the ether, smiling down and watching over their surviving relatives? Such ridiculous delusions were considered perfectly acceptable and even comforting during such trying times. I decided to let it pass. I made sure she didn't have any other psychiatric symptoms and then asked her to return in a week.

Naomi hesitated at the doorway, and turned back. "He sees through my eyes," she said. "He likes the TV. He always wants me to watch the news. He can't seem to get enough – sometimes he kicks me to keep me awake." She reported these events with a smile, informed with the enthusiasm of a proud mother.

"It's a boy, you know," she said. "I've decided to name him Adam."

Of course now I wish I could substantiate this account with a corroborative written record, but I made no notes in her chart about her bizarre revelation. If a social worker or lawyer ever needed to review her records, I didn't want a few off-the-cuff statements to potentially cause her trouble. Besides, I knew Naomi Johnson well enough and knew she was anything but crazy. I hoped the whole issue would just blow over, and never be mentioned again. And yet her story nagged at me.

After she had gone, I dug out the ultrasound images from her file. I had been targeting the intracranial anatomy during the exam. The forebrain was clearly absent, replaced in part by a large fluid-filled cyst, but the rest of the brain was also distorted – not simply shifted out of place by the missing tissue as one might expect – but markedly abnormal. What kind of aberrant functioning might that brain have? I was no neurosurgeon but I had learned enough in medical school to know that science doesn't understand one tenth of what our gray matter actually does. Was telepathy possible? I believed it was. Could this kind of morphology result in telepathy? No one could know.

The sonogram also confirmed it was a boy. Sidetracked by the momentous issue of the birth defect, I'd never gotten around to telling her. And yet she said she knew. Of course that didn't mean anything. Everybody and their aunt has an opinion on the sex of a baby. Fifty-fifty odds.

During her next few visits we went through the usual procedures as if nothing were wrong, she made no mention of the telepathy, and I didn't ask about it. Naomi was her usual pleasant self. She had a certain degree of apprehension regarding the labor since it was her first time, but that was definitely normal. She spoke glowingly about the fetus inside of her and its sometimes-painful acrobatic antics and that was normal too. She could pretend there was nothing wrong with the baby if it made things easier for her, but we both knew that wasn't true.

At her 36-week visit, I decided to broach the subject again, not so much out of duty to my patient but from an overwhelming curiosity.

Once I mentioned it, she became surprisingly talkative.

"He's very fluent now. Talks most of the time. He's got a lot of interesting ideas about all kinds of things. It's funny," she said with a slightly embarrassed chuckle, "it's like I'm not teaching him anymore. He's teaching me."

Now I regretted asking. I also regretted my gross negligence in this matter. I had ignored a bad situation and let it get worse. Just looking at her, it was obvious she had been going for long periods without sufficient sleep. She'd developed an entire delusional reality built around this magically-endowed fetus of hers. She was clinically diagnosable! She was also full-term, a ticking time-bomb that could go into labor at any moment. After she delivered I was sure this would all go away, but what was I going to do in the meantime? Should I just wait it out? I felt like I was covering up a mistake, ignoring a problem, and in medicine that course of action is always an error. What I needed was more information. "Why don't you keep a journal," I suggested. "Write down the kinds of things he says. I know I'd be interested in seeing them."

She hesitated, as if not willing to share this secret part of her life with anyone else. Then her expression changed completely and she began nodding and smiling. "He likes the idea," she said.

A few days later Naomi called. The nervous excitement in her voice told me she was in labor even before the words reached my end of the line. She thought her water had broken and there were contractions every five minutes. I remember leaving for the hospital immediately. Snow was coming down in big lazy flakes, the kind that are eager to clump together, and would quickly pile up. The roads were slick but I drove faster than was practical. Despite the pristine white swirls that sought to blanket the night in peaceful beauty, I knew what a horror show this was going to be. I wanted to get it over with as quickly as possible.

I admitted her to Mercy Hospital. Her labor was not a difficult one and for that I was grateful. Naomi proved to be as brave and strong as I had known she would be. She followed my instructions to the letter, she pushed well, and in just under three hours, I had the baby out. He was small for full term, with the head disproportionately large, which I attributed to the cyst in the skull. The facial features were mildly distorted with a predominant brow, low-set ears and an upturned pug nose. I cut the cord in silence; the baby did not breathe. He could not cry.

"It's a boy!" I exclaimed, but with quite a bit less than my usual enthusiasm. The pediatrician shot me a grim glance, shaking his head.

The pastor performed an emergency baptism with just one sentence. The need for expedience was well known to us all. Elapsed time: one and a half minutes.

We wrapped him in a warm blanket and lay him at his mother's breast. She coddled and cooed as any new mother would, but he was by then motionless. After a short while, she looked up. "He's gone," she said. As I was still busy wrestling with a stubborn placenta, the pediatrician pronounced the baby dead.

So that was the way it happened, but the story of Adam Johnson does not end with his death. Nothing I had witnessed in my career could have prepared me for what came next. Naomi had taken my advice and kept a journal of what she considered to be the baby's thoughts and opinions, feverishly filling it up in the last few days prior to her delivery. It was easy reading, written in simple terms with the lack of skill one might expect from a high-school dropout, but she gave the baby the by-line, claiming she was merely the ghostwriter. It's a short book, consisting of a unique social analysis from an unlikely but very unbiased source. It is a book born of one woman's determination to let her son have his small chance at life, and that son's desperate need to contribute in whatever small way possible and in what short time, what pitifully short time, allowed him.

Some people claim that within that slim volume is the answer to all of our problems, and I happen to think they're right. Within a few weeks Naomi's book was a bestseller in America and spread quickly throughout the Western World, its popularity fueled by internet versions available widely and at no cost. The Russians and Japanese have embraced it wholeheartedly and the Chinese translation is just now becoming wildly popular. Adam Johnson has become a phenomenon.

The book speaks eloquently and clearly, not through parable or metaphor, and the message is a simple one, and could be practically summed up in one phrase: share with one another. Share all that you have, not just your possessions but share yourself in all things. The end result is simple: the world can be a paradise for everyone. Of course I realize this message has been espoused before and by far greater and more noteworthy men than Adam Johnson, but little Adam Johnson went those great men one better. He tells us exactly how to do it, mapping out the process in a step-by-step fashion with a geopolitical awareness that far exceeds anything Naomi Johnson could have devised. The book is a roadmap to Paradise, deftly circumventing existing political tensions in a quest for peace and understanding.

The idea is a basic lesson we strive to teach each child by the age of two or so, but can't seem to learn for ourselves, but there was nothing simple about the intricate web of details, compromises and accords necessary to bring about the outcome. Mankind has never been very good at denying its consumptive self-interest, and even now, when a civilized country will burn excess grain in order to keep the price up while half the world starves, our selfishness is appallingly apparent. Perhaps from his unique perspective Adam Johnson could see what we, mired in the complexities of modern life, of cell phones and deadlines and lay-away payments, consistently fail to grasp. A simple truth. An essential one.

People everywhere have embraced the message, forming for themselves what can only be described as a sort of secular religion. Some are fanatic about it, and in our current age of telecommunication almost everyone is at least familiar with it. There is no mention of God or religious fervor. This is a religion of Man. Adam Johnson left us no one to worship except each other.

'Start with the food,' suggested the boy, and they are doing just that. I have a feeling when this thing really takes off there will be no stopping it.

The world is changing. The message is spreading and people are taking it seriously. Organizations have been set up, billionaires are donating money by the shovelful, governmental committees are even now in session with the cessation of hostilities a viable prospect. A truce has been called in the sands of Kashmir. The concept of multilateral nuclear disarmament has been transformed from a pipe dream to a looming prospect. After all, it's all right there in the plan – every detail, every political tradeoff. Adam Johnson has united people in a way nothing else has ever done before. Perhaps it's simply a case of perfect timing: a mother's compelling story, a perfect philosophy, a world-spanning technology capable of disseminating information instantaneously and to remote places never before accessible. Or maybe the world is finally ready to listen. I don't know.

You might think her story incredible; you might think she made it all up in some kind of overblown publicity stunt and there certainly are enough people, consumed by self-interest and greed, spouting such views across the airwaves. I can't help but feel an element of urgency here. Adam Johnson's plan is based on the current political situation and available resources. He has provided no contingency plans and, although I've never been one to take on the role of zealous crusader, I firmly believe we've only got the one shot at this. These days there are all too many fingers poised on the buttons of mutual destruction. More every day, it seems.

So to contribute my small part I present this account, and in the hopes of quelling the naysayers I offer this small addendum. I had been in that delivery room, I had held her newborn son for just a moment, and I had seen his eyes. I have delivered thousands of children, gazing into their eyes in the first moment of life just as I did with Adam Johnson. His were not the vacant eyes of a newborn; they were not the eyes of a child at all. There was awareness in those eyes, and wisdom. I saw it.

People around the world are fascinated by Naomi's story, but will it be enough?

Can the message of an unborn baby change the world?

Save it?

The wheels are turning, the message is spreading, and I have nothing but hope. I guess we'll just have to wait and see.

The End

Apple End

Author's Bio

Eva Burkowski grew up in England, and as a child played on the Lickey Hills, in the woods that inspired Lothlòrien. This may have something to do with her fondness for fantasy literature. She studied at Oxford, first Classics, then Fine Art; and then she fell in love with a Canadian philosopher. A shared Slavic heritage clinched it. Forty years and two children further on (after she spent a happy quarter-century teaching high-school English and writing novels and stories just for fun on the north shore of Lake Superior), Eva and her husband are retired. They enjoy study, travel, wine, theatre, film, and Gordon's massive book collection. Eva is actively involved in community theatre, and she directs Shakespeare plays whenever they let her—ten and counting. She still makes time to write—and, of course, to read from paper pages.

Editor's Notes

The idea that one does not have to be the elder generation to pass on knowledge is not new, but that is usually how it starts. In the end, maybe there is more than just knowledge to be passed on.

Apple End
By
Eva Burkowski

When Margery heard the horses, she was calf-deep in the stream at the bottom of the orchard. She held her breath to listen, and became the statue of a sturdy woman wringing out laundry.

Her brain raced. The sound of hooves usually meant the peddler's cart, or Lily riding over from Pig End to trade her bacon for apple-butter; but these weren't thudding village nags. These horses' feet went *tac, tac,* which meant iron shoes. Which meant King Rawn's Seekers had found Apple End at last. Which meant *Don't rinse the last dishtowel.* Which meant *Leave the laundry-basket; leave the apple-baskets; leave ALL the baskets.*

--Leave everything and RUN! GO!

Margery flung the wet towel into the laundry-basket as she leaped barefoot for the bank. But she took a frantic second or two to crouch by the other baskets that contained the last of her harvest, and grab up an apron-full of apples--the striped pippin apples so sweet that it was said King Rawn himself ate her apple-butter on his morning rusks.

--But he can hardly have sent his Seekers here looking for my apple-butter! Great Mother, I wish it were *that! Let them only stay up at the yard till I get there!*

Margery bolted across the tussocky grass, ducking beneath laden branches, clutching her apron-full of apples to her, and dodging between the trees. Her full breasts jolted painfully in her bodice, and she was breathless and tousled when her feet felt the hard flagstones of the yard in front of Apple End, and she saw three horsemen come to a jingling halt outside her door.

Her belly squirmed, because the horses were King Rawn's grey troop mounts, just as she had feared. She scanned the riders. Two of them were troopers all right; they looked like solid, unimaginative men.

--Nothing to be feared there.

--I know--but the other?

The horses had been ridden hard; their dappled coats had been turned into flat feathers by sweat, and their hides steamed. Their blunt heads hung to their knees, and the two troopers slumped in their saddles. But the third rider sat as stiffly as though he were on parade before King Rawn, and he narrowed his eyes, green as sea-ice, as he watched the cottage-wife approach them, picking her way across the muddy yard.

--That one has never tasted apple-butter in his life. Looks as though he dines on raw meat and drinks vinegar....

--Yes; that's the one that's to be feared, if it's Joris. He has the Blood, they say, Joris has.

--Great Mother! Do you think it is? If that is *Joris the Hunter, I'll never--*

--Yes. Yes, you will.

Margery dipped a wobbly curtsey, trying not to spill the stripy apples out of her apron. There was a long silence, broken only by the horses' steamy snorting and their jingling bits. Margery blinked up at the three men from under her mop of brown curls and tried to catch her breath, and tried not to fidget, and not to focus on their eyes, and not to let anything more than a peasant's dull alarm show in her own. And not to drop to the flagstones from the utter, utter terror that was making her knees unlock and her belly churn.

--Stay silent until they speak.

--I know, my love; you told me.

Joris the Hunter laid one gloved hand on the wooden pommel of his saddle, and other on his inlaid sword hilt. He drew his thin, dark brows together. Margery looked down and scratched the top of one bare muddy foot with the other.

"Where's your man!" Joris the Hunter demanded. "We've ridden two days to find him. Now--where is he?" It was the sort of voice that insisted on a response--clear and cold.

Margery stared dumbly up at the long attentive face and moaned.

"Come on! Where is he? The one they call The Sorcerer of Apple End!" He waved a hand towards the swaybacked cottage, and then to one of his men with a quick nod, and the trooper dismounted, clearly about to search the house.

Margery whimpered. The trooper turned back, and stood waiting, one arm thrown across the saddle of his horse.

"Well?" Joris leaned down towards her, his icy green gaze raking her face.

"*Please* you, Master; my man, he's de-ead!" She pitched her voice to a whine. "De-ead--more'n a year *since*!" She drooped her head and sniffled, and let a few tears roll down her round cheeks. It was too easy to let them spill; she was only afraid she wouldn't be able to make them stop.

The two troopers murmured to one another. Margery caught the suggestion one made, and heard the other shush him without much conviction.

--*Something about consoling the grieving widow, the wretch!*

--*Yes, I heard him . . . and making her forget some pasty-faced dabbler in the Art, and giving her. . . . I couldn't hear the rest. Animals!*

--*Yes, animals--but harmless. Not like the other. Not like Joris....*

"So he's dead, is he, your man?" Joris considered, his head on one side. He leaned forward again. "We heard at Pig End he was dead. But not all rumours are true. Especially where Sorcerers are concerned, Mistress."

His eyes grew narrow and seemed to gleam through their slits. "Or perhaps it is not your man we are seeking, but you yourself? Are *you* the one we are looking for? A sorcerer does not die so easily."

Margery forced herself to look straight up into the green frost of him. --*You! You? A Sorcerer?*

"Me! *Me?* A Sorcerer?" She goggled, her lips slack. Her tears stopped from the shock.

--*Don't overdo it. He's sharp as a starved hound, that one.*

--*Shhhh! If he has the Blood, he'll hear you!"*

"Nay!" she went on, shaking her curly head slowly side to side, making her expression dull and puzzled. "Na-ay, Master! I *told* you. 'Twas my man, Boyet, was the Sorcerer!" She blinked earnestly. "'Twas he as planted the apple-orchard for me, Master; all in one spring night, the trees grew, and in the morning, they was as big as you see 'em now, and all covered in blossoms, thick as snow!"

Joris snorted in scorn, and his men guffawed.

--*Oh, Great Mother, but they were beautiful, my love. You woke me with their scent, spilling blossoms all over the bed....*

She muffled the dear memory lest Joris's Blood hear it, and covered her terror with excited babbling, as she took a step towards the Hunter.

"Ay, 'twas Boyet was Sorcerer of Apple End--ask any of the folks round about; Lily at the pig-farm will have told you, her that caught the lung-rot my Boyet cured--or ask the men as work for her down a-ways--they'll tell you how my Boyet made those sows at Pig End farrow such litters that the whole valley got sick of bacon! Ask—ask anyone!"

"Hold your noise, woman!" Joris interrupted, and she flinched. But she took another step nearer to the big horse, and continued, her voice shrill, begging and getting forgiveness silently even as the hateful words spilled out, in their coat of truth.

"Ay, he cured the others right enough, but he couldn't cure himself! Even a silly Sorcerer will get sick, Master--and 'twas the very selfsame lung-rot as he cured Lily of, as killed him--last year it was, just as the fruit was setting. . . ."

She began to whine again. "'Tis the weather at the Ends, Master, here down by the stream where the meadows flood; 'tis never dry hereabouts. My Boyet took a fever, and he couldn't get strong again, after."

--Aye, after. But it wasn't the lung-rot that really killed you; it was what they did to you before, in King Pellin's dungeon, that took away your strength.

--Shhh!

--White, my love, as apple-blossoms, your poor body, all wound about with balefire as you writhed on the stone floor. . . .

Margery jerked herself away from the clarity of the memory, afraid lest the drops of Sorcerer's Blood in Joris's veins might really somehow see them too. But the memories wouldn't go, of Boyet's thin, clever, merry face.

--Never lie outright, if they question you; that's what you always said to me, my love. See how I remember? I remember every word you ever said to me-- so few words, and so little time to say them in. Three years with you, just three, to last me all my life.

Margery blinked stupidly, and stifled a convincing cough.

The big, gray horses twitched their hides and shifted their hooves, eager for King Rawn's stables and their warm bran-mash. All three riders were back in the saddle now. The troopers looked as eager to be gone, Margery thought, peeping at them through her lashes, and wishing they would just turn their horses' heads and leave. She sniffed and coughed again, plaintively.

Joris the Hunter looked round at his men, who sat up to ragged attention in their saddles as soon as his eyes fell on them--eyes full of green scorn.

"Well?" he barked at the one who had remounted. "What do *you* think?"

The man said what he thought his commander wanted to hear. "She's lying, sir," he blustered. "Sure to be. They always do, don't they? I think it is her, she is the Sorcerer. Like you said. I mean, just look at her."

Joris gave the man a withering glance. "Do you see the signs on her, then? At that distance?"

"Not from here, sir, no. But I bet I could find some on her, if close to."

The other trooper sniggered, and then turned it into a cough. The first got down off his horse again with a jingling of spurs and knife-belt, and swaggered towards Margery, who stood stock-still. He slapped the apples out of her grip with his open hand. The stripy fruit tumbled and bounced out of her apron, bruising on the muddy stone, twinkling bright, releasing the smell of summer. The falling fruit made the horses shy, but then they quickly dipped their heads to nose after the juicy apples.

The sound of their crunching drowned Margery's squeal. She hugged her arms across her breasts, cringing away from the large man as he loomed over her. She could smell acrid sweat—-his and the horse's--and wet leather, and lamb-stew. She prayed the Mother his nose was not so keen as her own.

He grabbed for her wrist, twisting it, and levered it away from her body. She did not dare resist. With his other gloved hand he ripped down the neck of her bodice, and made a great show of examining her full breasts for the tell-tale signs, the moles or raspberry splotches over the heart, that were said to mark a practitioner of the Art. Margery turned her head aside and endured the crude handling, trying not to wince when he hurt her.

--I suppose they still believe that nonsense here. Thank the Mother it is not Joris; for he would smell out the truth, so clever as he is, and his hands would tell him far too much. . . . " She stifled a shiver at the thought of those long hands on her flesh.

At last it was over, and she clutched her bodice together again with a sullen look, and tied the torn tapes as best she could, whimpering. The trooper shrugged and went back to his horse.

"Nothing, Sir," he reported, not quite meeting his commander's gaze. He remounted.

But Joris leaned down over his horse's neck, and fixed his eyes upon hers again. She felt like a bird before a snake.

"Well?" he hissed. "*Is* it you that has the Mother's power? Or shall we burn you with brands, and prove that you cannot die by fire?"

Her memories crowded again. She saw Boyet, his flesh rosy with flame as they passed brands over and over his skin--the white skin that could feel the agony of burning, but could not burn away--for the pleasure of watching him squirm and cry out. Slender Boyet, shaking in shock afterwards in her arms, and cursing the torturers and the evil they had wanted him to do. Poor exhausted Boyet, swearing that he would summon enough power so that he could escape before dawn and flee with her into King Rawn's kingdom and safety....

Safety. They had fled and been safe for a month, no more; then Boyet, his power still depleted, had cured Lily, who had the lung-rot; and then Jess the carter's daughter, who was almost dead of a fever. And then word had spread, and he had used up the rest of his precious strength, little by little, helpless to refuse in the face of so much sickness and hunger. He had raised the lovely apple-orchard, and made poor Lily's pigs flourish, so the Apple End farms would eat; but the power he shared with others weakened his own past recovering. And though the people hereabouts were close-mouthed, the rumours had at last brought the Seekers after him--a year too late, thank the Mother, to do *him* any harm.

--No need to fear; not for Boyet.

--But the fire! She had seen what fire could do.

There was no pretence in the fear with which Margery cried out,

"Not the fire, Master! I swear I am no Sorcerer, and I'll *burn*!"

Joris's eyes searched her contorted face. Margery could tell he knew she was hiding something, and he meant to find out what it was. She began to back away; she could not help herself.

"Hold her!" he barked; and in a split second he was down off his horse and at her side, and the soldier who had handled her jumped down again too and had her elbows pinioned behind her back before she could turn and run.

Joris took a padded fire-box from his breast and opened it, and grabbed her wrist, and laid the glowing, scarlet ember with his gloved hand upon her palm.

Margery moaned, and tried to separate herself from the pain. There was charred blackness, and the reek of flesh burning....

--Not like Sorcerer's flesh, which glows and smells fragrant at the touch of flame, like apple-branches on the fire; but a smell like pork roasting. . . a smell strong enough to mask all others from him, thank the Mother--Great Mother, give me strength--I can bear it--I can! *And you, my love, don't interfere. . .*

Joris flicked away the ember and clamped his damp gloved hand over the smouldering spot on her palm, so that she screamed shrilly at last with the agony, and slumped against the trooper who pinned her back against his chest.

Without looking back, Joris turned, strode back to his horse and remounted it, beckoning sharply to his men. The one who held Margery suddenly reeled and staggered back, releasing her, as he succumbed to a fit of coughing and sneezing so violent that he could barely stumble back to his horse and get into the saddle again.

Margery dropped to her haunches on the cobbles, her tangled brown curls veiling her face as she hugged her hand between her thighs and rocked herself and whimpered for the pain.

"*She's* no Sorcerer," she heard Joris say, scornfully, as he wheeled his horse. But as his man continued to sneeze, explosively, the Hunter turned his mount again towards Margery, his eyes suddenly narrow with suspicion.

"What did you do to him?" He pointed accusingly to the trooper, who was mopping his streaming eyes.

Margery stifled her sobs long enough to look up and choke out a desperate answer even as she rocked with the pain. "Me, M-master? *N-nothing!* What could I do? I *told* you, Master; it's damp in the valley here, and the air is full of lung-rot and fever. My man, Boyet, he started just like him there—sneezing, and with the cough and all—and it rained this morning--"

She still crouched on the muddy stone flags, nursing her hurt hand, and watching the men through the cloud of her hair, willing herself not to glance back towards the orchard.

Joris hissed, "If you're lying to me, *woman*. . . . " In his mouth the word sounded like a curse. Margery just kept staring blankly, staring anywhere but at his eyes, thinking of nothing, keeping her mind away from the river-bank, filling it with visions of apple-blossoms. She could feel the Hunter's eyes boring into her, as if he would burrow into her mind and fetch her secrets out.

--Go on and try! You're not Boyet; he could have done it--one look, and he'd know just what a person was thinking. No wonder King Rawn sent to find him. But, thank the Mother, he's beyond any king's power in the Five Worlds now. . . . And you're safe too, my dear, my apple-blossom.

Suddenly sure, the Seeker Captain wheeled his horse again. "Come!" he called his men. "There is no Sorcerer here." They rode off, *tac, tac,* through the dilapidated gate, and were gone.

Margery pulled herself unsteadily to her feet, breathing shallow breaths. She watched them until they were quite out of sight. Then she heaved a shuddering sigh and closed her eyes for a moment.

--My love; they are gone--for now at least. But when Joris has a chance to think clearly, he'll come back for sure. We haven't much time.

Putting aside the searing pain in her palm, as Boyet had taught her, for she could do it now that the immediate fear had passed--Margery crossed the yard and ducked under the heavy trees and began to run. In a few moments she was back at the river-bank. There, all was as it had been. Almost all. She wiped the worst of the mud off her dirty feet in the wet grass and slipped on her shoes.

--You used to wear jeweled kidskin slippers.

--Aye, I did—-before I fell under a Sorcerer's spell and ran away to find my heart's desire--and I had jackets and kirtles of quilted silk, and a jeweled coronet too--as if that matters now—or mattered then!

Stooping, she picked out of the sixth basket the only thing that did matter anymore. She wedged the bundle on top of the pile of dry, folded laundry, and hefted the loaded basket, carrying it tucked against her on one sturdy hip. Then she made slowly for the cottage once more, her free hand stroking the tree-trunks and the laden branches as she passed between and under them for the last time.

"We'll have to move on," she mused aloud. "Over the mountains, I should think, to the Freelands, out of King Rawn's reach. It was what we planned, after we had rested at Apple End. . . . I'll sell Lily the orchard and all the apples tomorrow, and my recipe for apple-butter, and we'll go. We'll go where they'll never find us--and even if they do. . . ." She chuckled.

Reaching the house, Margery opened the rickety door with one foot, went in, and laid the laundry basket with its burden on the scrubbed table. She unlaced the sheepskin bundle that lay upon the linens, and found, not at all to her surprise, that the baby it contained was not napping any more, but very much awake.

Margery picked her daughter up, and nuzzled the soft milky-smelling baby cheek, pretending to eat it; the baby crowed and blew bubbles, and batted at her mother's nose and tangled hair.

Margery hugged her. "Ah, Holly-my-love, what a fright you gave me! When that trooper started sneezing, I thought I'd die—Joris was that suspicious! --but how proud of you your daddy would have been!" Holly giggled and found her mouth with a fist and began sucking noisily. Her mother looked at her sternly and continued. "But there's a time for everything, my pippin, and sometimes it's better not to be too clever--though I thank you for the dry laundry, that I do!"

Margery lowered herself into the battered rocking-chair with a sigh, and looked round at the rough-cut walls. She would not be sorry to leave this place, dear only because Boyet's body lay beneath the grass under the apple-trees.

She undid her bodice with her free hand, and put her daughter to nurse, making aimless conversation to soothe them both.

"I thought for sure Joris would smell the milk on me--and then he wouldn't have left until he'd found you and dragged us both to King Rawn. . . ." She rocked steadily as she relaxed and felt her milk let down. Her voice slowed as lassitude filled her limbs and her tension dissolved.

"Ah, but you'd hate it at court--any court. All that ceremony, and 'Yes, Your Majesty; no, Your Majesty'--not to mention the unspeakable things they'd make you do for them. Much better a pocketful of your daddy's apple-seeds, and a nice cottage over the mountains, my pippin."

She yawned and changed Holly's warm weight over to the other side. Lulled by the aftermath of fear and pain, and the tug of the baby at her full breast, Margery dozed as she rocked comfortably, and missed the adoring twinkle in the baby's eyes as she suckled and kneaded at her mother with a pudgy hand.

And not until Margery woke later and looked down, to see her daughter--Boyet's daughter--now smiling in a sated sleep, her mouth slack around the nipple, did she find that the burned skin of her injured palm was pink and new; and that drifts of scented, snowy-white apple-blossoms (quite out of season) filled her lap to overflowing. . . . and were still falling slowly, like stars out the Five Heavens, from Holly's half-curled baby fist.

The End

Coming Round Again

Author's Bio

Jennifer has been writing in one form or another since she was a teenager. She currently writes from the sunny beaches of Jacksonville, Florida where she lives with her family, but loves the mountains of Virginia where she was born. Her writings include YA fantasy as well as poetry and short stories. Since completing Remeon's Destiny, the first novel in her young adult fantasy series, Realms of Chaos, she has been hard at work on the sequel. When she's not hanging out with her characters, her favorite activities are reading, running and spending time with family. For more of her work visit her publisher at
http://www.bhcpress.com/Author_JW_Garrett.html, or her website to sign up for her newsletter https://www.jwgarrett.com.

Editor's Notes

We can learn a lot, not just from just the previous generation, but from all of history. But first we need to find that connection to the past that allows us to convert facts into knowledge and understanding.

Coming Round Again
by
Jennifer Garrett

Barely missing her finger, Melissa slammed her locker shut. One *more paper to go and then I'm officially a sophomore.*

"Hey, Joanie, am I the *only* one going on this field trip, or are you too?"

Joanie turned to Melissa and laughed. "No way. I finished that project days ago," she said, as she looked down, finishing a text. "This is what you get for waiting, and that museum sounds disgustingly boring, by the way. Good luck with that."

Melissa rolled her eyes and groaned loudly. She turned around to survey the impending crowd clamoring through the hallway. "Cheri, how about you? Don't tell me that I'm really gonna have to go alone. I can't be the only one still searching for a topic. Do you wanna come with me?"

"Nope, gotta work. You're on your own this time." Cheri shouldered through the maze of students to move in closer beside Melissa. "I have it on good authority that Daniel isn't done," she said in a mock whispered tone, then she laughed. "He said in Calc today that he was waiting till the last day 'cause he does his best work under pressure. And look at your twelve o'clock, coming in hot," she said, loudly in one of Melissa's ears, eager to watch what happened next.

Melissa plastered herself against the row of lockers to avoid getting smashed, and readjusted her backpack as Daniel made a beeline in her direction. "Really?" she muttered to Cheri. "Thanks a lot. How many times have I turned him down this month? Get lost, Cheri. You're no help, and I need to catch that damn bus." Melissa pushed her way outside and on to the waiting bus and picked a seat.

As Daniel poked his head into the bus, she put in her earbuds and closed her eyes, her head back in her best relaxation pose. Seconds later she felt a poke on her shoulder. She ignored it. *Maybe he'll get the message. ...* Two seconds later another poke. *Ughhhhh!*

"Daniel, ... hi. .... Really not feeling well. Waiting for my meds to kick in. ... Actually I think I'll move to the front by the trash can, just in case."

"Oh, … sorry to …"

Melissa squeezed herself into the very front seat of the bus, not giving Daniel a chance to finish his sentence.

"Good grief," she said under her breath.

"Melissa, so glad you could join us today. This is an important grade for you, right?" Ms. Gnat glared at her from the seat across the aisle.

"Oh, hi. Didn't see you there." *Obviously ...* "I'm really pumped about this museum visit. Then tonight I'm going home to get my paper done, while it's still fresh in my mind."

"Do make it count. I see so much potential in you."

Melissa forced a cough and adjusted in her seat to cover up her laughter. "Absolutely," she responded solemnly, pinching herself to keep a straight face.

Shortly thereafter the bus lurched to a stop in front of the museum, and Ms. Gnat rose to speak. "Everyone, please, give me just a minute of your time. *Please*," she said a little louder and with more emphasis the second time. "Remember to take this tour at your own pace. Read the information as you pass the exhibits. Most of them have pieces you can actually touch, making your understanding much more meaningful. Hopefully you will all come away from the experience with a moving topic since your papers are due in *two days.* Meet me back here in an hour, and I'm sure I don't have to remind everyone to behave. I'll be walking around the museum as well. Let me know if you have questions."

Awesome. I just can't wait. ... Melissa stood waiting to be first off the bus. She quickly handed her ticket to the museum attendant and made a hard right past the first exhibit, then hid herself among the crowd, mulling through groups of people.

Ahead a line was forming; Melissa peeked around to see what was the holdup. A museum worker stood in front of an exhibit entitled *They Knew Better.* Intrigued by the title and the number of people waiting, Melissa stood in line. *Maybe this will give me an idea.*

Behind her someone began pushing. Then others joined in, pushing back.

"Hey, stop." She found herself moved forward by the group in herdlike fashion and then pushed aside into a table. Melissa picked up some pamphlets that had fallen and turned to replace them. Directly in front of her, an image caught her off guard. The painting was on a nearby easel and revealed the face of a young black girl. Her soulful eyes appeared to follow Melissa as she circled the stand. The girl's forehead was covered in sweat and her cheeks in tears. Her arms were outstretched in a silent plea, hands splayed open, as if she had just been permanently separated from one she loved dearly. Her mouth formed a permanent O, stuck in time, with the echo of the child's unheard scream reaching out beyond the years to Melissa now.

The crowd rustled around her, and she moved to the side again. On the table next to the painting were small items of clothing, tiny pottery bowls, and a butter churn. The sign affixed to the girl's painting read *You Don't Own Me.* Melissa picked up one of the small bowls and felt its rough imperfect sides. She marveled at the etchings there and wondered about their meaning. Pushed ahead again, she lost her grip on the bowl, and it fell into her open purse. Before she could retrieve it, the painting of the girl with the sad face was behind her. Melissa continued on with the force of the crowd.

Melissa rounded a corner and encountered piles of shoes of all sizes—large, small, women's, men's, and children's. The sign above read simply *We Were Here.* Confused, she read the small print. *Shoes recovered from those sent to the gas chambers at Auschwitz.* Her eyes were drawn to the smallest pair of worn dark leather shoes, maybe for a one-year-old; however, there was no way Melissa could know for sure. She pulled them from the stack and turned them over in her hands, feeling the crevices and strings that still clung to the shoes.

While envisioning the toddler, she imagined the horrors that poor little life had to endure before her existence was cut short. Melissa couldn't replace the small pair in the tall mound before her; she felt charged with keeping this miniature set safe. She wiped tears from her face and resolutely placed the child's shoes in her purse.

Melissa passed by the next few exhibits while she pulled herself together. Then she stopped at what seemed to be a new addition. This exhibit was focused on the business ventures lost in the 9/11 attacks. It was a new approach on information she had been told all her life. She had always lived in a post-9/11 world; she was born in November 2001, so it was very much a part of her heritage. The business list began at the top floor, with *The Windows on the World* restaurant as the first entry. She glanced at her phone and realized she was almost out of time.

The restaurant had occupied fifty thousand square feet of space, founded in 1976. Those who died in the restaurant were listed, their names engraved in a tablet made of stone. Melissa ran her fingers over the names as she looked at the picture of the restaurant with its all-encompassing view spanning Manhattan. She shuddered as she tried to fully fathom for the first time what it might have been like to be a prisoner on that top floor, knowing there was no hope.

A large basket on a nearby table was filled with odds and ends. They seemed to be old. They were charred, dented—some of them only lumps, unrecognizable as to their original use. She picked through them. Among the items were a handle from a cast iron skillet, a copper napkin ring, and heavy bits of steel. The basket was full of many such varied items. She continued on but stopped, mesmerized, when confronted with sketches of the doomed souls as they had been drawn moments before jumping to their horrific deaths. These images were not new to her. But it was the first time she had felt an intense human connection. Just like the other two displays, she was drawn to this exhibit. Melissa held the napkin ring tightly then decidedly placed it in her purse. She would bring all the artifacts back tomorrow, *try* to explain why she had taken them to begin with, and beg forgiveness.

Seated on the bus at the appointed time, Melissa was oblivious to Daniel perched across the aisle from her as he chattered incessantly. An hour later she was home, sitting at her computer with a blank screen and the three items from the past cradled in her lap, each representing a topic that weighed heavily on her heart. She was compelled by all three stories. Each needed a voice, yet she didn't feel she could give justice to any of them. Over and over she played the events through in her mind, but no words would come.

A loud bang grabbed her attention. She sat up with a start, immediately alert at the sound of a bloodcurdling scream. She felt disoriented and extremely hot. "Mom? ... Is there something wrong with the air?" she yelled. "Mom?" she said a little softer. Melissa opened her eyes wide but could see nothing in the pitch black. She drew her hands in front of her face but, seeing nothing, only felt the dark of night engulfing her in silent stillness. *We must have lost electricity.* She heard a rustling close by and turned toward the noise. "Mom? ... Who's there?"

"Child, what are you hollering at? Now hush up. If the massa hears you, he'll be out here right quick. Go back to sleep."

"What? Oh, my God, I must be dreaming—my paper—I fell asleep."

"I done told you once. Hush. Stop your foolish talking."

Melissa broke out in a cold sweat and stifled an urge to scream. Unable to see, she felt the space around her. In the place of her queen-size mattress she grasped a flimsy pad underneath her. Her hand came away damp. Exploring further she found a scratchy blanket that smelled like a mixture of sweat and urine. She heard heavy footsteps approach on creaky steps.

"Now you've gone and done it. Go now. Hide!" the woman whispered.

The door burst open. A figure stood in the doorway.

Melissa smelled the strong stench of alcohol as the moving figure collided with several pieces of furniture.

"Mabel, ... shut up that child of yours!"

"Yes, massa. Sorry, massa. Bad dream is all."

Melissa heard the sound of a match strike, and a small flame illuminated the space.

She blinked repeatedly, taking in the scene in front of her. From the corner where she sat, a white man staggered forward, plowing into the table as he reached for the woman, Mabel, behind it. Dishes clattered noisily as they fell to the floor.

Mabel sidestepped the items and moved toward the door.

"Everything's fine now, massa. Sorry to disturb you."

Melissa froze in her spot as she was finally able to see around her in the low light. She turned her arms back and forth, touching every inch. She felt her face and moved her fingers to the rough, tangled mat of hair on her head. Next to her was a water basin, and, behind that, a broken piece of glass hung on the wall. Panic threatening to stop her, she moved there while she still had the nerve, hoping she would snap out of this nightmare at any minute.

Reaching up on tiptoe, she checked out her reflection, only whoever stared back wasn't her. Melissa screamed, and the voice coming from her was foreign as well—youthful, scared, and childlike. She took another timid peek at herself. Melissa did recognize the face! She looked like ... like the child in the museum painting. Melissa backed away slowly and tripped on her bedding, falling with a thud to the floor.

"Shut up that brat," the man yelled, "or she's next. Make no matter to me. One's just as good as 'nother."

"Yes, massa. Please, massa, she's a good girl."

"Shut your mouth," he screamed as he smacked Mabel hard with his fist, sending her crashing on top of the table.

Mabel raised her bleeding head. Wordlessly she motioned for her child to stay. Melissa reached around, fumbling for anything she could use as a weapon.

"No, please, massa. No need for this."

"I say what I need," he bellowed, raising Mabel's body up by her hair and smashing her head again to the table. "You, then her," he said, pointing to Melissa in the corner. "I aim to teach Missy some manners. It's time she learned how to obey her master," he said, slurring his words together.

"Please, please ..." Mabel cried as he pulled up her dress from behind and loosened his trousers.

Melissa heard the rhythmic grunt of the man as he banged Mabel back and forth on the table, stifling her cries with his hand covering her mouth. Melissa made her way around the perimeter of the small room, grabbing a loose board as she snuck closer to the disgusting scene. *Pig!* She stopped as she neared the drunk man.

Mabel's whimpers had ceased. Melissa heard the man's groaning and could smell his rancid breath as he exhaled in heavy bursts. She steeled herself and poised in position. After a loud moan he pushed away and turned around, swaying, unstable on his feet. With no less than a foot between them, Melissa took the short end of the board and shoved it hard at his groin. He collapsed, doubled over with a yell, one hand groping for his attacker, the other his injury. Melissa dodged his first swipe, but he grabbed her ankle at his next try.

"You bitch!" he screamed. She moved awkwardly on the floor as she tried to pull away, but he held tight. He breathed heavily as he whispered, "You're gonna regret that." She tried to claw her way forward but he recovered and reeled her in. Then came a loud thud, and she felt the grip on her ankle release. Melissa turned to see Mabel, standing, an iron skillet in her hand. The man's eyes stared directly at Melissa, and she shuddered. Then they closed and he fell over, out cold.

"You silly, silly child," Mabel said as she reached down, enveloping Melissa in a hug.

She clung to Mabel, relieved they were both still alive. With Melissa's head resting on Mabel's chest, she felt Mabel's heart racing, her own breathing now normalizing.

"Help me now," Mabel said. "Let's drag him outside and leave him by the big house with his bottle. With any luck at all he shouldn't remember none of this."

Melissa nodded wearily in agreement as she assisted Mabel. After a shaky step forward Melissa stumbled and fell. The scene before her went gray, turning into blurry shadows as she heard Mabel yell, "Missy!" Then all went black.

She woke, shivering, lying on a cot. Melissa blinked to orient herself, realizing this was not home either.

Others around her stood and appeared to be leaving.

"Hurry now. If you're late, we all pay the price," the woman next to Melissa hissed.

As she rose, she tried in vain to pull her loose clothing over more of her body.

"Okay, I'm coming," she answered. She exited the tent, followed by a trail of other women and children. On all sides were men in uniform, poised and ready to shoot. Melissa recognized the insignia immediately. Her heart sank. She choked and gagged as the smell of raw sewage and rotting flesh filled her nostrils.

Behind the uniformed men on one side were other men with

bandannas over their faces. To her horror they were throwing lifeless bodies into a ditch. She forced her gaze away from the scene, willing her eyes forward. Her group entered a building. The line of women filed behind rows of tables littered with clothing, separated by type. Melissa saw shirts, dresses, pants, socks, and then she came to stop in front of a large pile of shoes. Shoes! *Was she being forced to live the nightmares of those she saw at the museum? I'll never steal again—not ever*! She caught a glimpse of herself in a discarded broken mirror on the table. The face staring back at her was barely skin and bones with disheveled hair. Sores marked her drawn face, and her blonde hair was dirty and stuck to her cheek. *Who am I?*

Behind her at the main entrance, families disembarked a train, then were separated. Their belongings were left behind as they were forced into various lines for processing. Those deserted suitcases contained mostly clothing and items of little monetary value. All pieces were gathered and dumped onto tables then sorted for use in the camp. Beloved pictures and keepsakes, chosen in haste by the passengers who departed quickly from their homes, represented all they owned in the world. These collections which defined their lives now filled the trash bins. There was no past or future at the camp only the painful immediate torture of the present, to be endured, or not; thus, these treasures had no place here.

Screams could be heard as the people panicked in realization of the horrors they were about to face. Melissa tried to numb her mind to the activities around her so she could sort the clean clothing being brought to her from the newest passengers' baggage. But she could not silence the wailing.

A shrill scream, different from all the others, rang out as a young mother lost control of her child, who careened between the tables, her giggling incongruent with the atrocities taking place around her. She was quickly followed by a man with a stick, raised to beat her.

Melissa jumped forward and intercepted the child as the uniformed guard pulled up short, threatening to hit them both.

"Please, let me take care of her clothes. I will bring her back to the line after I've dressed her in something more suitable," Melissa said, quickly undressing the child, leaving her shoes for last. "No harm done. See?" Melissa said, carefully avoiding the soldier's gaze as she looked toward the floor. She stroked the child's face and placed her little shoes on the appropriate stack, leaving the girl barefoot, as disgust filled Melissa.

When she walked back to the line, the child's mother was long gone, and Melissa knew by the direction of that line that the mother would not be returning. After pulling a ragged shirt over the child's head, she placed the little girl in the line moving in the opposite direction, giving the girl to a woman with kind eyes. The woman distracted the child, and thankfully she was quiet for the moment. Melissa watched their progress as the group with the young girl passed through the final gate into the camp. Melissa sighed. For now, even if only for the day, this little one would live.

"You!"

Melissa turned to face the man who had yelled.

He grabbed her arm, exposing a number there. In a low voice he mumbled instructions to a nearby guard. "And confinement after." He circled her and, from behind, tore off her dress, exposing her body, simply skin hanging on a skeleton frame. The guard dealt one excruciating blow. Then beat her repeatedly, the long wooden stick leaving a trail of marks down her back where pieces of flesh now lay newly exposed. Next he pounded on her head, winding up before each hit for maximum impact. She fell to her knees, and blood flowed from her multiple head wounds into her eyes. After a final blow, she lay in a pool of her own blood, unconscious.

"Mother? Mother, are you okay? Mom?"

Melissa raised her head and stared into the faces of two adult women then looked around and took in her new surroundings. Just to her left, out the expansive window, she could see a wonderful view ... of New York.

"Where am I?"

The two women in front of her exchanged glances. Then one of them spoke. "Here we go again. Mom, you remember. We're celebrating. My birthday is tomorrow," she said with a pained expression on her face. "We're here at my favorite restaurant for breakfast. You remember now, right? On the top floor?"

Melissa stood for a better look. "Oh, wow. ... Oh, no. What day is it? And what year?"

"It's the eleventh of September, 2001, the day *before* my birthday, like I just said."

"The time, what's the time?"

"It's 8:20. Mom, you're getting all agitated. Sit down, please. I'll give you some more medication." She turned to her sister. "The nurse said this wasn't a good day. I should have taken her at her word."

"Jess, look at her eyes. She's scared. Maybe we should take her back. We can return next week. We'll break tradition and do this *after* your birthday."

Melissa energetically nodded her head in silent agreement and pushed back her chair, swinging her legs around the side to leave. She hit an obstacle. In front of her was a walker. Melissa looked at her arms and legs which weren't moving fast enough. "Good God, I'm old."

The two women laughed, with one of them saying, "I think she's coming around again."

"No, I've been around and around," she said, as she focused intently and moved her legs in unison, upsetting the table. Silverware, plates, and dishes toppled over and crashed, breaking loudly as they hit the ground. "We're all leaving, so I can come around again, at least once more."

"Mother, you're not making sense."

Melissa maneuvered her walker, willing her slow limbs to keep pace. She continued mumbling as she walked, hoping her daughters would keep up.

"The time, the time? Leave! Everyone leave!" she shouted as she rolled toward the elevator.

"I'm sorry, everyone," Jess said. "I apologize for my mother. She has Alzheimer's. We're going. Sorry for the mess. This should cover it." Jess handed the waiter a wad of cash, then rushed to keep up with her mother and sister.

"Leave! Now!" Melissa screamed as the pair pushed her into the elevator. "Time? Time!"

"Mother, five minutes later than the last time you asked, ... so 8:35."

"Oh my, we're not going to make it," she said, as tears streaked her face.

"It's okay," Jess said, patting her hand.

"No, it is very definitely not okay, and it won't be okay ever again!" Melissa sobbed. The elevator dinged as it finally reached the lobby. Melissa burst through the elevator doors and screamed, "leave, NOW!" as her daughters followed her to the street and hailed a cab. "Time?" she asked meekly, as they piled in the cab.

"It's 8:43, Mother. Here, hold your purse so I can get in."

Melissa held her purse on her lap, and the sun's rays shone on her face. Squinting, she fumbled through the items inside her purse and pulled out a napkin ring—a copper napkin ring.

She heard the roar of the first plane flying low, and she screamed and ducked her head.

Just an hour later Melissa was alone in the guest bedroom and overheard her daughters' conversation from the kitchen, the TV blaring in the background.

"If not for Mom, we'd all be dead."

Melissa explored the guest room while the conversation elsewhere continued. Pictures of "her" were prominently placed about the room, and copies of worn books littered the bedside table. She continued to hear snippets of the sisters' conversation.

"You'll sound crazy."

"They'll arrest her. How did she know anyway?"

How will I get home now? Will I ever get home? Was I meant to die today? Throwing open the guest room closet door, Melissa dug around in search for some unknown clue. After another hour had passed, she found a little box tucked away in the back of the closet. She took a deep breath then and hurriedly pulled off the box top. Melissa froze. In it were two items: the small pair of leather shoes and the tiny pottery bowl. *I've been here before.* Tenderly Melissa took out each item. *But I found these only yesterday at the museum—or did I?*

She picked up the napkin ring that had fallen in her purse at the restaurant earlier in the day and added it to the box. As she stepped back into the bedroom, something odd in the mirror caught her attention. She walked tentatively toward it and peered in, studying her own image. The now familiar facade of the old woman stared back but immediately faded in front of Melissa. She watched, transfixed, while the colors swirled and transformed into another image … into her! There she was. Melissa groped the mirror, confirming it was her real self.

Then the reflection became murky, faded, and changed again. She reached for the bed behind her and perched on the end, impatient to see who would appear next, still clinging to her box with its precious memorabilia. That vision cleared, and she saw Missy, the young slave, then the thin blonde woman from the concentration camp. Lastly came the elderly woman again from the twin towers, followed finally by Melissa. The visions continued to parade past her, each representation a little different than the one before.

She felt the connection of all three women pumping through her veins, and they were no longer strangers to each other. The veil was broken. No longer was one female's life experience dulled to the others who lived within Melissa; instead, they all invigorated and empowered her. Instantly she knew what she had to do in order to get back to the present, back to the life she was now meant to live—back to being Melissa.

She had to die.

It had to be quick, before she lost her nerve. Her gaze darted around the room, and her mind raced; her heart pounded in her throat. *The window—that was it.* She moved as fast as her aging limbs let her and yet easily slid open the window. Nothing was in her way, until the blacktop below. *If I'm right, I'll wake up at my computer, and, if I'm wrong, well ...*

"Mom, dinner."

Melissa heard a scream behind her as her feet left the ledge.

"Melissa, wake up. You'll be late for school. You fell asleep at your computer."

"Mom? Mom!" Melissa blinked and opened her eyes wide, then clung to her mom. The items in her lap fell to the floor.

"I wasn't sure I'd see you again," she whispered.

Her mom pulled away and gave her a worried glance.

"Are you okay? I'm right here," she said, as she patted her daughter's back. "That must have been some dream. Get ready and come downstairs. We'll talk." Her mom closed the bedroom door as she left the room.

Melissa reached to the floor for the three precious items, wrapping them in her arms, and ran to the mirror. She held her breath, waiting. The images began. Familiar now, they faded in and out, and her eyes filled with tears as she reached for the mirror and touched each one. *They're me. I'm them. They're calling me.* She gasped and fought the fear building in the pit of her stomach as she tried to internalize the meaning of all she had witnessed. *I must tell their stories, my stories, the lives I've lived, and all that has been overcome—my story throughout time.*

Bound together by tragedy, loss, and fear—but also triumph and grace—the figures from the past continued their eternal march into the present. But now they had a voice.

The End

Half Remembered Beaches

Author's Bio

Kelly Sandoval's fiction has appeared in Strange Horizons, Uncanny, and Best American Science Fiction and Fantasy. She lives in Seattle, where the weather is always happy to make staying in and writing seem like a good idea. Her family includes a patient husband and daughter, an anarchist tortoise, and a put-upon cat. You can find her online at kellysandovalfiction.com.

Editor's Notes

Remembering the past can build the future. But what if remembering the past also builds the present, and make us who we are.

Half Remembered Beaches
by
Kelly Sandoval

The entire way there, my brother and I argued about the existence of the beach.

"Listen," Aaron said, his gaze fixed on the wispy city reflected in my car's rearview mirrors. "I'm not saying we didn't have fun. I'm just saying it wasn't real."

"You remember the time we forgot to pack the hotdogs?" I asked.

"Dad was shouting." Aaron picked his nails. "Mom just walked into the waves. Stood there up to her neck and refused to come out until he apologized."

God, how I'd sobbed that day. Seven years old, too big for tantrums, and I'd thrown myself on the sand, screaming that she would drown.

I could still remember the taste of the sand, the weight of the sun, and the raw desperation I'd felt watching the waves crest over my mother's head.

Aaron had sat with me. Patted my shoulder with awkward big brother affection and promised Mom would be okay.

"That happened," I said. "Who'd make it up?"

"This is what's happening now." Aaron pointed to the trees, which were more like the ideas of trees these days. No more oak, aspen, or pine. Just an indistinguishable green smear drifting like smoke in the breeze.

I drove. Unlike trees, roads are wonderfully solid things. Built and maintained, recorded obsessively, memorized and talked about on every rush hour traffic report. Roads were remembered, and it showed. My car, on the other hand, was a little soft along the edges. It still drove fine, but it'd begun to lose distinction, looking like every other white, four-door sedan still on the road. It'd been green, but the color had gone months ago. People don't think of cars as green.

If only I'd had one of those iconic American muscle cars, all orange and chrome. Leather seats. A car to remember.

"How's Lisa?" I asked, as we turned the last corner and the ocean came into view. An endless stretch of blue-gray, with white waves stretching for the shore. Just as I remembered. As it'd always been.

"We broke up. Two years ago."

"Sorry," I said.

Had I known that? Should I have? I sent Aaron cards at Christmas, but we'd never been much good at talking. But when I'd called him up, told him I needed him, needed to see the beach that had been ours every summer, he'd said yes. Just yes.

It was only after he got in the car that we started arguing.

"Nevermind," he said. "Still with Taylor?"

"Long gone."

"Oh." He tried to smile. "We're not good at this, are we?"

"I'm doing my best."

"Points for effort. You're gonna miss the exit."

"I know where I'm going." But I'd needed the reminder. I followed the exit road, until it spilled out into the same parking lot we'd used every summer. When we were little, we'd had to sit in the car, waiting for seeming hours while our father drove in circles, looking for a spot.

Now, it was just us. I drove straight through the lot and out onto the beach. It should have been a problem. My little four-cylinder should have dug itself in and given up. But I was driving the idea of a car onto the concept of a beach. We drove straight up to the water, Aaron and I both laughing just for the release of it.

"See," he said, getting out as the waves lapped the tires. "It's not real."

"Shut up." I pushed my door open and breathed in deep. The seaweed stench hadn't changed. "Look around, Aaron. Just take it in."

He came around to my side, leaning against the car as I slid out. "So this is what you wanted to see?"

The water was cold, uncomfortably so. I remembered that, too. "I just need to believe in something. Just for a second."

But we'd all stopped believing. Me, Aaron, the whole damn world. They called it the Verisimilitude Plague. Reality breaking down along the edges, and it turns out none of us had been paying enough attention to the details.

"Crap!" The ocean floor had the rough, even texture of a hotel pool. It hadn't always been that way. Had it? I took a step forward, then another.

"Jessie!" Aaron splashed behind me, but I didn't turn. If I kept my gaze locked on where the water met the horizon, everything looked like it should.

He caught up to me when the waves were at my shoulders. Grabbed me by the arm and just held on.

"I'm not coming out," I said. "Not until the world's real again."

"You're such an idiot." Aaron's fingers stayed locked around my wrist. Not pushing or pulling, just waiting.

I turned to look at him. He looked back, his eyes no longer any particular color. Why hadn't I bothered to remember the color of his eyes?

"I don't have toenails anymore. Or freckles. There's just you." I shrugged, trying not to make a big deal of it. We weren't close. Couldn't spend ten minutes in a car without fighting. "I won't last long."

"You've got a birthmark above your left ankle," he said. "The one that looks like a squashed fly. And your front teeth are crooked."

"Your eyes are green." I turned back toward the featureless beach and watched the waves swamp my generic white sedan. "Same color as my car."

He tugged my wrist. "Let's go. I brought hot dogs."

"Solid!"

"America's favorite F-ing treat." He started walking, and I let him pull me along. "Hot dogs and cockroaches, they'll be the last to go."

"What about us?" I asked.

"Us too," he said. "You remember that time you lit grandma's couch on fire? Because I'm never gonna forget it."

"I didn't!" I shoved him, and he stumbled forward onto the beach, laughing. "The cat knocked over a candle."

"The cat *you* were chasing." He grinned at me, that familiar, superior grin. His eyes were the green of a newly painted car.

The End

Undermind

Author's Bio

Marc Vun Kannon, after surviving his teen age years, entered Hofstra University. Five years later, he exited with a BA in philosophy and a wife. He still has both, but the wife is more useful. Since then he almost accumulated a PhD in philosophy and has acquired a second BA in Computer Science. After dabbling in fulfilling pursuits such as stock boy and gas station attendant, he found the spiritual home of his current self as a software support engineer, for CAMP Systems International.

Marc puts his degrees in Philosophy and Computer Science to good use writing stories about strange things that happen to ordinary people. His wife and three children think it's harmless enough, and it keeps him out of trouble. As a philosopher (his first novel demanded he write it while he was in Graduate School), his main interest is in the characters, and as a Computer geek, his technique is to follow the character's and story's logic to 'grow' a story organically. His main rule when writing is to not do again what he's already seen done before, resulting in books that are hard to describe.

Editor's Notes

The idea that what we remember can make us who we are is within reason, but sometimes what we do, or why, is not. Sometimes there is more to us, and everything around us, than we can see.

Undermind
By
Marc Vun Kannon

The man with the strange and unlikely name of Anzarel lowered himself to look out the window, a simple thing of glass and wood, and observed the world around him. The dark clouds moved and the wind blew, in different directions. Pieces of paper moved in the road. They tumbled to the nearest intersection, where they were blown up into the air by a cross-breeze. When they came down there was one less than before. He turned away from the window, as concerned as one of his kind ever got.

Some would have called him a mystic, a scientist, a craftsman, or a philosopher. He himself would have scorned the use of such titles, although they were all true enough. His science was mental, not physical, in which the world was not an object to be known but a filter for his understanding of himself. His craft, the making of specialized glass and mirrors, was a tool whereby he could see the mold that shaped his thoughts, the mask he currently wore, that he could the more easily remove it. Inevitably he would find another, finer, subtler mask beneath, and then he would make himself a new, finer, subtler mirror.

Other words also applied to Anzarel. He most deplored the label of *Psychic*, which only showed that the speaker had no cogent ideas whatsoever about the mentalist sciences. On the other hand, terms like *Observer, Missionary*, and *Time-traveller* were equally applicable but less objectionable. Like all words and masks, though, they fell far short of conveying the truth. As an observer he was part of the experiment; as a missionary he had no faith to spread to others. He was a self-reflecting mirror, of infinite dimension, and his sacred calling was to explore those dimensions.

But not tonight.

His dwelling was dim, the world's light fading faster then it should. His crystals and glasses, when he had called them up, had been clouded, foggy, forcing him to use the window. This condition had not changed. There was no illumination to be found in them, not tonight. He would have to look within.

His crystals, though muted, nonetheless lit his way across the floor of his study, to a closed cabinet carefully mounted on the wall. A shield, for the user's sake, since nothing merely material could break his creation. If anything the opposite was more likely, unless the user was another like him, and even they had to be careful.

Anzarel opened the cabinet doors and gazed at himself in the mirror, the first precept focusing his thoughts. *All knowledge is self-knowledge.*

The room in the mirror was dark, his crystals merely toadstools and chunks of stone. His reflection, the image of his own undermind, did not gaze back at him, looking anywhere else, remarkably mobile in the confines of the frame. It noticed the state of his fire and left, turned its back to tend its own reflected blaze.

"So, it's like that, is it?" muttered Anzarel to his unreflecting self.

One of *those* nights.

Knowledge was power. Tonight the humans of this time and place, neither dark nor light, would grope again toward power, and he must be ready. He shut the doors, and then covered his lights as well. He should be in his shop. Tonight he would not be the watcher, but the lens, and the humans would see...what they would see.

As he closed the door, the room flooded with light as the thunder crashed.

Doris Grey jumped backwards with a scream of surprise and almost-terror, as the lightning revealed the gargoyle in her bedroom and then abandoned her. Frantically she scrambled back to her bedside table, blinded. She hadn't yet found anything useful to the cause of self-defense when a second burst revealed nothing to defend against. No monsters in the corner, just the dressing mirror she knew was there, its shadowed glass reflecting only the ceiling to someone crouched on the floor.

She stood, and it reflected her just as it always had, even when she looked like a gargoyle as she did now. Her hair was a mess, naturally, and she was still dressed—Still dressed? Oh yes, she and Davis had been working late, achieving nothing. Davis. Working.

The light dawned, or it may have been a last flash from the quick-moving storm. Where was her cell phone? Ah! Purse, table, hallway. Where she'd left it as she dragged herself in, what? She looked at the clock. A whole 45 minutes ago?

She left the mystery in her bedroom and went to where her phone was. Speed dial was a wonderful thing. "Davis!" Of course it was Davis, no one else ever answered his phone.

"Dag?" No one else ever called her that, just as he never used the nicknames that others used, names she loathed.

"Davis, listen," said Doris Anne Grey, "I had an idea…"

Davis listened, amazed at her force and lucidity. She'd looked like a dead thing when he'd dropped her off. Now her voice alone brought her image searing across his mind, and he almost lost track of what she was saying. "You want another mirror, dark glass." He opened his briefcase and got out his notepad, still folded over from tonight's session. "Why? Oh, symbolism. Of course. No, I think we can swing it." Well, their fellowship could *swing it* with some help from his checkbook; his food budget wouldn't mind. He'd resolved to lose weight hundreds of times. He made a note in his book. A research assistant always made notes. "I'll get right on it," he promised, and hung up. *Tomorrow?*

It wasn't like tomorrow had a lot going for it. The grant money had gone out and success had not come in to take its place. Assistants had followed the money, and even more success had not come in. Now there was only him, and without his food budget there would be less of him as well.

The lease on the lab expired tonight, so their final session had had only him, her, and a mirror that had showed even less than was there, according to Dag.

"She wouldn't speak to me."

He looked at the sparse notes, memory supplying all that they didn't. "Not speaking? That's a first, isn't it?"

Doris had nodded. "She wouldn't even look at me."

That wasn't something you heard every day. "She's your own reflection. How could she not look at you?"

"Don't ask me," said Doris. Then, just then, Davis remembered her looking very tired, suddenly. "Ask her."

"Dag, the mirror only shows you yourself. The image may take different forms with the hypnosis, but it's still just you."

Her sigh sliced through him, even in memory. "I thought so. I hoped so."

"Most people don't hope to find their dark side, Dag."

"Most people don't have to, Davis. I've been called 'White Queen' and 'Ice Princess' all my life."

"By who?"

"By people who don't look at me the way you do." She'd reached out to touch him, but stopped short of actual contact. She never touched him, never touched anyone. "I'm sorry, Davis, that was cruel of me. But I'm not a saint."

"You don't have to tell me that, Dag." He didn't believe her when she did.

He'd driven her home, and by the time he got to his own place she was up, around, and on fire again. Something about tonight had set her off, and she'd want to strike while that iron was hot. She'd want this tomorrow.

She *would* want this tomorrow, wouldn't she? Personal lack of demons aside, time was getting short. He'd need something to show for tonight. Phone book, phone book. Regular mirrors they could get anywhere. Specialty mirrors had to be ordered. They probably couldn't get one soon no matter what, but he had to try, and it's not like there were that many suppliers to start with. One name on the page jumped out at him, and he entered the number without even looking at the pad. Someone answered on the first ring.

"Anzarel's Glass and Mirror. May I help you?"

"By morning, very good, sir." Anzarel stared at the buzzing handset for a moment, troubled by more than the noise. He could end that by hanging up, which he did. But the order…a dark mirror? Dark glass, tonight of all nights? Did they even know what they were asking for? Equally troubling, either way, but…warning them was not an option available to him. They wouldn't understand his warning even if he tried.

In this matter, as in all others, they could only learn by doing.

It was not his decision. Dark glass was needed, dark glass would be supplied. In one night! Frame and materials he had in his stock. His physical minions were ready as always: fire to melt the sand, air to cool it. The darkness would be a problem. Merely physical minions couldn't touch the stuff. He'd have to create a Named Agent, probably a Pogli, to distribute that part. Named Agents were tricky, pieces of himself, given the smallest masks of self-identity. Much more autonomous than a physical minion. He'd better put that off until the time was right. Minions, agents, darkness -- all at the same time? The time itself was short. The mirror would be small.

"Kind'a small, isn't it?" asked Davis, when he saw the size of the parcel the delivery man brought in. Dag might be able to see her whole face in it at one time.

The tone was neither accusing nor mocking, so Anzarel decided to take it at face value. "Limited options, sir," he replied. He walked slowly, carefully placing the wrapped item on the table as if it wouldn't reflect a nuclear explosion. Which it would, once he'd sealed the thing. Basic Psychics would do it, but the people of Earth were still struggling with materialism. *Those nights,* caused by mentalist events in the physical world, were still pretty rare.

Anzarel turned to find Davis looking at him. "You know," said the research assistant hesitantly, "when we spoke on the phone last night, I had an instant picture in my head of what you looked like."

Anzarel felt hope bloom, rather more than he usually did. "And did it look like me?"

Davis smiled a strange smile. "Exactly. Exactly like you." *Right down to the tweed vest and bushy hair.*

Anzarel nodded, keeping his satisfaction contained, as always. "Well then, that's good. Like to think I sound like myself." He wiped his completely clean hands on a spotless cloth. "I had a similar impression of you, I'm glad to say." Which was much more surprising. Most humans didn't know themselves that well.

Doris walked into the room. "Let me see it, please," she asked, all business, and Anzarel quickly unwrapped his creation. The glass gleamed black, the image of the room within not just dark but...off, somehow. The angles, not quite right. Davis, standing farthest away, was glad of the distance.

"Oh, that is a beauty," breathed Doris, oblivious but entranced. She reached to touch it, but her fingers stopped short of actual contact.

"Indeed," replied Anzarel quietly, observing the pair of them. These humans had potential. As an observer he still wore the mask of sympathy, and he sympathized. She in particular didn't seem quite right, but perhaps that was necessary for this iteration of the experiment to bear fruit.

"This...is what I wanted. Just precisely what I wanted." Delight sparkled in her voice. Anzarel only nodded his appreciation.

"Pay him, Davis," said Doris absently, but Anzarel started moving to the door before Davis could get his checkbook out.

"I will return later," he said. "If you are satisfied, you may pay for it then." His part was done, for now. He could only wait on the success, or failure, of their enterprise.

Nothing Davis could say or do would get him to accept payment now. He couldn't even get him to accept a tip. "What a strange little man," he said, closing the door behind their rapidly departing guest.

Doris didn't even hear him. "Let's get started right away."

Anzarel returned to the familiarity of his study with great relief, not bothering to rouse his crystals. His night's labors had gone well, despite the risk. An interesting pair, mired in materialism though they were. A long night, for its kind, and well over. Time to seek rest. This world could get along without him for a short time.

"...three, two, one."

The elevator stopped and Doris got out into an empty room, its only decoration the mirror she'd been looking at when they'd begun. This was her place. Her private place. No one ever came here, not even Davis. *Hmm.* Davis. The room warmed. Maybe she should.

Nobody ever came here, nobody ever would. This was her place. Plain. Cold. She heard Davis' voice again, asking the usual routine questions.

"Can you hear me, Dag?"

"I can hear you, Davis."

"Do you see the mirror in front of you?"

"I see it."

"Do you see anything in the mirror?"

"Yes."

"What do you see in the mirror, Dag?"

"I see me." She saw her mirror-self looking at her. She saw her mirror-self say 'I see me.'

"Would you close your eyes, please, Dag?"

"Yes, Davis." Her private place became dim. The lights weren't enough to let her see the mirror.

"I'm putting a new mirror in front of you, Dag. When I tell you to, open your eyes and look into the mirror."

She made no response, since he did not ask a question. She waited. She saw the mirror being placed in front of her, darker than the lack of light in her private place.

"Look."

The lights in her private place came up, but the mirror became darker, if anything. She looked into it.

"What do you see?"

Doris Grey fell over backwards with a scream of terror, as the mirror revealed the gargoyle she had seen in the corner of her bedroom.

"Dag! What do you see?"

Doris Grey scrambled backwards, away from the hideous thing that looked like her but wasn't her, couldn't be her...

"Dag, can you hear me?!"

Doris Grey stopped, paralyzed, as the monster wearing her face began to...flow out of the mirror. Into her private place. "Oh, I hear you, Davis," it said. In her voice, in her *caressingstrokingsoothingseductive* voice—

"Dag! Close your eyes, stop looking into the mirror."

Doris Grey ran out of room, and lashed out desperately. Having found herself at last, she fought herself, unable to comply with the directive. Her hands passed through the thing, the creature, unable to feel a difference between them. Its warm burning self stuck to her, tainted her, staining her Grey in truth as it followed the lines of the White Queen's heart. Sensation exploded within her: anger and sadness, pain and joy all at once.

And loneliness, so much loneliness.

Something happened, something blocked the mirror, but it was too late. "I don't think she can hear you," mocked her other self. No, not her self, never her self. She tried to refuse, to deny the lie, but the other owned her hands, her voice. It flowed up, covering her face like a mask. She wiped at it, but that only spread it faster, got it in her eyes.

It couldn't be a mask, could it? It was her. Or was she the mask? She couldn't think, couldn't remember the structure of the...of the...

Her vision began to dim, but she could hear Davis' voice still.

"Doris Anne Grey, get into your elevator now."

Doris Anne Grey stood in her elevator, wholly and gladly responsive to Davis' use of her full name, an emergency imperative. She carried the stain with her, couldn't see or speak, but she could hear the doors closing. She would be safe, he would protect her. The horror would be—the doors opened again. *"Room for one more?"* purred the thing as it flooded into the elevator and into her mouth and ears and . . .

"...eight, nine, ten."

Davis snapped his fingers. Doris Grey took a deep breath, and then another. Her gaze never left Davis' face as her arms lifted, her hands rose up and her fingers started touching gently on her own face, her cheeks, her hair. Her hair, sleek and kempt until she pulled unflinching on the clips that held in place, until some of the hair ripped from her head. She dropped them and started touching herself, her hands stroking down over her shoulders, her arms, her...Davis captured her hands in his, ending her self-examination. "Dag?"

She looked at him, uncomprehending.

"Dorrie?" he asked. She hated that name. Hopefully she'd slap him for using it.

She smiled. She reached out for his face instead.

He pushed back, aching to be touched by her but not in these circumstances. "Who are you?" he asked. "What is your name?"

She looked confused. Her lips moved a couple of times, but without making a sound. Then her expression firmed, and they moved again, differently this time. "Pogli." Her hands moved...

Anzarel woke a short time after he went to take his rest, feeling very good, very right, and that was just wrong. He was, should have been, beyond such extremes, unless he chose not to be, and he had not so chosen, pleasure being such a difficult mask to remove. He took himself off to his study with haste, but the crystals were still dim. From the window, he could see the nosy neighbor, scribbling frantically as he opened his curtains twice in as many days. The wind blew south, the clouds rolled east. There were no papers in the road today. In the mirror, his reflection was at least looking at him today, although it lacked its left hand. Anzarel didn't waste time cursing. He didn't know how.

Davis wasn't thrilled to find the odd little smith back on his doorstep, but he wasn't really surprised, either. "What do you want?" he said.

"I want to help," said Anzarel, who didn't need to see Davis' disheveled clothing, unruly hair, or disturbed mental state to know that they needed his help. "An error has been made."

Davis gestured him inside, not sure he could stop himself from shouting his problems for the whole street to hear. "You got that right. No money, no jobs, no future, no results, and all we've got to show for our efforts is a black mirror and at least one of us is out of our minds." He ran his hands through his hair, trying to make it less unruly but not succeeding very well. "I'm not too sure about her, either."

Anzarel was tremendously relieved. Irony was good. "And what is the nature of her…difficulty?"

Davis shut up. She'd never forgive him, if she ever came to her senses. It was personal, probably confidential, and definitely very embarrassing. For both of them. He tucked in his shirt.

"It's like that, is it?" Anzarel sounded rather disapproving.

"It might have been," said Davis defensively, "But I wouldn't, we didn't, and now she's in the kitchen tasting everything on my shelves." Including the molasses, and the hot sauce.

Anzarel smiled. He didn't doubt, and he did believe. Davis smiled back. "That's excellent, young man, excellent," said Anzarel, "That means there is hope." He didn't say for whom.

Davis turned to lead the way to the main room, strangely heartened. "What can you do?"

"Nothing, young man," said Anzarel and Davis stopped. "You shall have to do it."

"It?" said Davis. "What 'it'? I mean, why me?"

Anzarel looked either sad, or annoyed. He raised his empty hands. "The mirror is my creation, and I'm afraid your lady's affliction mirrors my own. Or mine reflects hers, it makes no difference."

"She isn't my lady," replied Davis unhappily.

"Of course she is," said Anzarel brightly. "Why else would she still be here?" He looked around, and pointed to a table. "We shall need my mirror, here."

Davis lifted the oddly heavy mirror from the floor, touching it as little as possible. "For what?" he asked as he positioned it.

"Your lady is afflicted," explained Anzarel in professional double-talk-ese, "With a Negative Aspect Manipulator, a Named Agent called a Pogli. It was left in the mirror by accident, and your work gave it entry into her mind. You must call it out."

"Call it out. A Pogli." Davis looked up. "That's what she called herself."

"If it helps, think of it as a demon, and she's possessed."

"Ah," said Davis in mock-enthusiasm. "We're in fantasyland now, that's so much better!"

"The alternative is to watch her go mad for real, for the rest of her short life."

Davis gulped. Fantasyland it is, then. "What do I do?"

"Everything you have seen today is her. There is nothing to a Pogli beyond the name, and its purpose. It will respond to a strong will, and a more defined purpose."

Doris had wanted to see her dark side.

"Where will it go?"

"Back into the mirror," said Anzarel, as if it was obvious. "I will take it from there."

"And Doris?"

"Will be what she was, if not *as* she was." Pogli distribute darkness, and her darkness had been very much un-distributed. "Ultimately, a good thing, I think." He switched positions with Davis. "Call her in."

"How?"

"Offer her something she wants more than what she currently has. When she comes, hold her, make her look in the mirror, call it out."

Davis nodded, wiped his sweaty hands on his pants. "Doris," he called, "Come here and be with me."

Doris came running down the hall and threw herself into Davis' arms. He gripped her and spun her about, not letting go as she came face-to-face with the mirror and its maker. "No," whimpered something, with Doris' voice.

"Pogli," Davis said into her ear, "Get out."

Nothing happened. Anzarel made a gesture for more forcefulness.

"Pogli," said Davis again, "*Get. Out!*"

Still nothing. Anzarel looked dismayed.

Davis saw it. He stared at Doris' face in the mirror, and had an idea. "I will give you to the count of ten. Ten. Nine. Eight…" As he counted down in the familiar cadence, Doris grew still, her eyes more focused, meeting his gaze in the mirror. "Doris Anne Grey, do you hear me?"

"Yes, Davis."

"Do you see me?"

"Yes, Davis. You are here with me, in my private place. You are standing between me and the mirror. You are protecting me."

"I am," said Davis. "I always will." He wrapped an arm around her, pulling her unresisting into an embrace. "Do you know that I love you? More than anything in this world? More than life itself?"

"Yes, Davis."

"There is no room for a Pogli between us." He put his other arm around her, pulled her in closer. "You don't want it in your private place."

"No, Davis. I only want you."

Davis stared into her eyes, into Doris' eyes. He saw her strong will, her defined and defiant purpose. "Pogli, get out."

The mirror shattered, fell into pieces, into fragments. "You broke it," said Anzarel in amazement. Had it not been for the sudden influx of negativity as his Agent returned to him, he might even have smiled.

Doris collapsed in Davis' arms. Awkwardly, he scooped her up, her arms going around him in a death-grip, and he carried her to his bed. He didn't come back. She wouldn't let go, and he wouldn't leave her alone.

Anzarel didn't wait. He gathered up all the remains of his mirror–they broke it! How extraordinary!–and let himself out. He could go now, go completely, go for good. Now that these humans had demonstrated the barest capacity for the mentalist sciences, they would need guidance. Not his thing, guidance. His work here was done.

Davis tapped on the door of his own bedroom, and Doris looked up at him, too tired to raise her head from the pillow. "Did you find him?"

He shook his head. Neither the man nor any trace of the mirror, but he expected that. "Nowhere in the phone book, and you know there's no way I'd forget a name like Anzler. I can't remember the number, and it's not in my online phone bill." He'd even forgotten to make a note. They'd never find him, never know how he knew to show up when he was needed.

He stepped closer, to her and to the light. "Found this in my mail slot, though." He held up an envelope, with their names written on the outside. He opened it, pulled out two pieces of paper, one large and one small. He glanced at the small one and read from the large one. "It says 'Congratulations.'"

"Why?"

"No clue. 'I'm going now, and you won't be seeing me again.'"

Doris muttered, "Probably thought we'd sue him."

Davis continued, "'I was responsible for what happened today, so I am leaving you a little gift, by way of apology.' Not another mirror, I hope. 'I am enclosing one of your financial documents for an s-load of money'—my words, not his—'since your people insisted on giving it to me—'"

"'Our people'?"

"Mirror-buyers? Psychologists?" Davis offered with a shrug. "Humans? '—Your people insisted on giving it to me when I gave them my mirrors and I have no idea what to do with it. I leave it to you, to continue your excellent work.'"

"What work?"

Davis folded the check inside the letter. "I think he means you." At least. *Ultimately a good thing* was not *right now a good thing*. There would be therapy, bottoms to be gotten to. Understanding. He went to the bed and sat by her side. "How do you feel?"

As an answer she took his hand, not yet tired of the sheer novelty of unclouded sensation after a lifetime wrapped in gauze.

The papers went on the table, merely money. "So, it's like that, is it?" He lowered himself to lie flat on the bed, weary, yet careful not to take his hand away from her.

Mmm-Hmm, she hummed happily, rolling over.

Good, he thought, and dozed off. Anything else could wait until later. There would *be* a later; how extraordinary. The rest of the world could get along without him for a short time. Time to rest.

It had been one of *those* days.

The End

The Hearse Twins

Author's Bio

Soren James is a writer, poet and visual artist currently living in London. An intensely private person, little is known of this Soren character except that he recreates himself on a daily basis from the materials at his disposal, continuing to do so in an upbeat manner until one day he will sumptuously throw his drained materials aside and resume stillness without asking why. He has been published in: Strange Horizons, Grievous Angel, Cafe Irreal, The Future Fire, Freeze Frame Fiction, Every Day Fiction, and many others. More of his work can be seen here: https://sorenjames.wordpress.com

Editor's Notes

Sometimes it is like we are more than one person. What if we really were more than one person, or used to be, or will be? Let's take a little time to explore this with The Hearse Twins.

The Hearse Twins
By Soren James

In the living room of her converted barge, Jinny spoke at length about winter; the whining cadence of her voice slipping downhill as each word's cumulative effect drained our lives. It was like listening to hundreds of dogs expiring in a gutter, and after a while we all wanted to die.

It was only when George interjected – mentioning tomorrow was the first day of spring – that the conversation lifted itself from the floor. That was when we made our fateful plan to hold up a bank.

We weren't professional robbers by any means: two of us had been involved in fraud; George was an ex arms-dealer; Jinny was so full of confusing reports about her past, that I can't really say where she stood; and I was a tax attorney. Other than that, we were respectable people.

Tracing my thoughts back to that moment of the initial idea, I can see now that Jinny's involvement was a mistake. She'd been in and out of various institutions, repeatedly proving herself the most unstable of our group.

Added to this, two weeks earlier Jinny and George had drifted into a relationship, their enthrallment growing increasingly volatile right up to the eve of the robbery – when Jinny insisted George have an immediate vasectomy. With these two as gang members, the future of our plans didn't suggest themselves with much hope.

The day of the robbery was a disaster: George couldn't walk very well; Jinny was half comatose on tranquillizers; I was hung over; and the other two members of *The Hearse Twins'* (as Jinny had insisted we call ourselves the previous evening) were late due to a blown tire.

Not that any of this stopped our plans. We entered the bank at 12:15, an hour later than intended, only to be faced with the most curious scene. We were already there. The whole gang of us were sitting cuffed, and in conversation with the police. This was a shock, to say the least.

Even now, ten years later, watching sunrise ache its way into my prison cell, I can barely believe the scene that befell us that day.

Neither, thankfully, could the police. Distracted from questioning the earlier – presumably on-time versions of ourselves – they stared blankly at us as we stood confused in the doorway with guns primed.

Their eyes scanned our faces in horror – turning occasionally to compare our features with those of their captives. This scene seemed to continue for ages –everyone frozen in a farcical moment of bemusement – until Jinny screamed, "I'm sorry!"

This exclamation provided us, the non-handcuffed *Hearse Twins*, with a much needed wake-up call.

We ran to our getaway car, drove to the plane, and flew to Buenos Aires – all as planned, except without any money.

During the journey we said nothing. We sat on our confusion, silently pondered Jinny's apparently aimless apology. We wanted answers, but deep down I suspect each of us knew that Jinny was Jinny – and therefore, the least qualified person to explain herself.

Settling into the back room of a bar in Buenos Aires, the *Hearse Twins* soon rounded on Jinny for an explanation. Still drugged and listless, she slurred: "I remember time-travel before it began. It was simple then. But once underway, I began recalling more and more events. Soon I was remembering exponentially, recalling infinite lives and possibilities. There was too much. I had to give up control." She stopped, appearing to brush something from the side of her head. As she brought her hand in front of her face, we saw that she'd caught the fly by its wing. She became lost in analysis of the struggling insect.

"The details are fine," Jinny eventually continued, and let the fly go. "But putting any two things together creates the hell of belief and opinion. I've given up on that."

Anxious for her to stay on subject, I prompted, "Who were those people? Who are we?"

"Does it matter? . . . I guess it does. My barge is a time travel device. I informed myself to convert it twenty years ago. Then I decided to leave it on all the time – no longer caring where or when I ended up, or how many lives and memories I created. It was all so confusing. Still is. I don't know if I'm here now, or in some ancient civilization – drowning in milk while trying to influence the future, hoping tomorrow will be born anew each night. Or if everything's dead, and all time is spare."

We nodded impatiently, then tried to broach the subject again. After a long and confusing discussion we could only conclude that our other selves, if they exist, must be in prison by now.

Years later, the coherence of my life is deteriorating. I understand now why Jinny often looked as if she were falling apart. She was – from the inside out. Now the same is happening to me.

Still hiding out in South America, I'm having vivid hallucinations of another, an imprisoned life. Experiencing – or maybe even living – these two lives, I try to assimilate them, but such attempts feel meaningless. The only thing of which I'm certain is an increasingly confused sense of time and identity.

My parallel existences: a nomadic on-the-run urgency, and a cell-induced indolence making time pass ever slower, are tearing me apart and opening a well of nothingness beneath me. Meanwhile my inner world expands infinitely, engulfing the scraps of identity I thought I had.

When I think of Jinny, I'm thankful I have only two versions of self to assimilate. What must it be like for her with all those thousands of alternate selves? But then, perhaps it's more interesting.

The End

Core Beliefs

Author's Bio

Jim Gotaas started reading and writing science fiction as a teenager. He managed to sell a novelette way back in the last millennium to If Science Fiction. He then took a little time off to explore life as a draftee in the US Army, followed by PhD study and subsequent research and teaching in Physics. That short break unexpectedly lasted until he retired. Now devoting more time to attracting the elusive muse, he has so far failed to discover that special, magical lure that will keep her hanging around. Nonetheless, he's managed to sell stories to Daily Science Fiction and Pulphouse Magazine (one appeared in Issue 2, with two more in the pipeline). Though Jim started off as an ordinary American, he currently lives in England with his beloved wife, who coincidentally is English

Editor's Notes

What if being more than one person was not just a paradox, but a skill required to survive? In Core Beliefs we explore this, and what seeing from the perspective of other minds might be like.

Core Beliefs
by
James Gotaas

The room was comfortable enough, six walls in shades of green and pale orange, light and airy, the atmosphere laced with a faint neutral fragrance that didn't quite mask the peppery undertones when Lathan was seated across from the alien. The temperature varied from seat to seat, each member of the team feeling completely comfortable, no matter what their preferred temperature was. Originally, there had been twenty-six members of the human team attending, but the scientists and engineers had given up and now sat waiting in their ship for something to change.

Griegson touched his arm. "Lathan."

He turned to look at the senior. "Sir?"

"Any progress on why they won't talk to us?"

Lathan fought a surge of irritation, drew in a deep breath before responding. "I'm trying, but I just keep getting some sort of jumbled sense of rejection. It seems to be something that isn't covered by our existing translation data."

Griegson shook his stony face. "Well, you've got to do better. We're just wasting time now. If they're not willing to talk, they could at least let us start some of our survey work."

Lathan raised a hand helplessly. "Sir, that's one thing they're absolutely clear about. Nobody is allowed outside this room or our ship until they make some sort of decision."

Griegson subsided into his frustrated silence again. The telepathic channel to the alien was also silent, except for the ever-present background sense of the alien's body. Lathan's attention wandered again, darting around different aspects of their contact.

Each morning, the human team was escorted from their ship through strangely empty streets by a phalanx of impassive Breklori. They sat in the conference room all day, while Lathan passed messages to the Breklori representative and returned the incomplete answers to the others. At the end of each frustrating day, they returned in the same way to their ship.

Lathan had requested additional data on Breklori customs and history, careful to avoid possible awkward demands about technology or even politics. The Breklori didn't seem to have entered space at all, not even with satellites, but much of their technology hinted at being more advanced than the humans. The humans had carried out thorough passive scans of the planetary surface before landing for the contact procedure, but they'd seen no signs of communication towers, power stations or organized transport, despite what seemed to be a large urban population.

All requests for additional information had been turned down.

Griegson thought they were stonewalling. Lathan didn't. The sense he got from the nameless Breklori was that they were patiently waiting for an important decision.

In frustration, Griegson had gone so far as to order the ship's crew to carry out scans of the city, risking an incident. Lathan had objected, but been ignored. But the human sensors hadn't worked, although it wasn't clear why. Their range simply stopped at a distance of about ten meters from the ship, another hint at advanced technology.

The Breklori hadn't even mentioned the attempt.

Lathan felt an abrupt change in the telepathic connection, almost an electric charge coursing through him. He looked at the Breklori, who had suddenly stood up. The alien gaze swept past Lathan and over the other humans.

A telepathic conviction hit Lathan: a decision had been reached.

He was about to reach out telepathically for the Breklori, seeking clarification, when he sensed a change in the room. He looked around, and saw that every other human in the room had been enveloped by a pale, pearlescent white cylinder. Given the emergency, Lathan risked violating telepathic protocol and reached out for Griegson's mind.

He couldn't reach it, nor any of the others. Whatever the cylinders were, they cut off telepathic communication.

At least, Lathan hoped they had. The alternative was that those inside were dead.

He looked back at the Breklori, who was about to leave the room.

Damn. He pushed down burgeoning panic.

He had to take a risk. He sent a desperate telepathic demand toward the Breklori. The alien turned to look at him, finally some sort of expression on his face. But he didn't answer the demand. Instead, a tidal wave of rejection crashed over Lathan's mind. He couldn't bear the weight, and consciousness slipped away.

Lathan slowly regained awareness, against a backdrop of a severe headache. He checked his watch -- almost an hour had elapsed. He looked around the room, saw the same white cylinders where his collages had been. Once more, he tried gingerly contacting them. Nothing.

No sign of the Breklori contact.

Lathan rubbed his aching head. *What the hell could he do?*

He decided to notify the ship, even though he didn't know what was going on.

There was no response to his call. Were the humans on the ship affected as well?

But why not Lathan?

The obvious answer came almost immediately. He was a telepath, they weren't.

But they already knew that most of the aliens weren't telepaths either. So why the sudden action?

The decision. Of course, the last message had been that a decision had been reached. And the immediate result had been the cylinders. He needed to find out exactly what that decision had been, and why it had resulted in the encapsulation of the rest of the humans. Unfortunately, that meant that he had to try telepathic communication again, this time at an unknown distance. Telepathy didn't necessarily fade with separation, but it often made contact more difficult. And the Breklori response to his last attempt had been immediate and painful. But he had no choice.

Lathan leaned back in his seat and closed his eyes again. He found himself shaking slightly, but tried to ignore it. He carefully constructed a mental image of the Breklori representative's icon, overlaid it with the human sense of apology and the need for contact. He imagined it radiating out from him, searching for the mind of the alien. The process was a bit like dropping a stone into water, waves spreading out from the impact, but he had to keep reinforcing the image, gradually building up the amplitude of the wave to the point where, if he were lucky, the alien would sense it and respond.

And he finally did, his face appearing in Lathan's mind, surrounded by a faint aura of curiosity.

Lathan carefully constructed a message and wished it toward the image in his mind, words that were shadow pairs of human and Breklori languages, carrying both meanings.

What has happened?

Decision, came the single word response, again mirrored human-Breklori meanings.

Can you explain? What was the decision about?

Whether to accept your presence, when the non-thinkers were alone.

Lathan struggled to understand. The non-thinkers referred to a very particular form of thinking -- it meant the non-telepaths. Lathan gingerly probed for understanding. *Alone?*

They ... are not elements of a whole. They are not bound by collective responsibility. They act alone, without understanding.

Lathan understood the words, but was missing the connotations, emotional side-channels to the telepathic communication. He concentrated again. *Can you teach me about the whole?*

In response, a complex image slowly formed in Lathan's mind, of a telepath as nexus in a form of social grouping, connected by mental links to non-telepaths, providing an element of group agreement and reinforcement for individual actions.

Lathan struggled to hold the image in his mind. He pushed back with a need for further explanation.

Gradually, meaning became attached to the mental web, tags that had more meaning than simple words.

Breklori individuals had to be part of such a linkage to participate in society. The groupings were the fundamental foundation on which social and cultural interactions took place. Individuals grew into these linkages with time, starting out as children in their parents' network, then moving into others as they matured and were educated.

Occasionally, someone failed to make this transition. They were isolated, as his human colleagues had been. It was a form of stasis, where time didn't pass unless contact was established from outside. Other groupings could attempt to form linkages with them over time, but if they were never successful, eventually the individual would be painlessly put to death. Such a failure reflected badly on the nurturing grouping. The Breklori society refused to accept the potential danger of allowing the existence of individuals who acted completely alone.

It wasn't a hive mind, but it was a complex mental and emotional resonance that meant the Breklori society had fewer problems with disagreement.

Lathan guessed that it possibly also slowed their technological development, but it was clearly a price they were willing to pay for stability.

Lathan kept a slight connection with the other, but withdrew into his own mind to consider his options. Could he persuade them to accept the difference of the humans?

No. The Breklori people of wisdom had considered that long and hard, and rejected the possibility.

Could he persuade them to allow the humans simply to halt the contact procedure and go? Maybe.

He took a few moments to center himself, relax his body against the hard seat, breathe in cool air, gather his mental energy. He settled his hands atop his thighs below the tabletop.

Finally, he expanded the mental channel again and put the question to the alien.

May I take my colleagues and leave?

No, was the simple reply, but the side-channels carried additional background. That had been part of the decision. The humans could not leave, and no others would be allowed to come.

Can I leave by myself? He didn't want to, but there was a chance that he could somehow return and negotiate once he'd reported to the Alien Contact Authority.

Again, *No.*

Again, the side-channels: they were less certain what to do with Lathan. Some were horrified that he wasn't acting as a nexus for the human mental linkages. It was an unforgivable failing in their society, and he should be punished. Others were willing to accept that the humans were different, but still weren't certain what to do with him. None of the voices would accept him simply leaving.

Lathan started to despair. Rather than share that with the alien, he cut off his communications and opened his eyes. He rubbed his forehead; he was sweating despite the comfortable temperature. He was also shivering, some unusual physical consequence of his telepathic efforts. His stomach was knotted, his hands had clenched into fists pushing against his thighs.

He was running out of ideas. He could even understand the Breklori attitude, if not agree with it. He wondered: should he have picked up on that fundamental difference somewhere during the contact process? He wanted to blame himself, but that was too much like giving up. Aside from the possible cost to himself, he was sure that would mean the eventual deaths of all his fellow humans here.

Unless ... could he actually *be* a nexus for a human mental network? He had rudimentary training in the task of being a negotiator between two minds, serving as a temporary link to establish trust and agreement between two people. He hadn't been especially good at it, not really comfortable with helping two minds to connect, which is why he hadn't been offered that as a specialty. But could he try to do that here? He had no idea how to expand a network of two minds to a larger network, not even sure if any human telepath had ever tried it. Realistically, he didn't even know if he was strong enough.

But it was the only chance he could see.

He sent out the telepathic tag again. He was answered almost immediately.

Yes?

This time, feelings of sympathy and support seemed to expand around the simple word.

Can I try to form a network?

After a short delay, *Yes.*

Will you help me?

How?

My people do not form networks such as this. Can you show me how you do it?

Silence greeted the request. Lathan wondered if he'd gone too far. But surely even Breklori telepaths needed to learn how to handle the task?

Can try. Our thinkers spend years learning. The doubt came clearly through.

I must try.

Will take you in.

A mental wave lapped against Lathan's mind, surrounding it, leaking into it, then floating it away from his sense of body. A stream of consciousness pulled him deep into the alien's mind, toward a central core that he'd never sensed before. Once there, he could sense dozens of strands leading away, pulling him in different directions, like an assault of flickering images and barely heard words that confused him, leaving him lurching out of control along one strand, then another.

Then a wall formed around his sense of being, filtering out the worst of the tensions from the strands. Slowly, a gentle pressure pushed him along just one of the strands, stretching him out, leaving his sense of self centered in that core, but with part of him rushing toward the mind that lay at the end of that strand. It took no time, and once there, Lathan could sense the clean, clear structure of the anchor points of the network. The alien mind remained complex and confusing, but the way in which it was joined to the strand became ... obvious. He was nudged into sending part of himself into the anchor points, leaving some small essence of himself, so that even as they withdrew to that central core again, he was stretched to become a small part of that connecting strand.

The process was repeated.

And again.

Each time, Lathan felt more of himself being left in the strands. He struggled to maintain his sense of self, of essential humanity, even as it was woven into the alien network of minds.

Remember your body, came a helpful prompt through a side-channel While still connected to the alien network, he was once more aware of his physical form, of the tension in his muscles, of his slow, steady breathing.

But the sense of body slipped away again as they pushed along another strand.

Again. Pain was forming a knot in his mind, twisting his sense of self. He was being torn apart by the network.

Again. Again, this time with more sense of tearing, his memories and feelings being scattered around the nodes of the network, no longer able to cohere into an ego. Along one strand was a bitter memory of his mother dying, a memory he simply lost as he retreated to his core.

Once more, and he broke apart. He was no longer a person, no longer a self, but simply a vibration along the alien strands, a disturbance which would die away, and when it had, there would be no more Lathan.

Then the alien at the core pulled his parts back together from the strands, reassembled a human self in the core, but a self that had changed. It pushed that self, tenderly back into the mind of the human Lathan, then left it there to heal.

For a while, there was no consciousness in Lathan.

Lathan was never certain how long he'd spent in the alien network, being torn apart, then pulled back together, finally cushioned from the outside in his own mind.

The watch on his sleeve showed almost eight hours elapsed.

He drew in a ragged breath, looked around the room. Nothing had changed, except for his overwhelming sense of failure. It wasn't just the pain of his mind being torn apart by the alien network, it was losing all control, being reduced to fragments of mentality residing among other minds, until he'd been rescued.

It took all his effort to avoid slipping out of the seat. His mind felt like quicksand, hindering any thoughts or decisions.

But he had to do something. He reached with a shaking hand for his belt pouch, pulled out a stim-tab, slapped it against his neck. Then he withdrew a ration bar, shoved it into his mouth, started slowly chewing the flavorless chunk. He closed his eyes again and just sat breathing, waiting for the combined stimulant and nutrients to restore some sense of capability.

After a few minutes, he could just about frame a coherent thought again. It would have to do.

He cautiously sent out a probe for the alien mind.

The other responded immediately.

I'm sorry, Lathan sent.

The alien voice was clearer in his mind, with the query: *Sorry? I failed.*

No. This one pushed too hard. With young thinkers, nodes are added slowly, over weeks, allowing strength, experience and stability to form. None have networked so many, so quick. Apology. Your mind seemed strong enough, but reached breaking point.

Lathan swallowed. *How long will I need to train to be able to help my people?*

Perhaps no time. A sharp command came to him. *Visualize network, visualize strands stretching out, reaching anchors.*

Without thinking, he did it. All human telepaths had to be able to construct an imaginary representation of their own mind, sharp and clear and stable, before they could reliably reach out to other minds. Now there was a new sort of space in his mind, in his internal map of his own consciousness. He was tied into the core of it, but could feel the strands reaching out, could see the structure of the anchor points even without a real mind being present there.

Follow.

Lathan obeyed, sent a strand of that mental network out along the path created by the alien mind. It came up against a barrier, but the path curled in space-time and slipped beyond it. The alien path stopped short, but urged Lathan on. He reached a human mind.

His immediate impulse was to pull back. It was a fundamental precept of telepathic training: the human mind was sacrosanct, owned an inviolate privacy against telepathic intrusion, unless specifically requested. Going ahead would violate the Telepathic Code of Ethics.

But he couldn't allow that to stop him. He had to intrude, to make contact, to ask the human to accept his presence.

Gingerly, he slipped into the mind. It was a much more comfortable experience than exposure to the networked alien minds, like calling to like. The target mind was confused, on the edge of panic, its physical form trapped in a small space that it didn't understand.

Lathan identified the mind. It was Griegson. He remembered his training, simple techniques to help calm another's mind. He hadn't been comfortable doing it in training, learning to negotiate and help a mind to control itself. But he had no choice. He pushed against Griegson's mind, forced it to be calm, than slowly made it aware of his own presence.

Lathan? What ... what's happening? Why are you doing this?

I'm sorry, sir. It's the way the Breklori function. We have to connect our minds to ... satisfy their sense of ... properness. All Breklori are all linked to telepaths, and they don't trust individuals who aren't part of a mental network. Lathan tried to embed his understanding in the other. He sensed the fear and uncertainty.

What if I tell you to just get out of my mind?

I'll do it, but the Breklori won't release you from their stasis trap.

Is this permanent?

No. But we have to try to maintain it while we're here. Otherwise we won't be accepted by them.

How much of me do you see?

Lathan felt the other's primal fear of having someone else know your deepest flaws and weaknesses, with the potential to use them against you.

All I see is your surface thoughts, sir. I have to ... maintain a link with your mind, but it will only communicate basic surface thoughts and emotions, nothing you don't want to share.

Lathan was lying. The essential aspect of the group networks in Breklori society meant that the network stayed deep, able to communicate and affect fundamental beliefs and ideas, to share those, to ensure stability and trust. But the humans in the network didn't have to know that.

Lathan went on, *It's your decision. I can try to create a human network that the Breklori will accept. If I succeed, we can dissolve it as soon as we leave the planet.*

Griegson struggled with the decision. Humans didn't trust such vulnerability. It went against everything their society believed was right in the use of telepathy.

For a moment, Lathan considered nudging him in the right direction. He could see now, see how he could slightly tweak the structure of the node within Griegson's mind, push it in the direction he wanted. Push it toward the necessary agreement. The temptation was strong for a moment, made stronger by the desire and need to save his colleagues, even against their will.

No. They had the right to make their own decision, even if it cost them their life.

So he didn't nudge, he didn't compel, he simply asked, *Sir?*

He waited patiently for the answer, maintaining the barest link to the other's mind. It seemed to take hours for Griegson to make his decision.

All right, go ahead. But as minimal engagement as possible.

Yes, sir. Can you please concentrate on your acceptance of this. It may help with the others.

It should be an individual decision.

Lathan pointed out, *Anybody who refuses will be stuck here in stasis.*

He could feel Griegson's fear and uncertainty, in a way that he'd never been able to before. The contact with the Breklori mind-web had changed him, changed how his telepathy worked with others.

All right, Griegson finally sent.

Lathan fell back into his telepathic core, while maintaining a thread of awareness of Griegson's mind. He pushed out a sense of confidence and well-being, and felt it being returned along the mental strand, felt it strengthening.

The white cylinder suddenly vanished from around Griegson.

Lathan felt a burst of confidence. He could do this.

He gingerly reached out for Anne Kelly, came up against the barrier, slipped around it.

He made contact, careful to bury any of his previous awareness of her psyche, explaining the situation, offering to just withdraw again. Anne had previous experience with deep telepathic contact during her studies, and she was less leery of Lathan. She grabbed at the mental strand, pulled it taut. Lathan sent the memory of the mental web construct as an image, along with reassurance, combined with appreciation of the warmth in the mind he was touching. To his surprise, linking with Anne actually made his linkage with Griegson stronger, reinforced his own core with Anne's confidence.

After connecting to Anne, he spared a thought for his body, a sense of physicality that added substance to his mental strands.

Next came the other linguist, Singh. He was less experienced, but still accepted the telepathic link as a necessary evil, accepted his place in the construct, stabilized the node structure still more, despite his aggressive tendencies, subsuming those beneath a drive to succeed and survive.

Lathan realized that the construction and stability of the mental nexus didn't depend on just his strength, but could actually draw on the power of the multiple minds connected.

Slowly, he reached again, added Frasier, then Sanchez, then Cheng.

By now, they were all free of the stasis cylinders, looking around at each other in amazement, actually drawing comfort from the mental links that connected them all.

What's more, they were all filled with belief in Lathan, even Griegson. Their belief suffused his core, enhanced his stability as the nexus of the human web.

For the first time in his life, Lathan found himself actually believing in himself, his core of belief nurtured by the manifold contact. He let a profound feeling of gratitude flow out along the strands to the different nodes.

As an experiment, Lathan pulled enough attention away from the core nexus to speak aloud.

"Are we ready to try for the ship's personnel?"

As he studied everyone's faces, feelings of agreement and reassurance flowed from the nodes into his core, matched by physical nods. Anne even had a smile aimed at him.

Together, they reached out. One by one, they gathered in the other humans. Some were more difficult, some panicked, but the human telepathic web had a strength and resilience that could cope with such problems. Eventually, every human on the ship was also a node in their web.

Lathan became aware of an alien thought.

Your network is large. You must be careful. But well done.

Lathan sent gratitude and a sense of agreement back. *Thank you.*

The alien representative physically entered the meeting room again, approached the usual seat and settled into it. This time, he gently reached across the table toward Lathan. Lathan picked up his telepathic request, and placed his own hands against those on the table, forming a physical nexus. The contact with the alien seemed to add strength to Lathan's human web.

Only then, the Breklori turned to face Griegson. The Breklori mouth twisted in a new way, narrow lips forming an inverted vee. A sense of pleasure and welcome reached Lathan's core and spread out to the human nodes.

The alien spoke out loud for the first time, in Standard HumLang.

"I am Councilor eKaporza. Welcome to Breklor."

The End

The Elephant in the Room

Author's Bio

D. Avraham writes fiction and poetry, from children stories to adult humor; from spy thrillers to science fiction and fantasy. He is the author of Blight Crossing (Shirtsleeve Press, 2017), and The Shepherd King Chronicles: Foundation Stone (Beith David Publishing, 2010) D.'s stories have appeared in *Silver Blade*, *AntipodeanSF*, *Nebula Rift*, *New Realm,* and *Heater* among others. He currently lives with his family in the Hebron Hills of Israel, where, aside from writing, he teaches at the Jerusalem College of Technology, raises sheep and chickens, home schools his own kids, and tries to stay out of trouble. Sometimes he's successful. You can visit D. Avraham at his blog at davraham.com, on Facebook (Author.D.Avraham) or on Twitter (davraham818).

Editor's Notes

Often it is hard to tell what is real and what is not as sometimes the most unbelievable things can be true. In The Elephant in the Room we explore the idea that what is real might just be what we choose to believe.

The Elephant in the Room
by
D. Avraham

It was pretty clear that the elephants didn't mean any harm; they were not conspiring.

Even so, Floyd Dorfman, who discovered them, was convinced that they were, in fact, *conspiring in the corner*. Floyd was a bit of an alarmist and a confirmed conspiracy theorist. He had a very active imagination.

It was also just as clear that these particular elephants had crossed some sort of sentient barrier and were acting, as Floyd put it, *human*. It caused a considerable amount of excitement. Social media was abuzz.

They were small for elephants. The biggest wasn't much bigger than a medium sized brown bear. Floyd thought that they even *resembled* a bear in their overall bearing -- that is, aside from the the loose gray skin, and the standard issue elephant head and trunk. Floyd found them sitting in a circle, erect on their backsides, with their front legs resting on their round whitish bellies. The whole thing was weird, and made Floyd wonder if he was just imagining things. He had imagined elephants before. He dreamed elephants. He saw elephants everywhere. It came with the job.

Floyd started to get really nervous when he caught them standing erect, and walking on their hind legs. As Floyd put it, even a circus trainer couldn't have gotten elephants to walk around on two legs like everyday people. Moreover, they seemed as surprised as Floyd was when he caught them dancing the two step. Floyd finally decided that either he was crazy, or they were real. His medical insurance didn't cover mental illness, so the elephants must be real.

No one knew where the elephants came from -- not even Floyd. They just showed up one day in the Elephant Cave. Floyd, who was only barely holding onto his job as an elephant caretaker, assumed that they were acquired through all the normal processes. Since the Convention on International Trade in Endangered Species was updated to include elephants, Wade Park Zoo could only have acquired them from some other zoo, at least legally. Floyd decided that it wasn't his job to worry about where the elephants came from. He was only there to make sure they were fed and to sweep up the dung.

It was only after Floyd started making noise about the elephants, that anyone bothered to check, but nothing was found in any of the registries. This fueled the speculations; the conspiracists had a field day. The topic was the number one trending for months. Some people claimed they weren't elephants at all, but some ancient alien race. Of course, there were always people who claim such things.

The elephants weren't talking.

That wasn't precisely true. They were talking -- quite a bit now -- but they weren't saying much about where they came from. Anytime one of the talk show hosts asked, they artfully dodged the question.

"So, the keeper Floyd, who I guess, *discovered* you, told us that he doesn't know where you come from," began Gerry, the talk show host.

"Well, Floyd, as you might have noticed, is a little bit paranoid," offered one of the elephants to the delight of the studio audience, his diction slow and precise.

Floyd was offstage, and the stage personnel had a tough time preventing him from trying to reinsert himself into the discussion.

"But I discovered them!" he shouted from offstage. "They're my elephants," Floyd pleaded with one of the producers. "They're mine. The people should be cheering me," he complained.

Floyd had been on earlier, but the elephants refused to appear at the same time as him. They said he made them nervous.

Gerry smiled along with the audience, but when the laughter died down, he shifted his position and asked again, "So, were do you come from then?"

The elephant, who called himself Anika Bator, raised his trunk to make a point. "Where do any of us come from, Gerry? Would it really make a difference if I was born in Africa or America, India or Indonesia? I mean it's not like I'm going to run for President or anything, right? And, aren't we all made up of the same star stuff anyhow? Aren't we all part of this great wonderful world?"

The audience went wild with applause.

Gerry raised an eyebrow, but went on to another question. This wasn't a news show, and it wasn't only this studio audience, but the entire world, who had fallen in love with the elephants. He wasn't going to risk his ratings by being too confrontational. Besides, Gerry conceded, Anika Bator had a point. It wasn't like they were running for office, nor was anyone from the INS waiting offstage to deport them. What difference did it really make anyway? The attention deficit television public would revel in the elephants for a few days, maybe for a few weeks, and then move on to a new craze.

Colonel J.A. Hunter (retired) wasn't so sure. Something bothered him, as he watched the high definition images of Anika Bator, and his mate -- as he called her -- Hattie, with their young calf, Tyke. Something tickled at the base of Hunter's neck. Something smelled afoul. If only he could put a finger on it. He decided to give his old friend, Fred Treves over at the Pentagon a call.

"Fred, have you seen these talking elephants they're parading on the talk show circuit?"

"Yes, I have, J. Really incredible, huh?"

"Incredible?" Hunter pulled the phone from his ear and scowled at it. "Don't tell me you've been taken in by all this too?"

Treves laughed. "J., I think you have too much time on your hands. I hope you're not making this into something it's not." He didn't say the word, "again," but, nevertheless, it hung there on the line.

Hunter nearly burst. "Fred, if you're talking about that incident with Musk and those Chinese Pandas ..."

Treves realized his mistake and quickly backpedaled. "Now, now, J., don't get started on that again. It's a closed case. That ship has sailed, or launched, or ..." Treves paused. Hunter could hear the wheels of his brain spinning. "J., you didn't have anything to do with --"

"Don't be silly, Fred," Hunter scolded. "That was a simple technical error, a shame really." Hunter redirected the conversation back on topic. "Fred, but this is different. Have your people checked out those elephants? Are they legit?

"Martha took the grandkids to see them when they appeared on *Good Morning America*. She thought they were delightful."

Hunter barely contained himself. "Fred!"

"OK, Okay, J., Calm down," Treves defended. "Yes, we checked them out, but I can't tell you anything, not on an open line."

"Very good. I'll buy you lunch." Hunter wasn't asking.

"Okay, J., I'll humor you. Tomorrow, at our usual place."

"See you then."

Floyd Dorfman never imagined that his elephants would run for President of the United States, but by the time Hunter and Treves met for lunch, Anika Bator's offhanded comment about him not wanting to run for President had created a firestorm. The idea went viral. It became the most popular topic on the web. And, most people were in favor of the idea. Hell, an elephant couldn't be worse than the politicians they've been getting.

The media also loved the idea, especially when the mere mention of it drove ratings through the roof. All the more so when they could get Bator into the studio to discuss it. Even Morning Joe was parsing the possibilities. Did the Constitution preclude sentient non-humans from the Oval Office? The Founder's language simply said *person*. Even though he wasn't human, didn't everyone consider Anika Bator a person?

"Those elephants hadn't been wearing pants less than a month ago, and now the public wants them to be our President? What's the world coming to?" Hunter greeted Treves with his complaints.

Treves chuckled. Well, J., it's not like all of our Presidents have been able to keep their pants on, you know. I'm not sure it's a disqualification."

"Don't make light of this, Fred."

"You don't think that these elephants can actually get on the ballot, J? It's a joke, like that guy with the orange hair."

"People took that seriously enough."

"And we' survived it. We're still here, right. It takes a lot more than a few crazy candidates to break the system, J. Don't be such a worrier."

"I can't help it. It's my nature." Hunter clasped Treves' forearm. "Please tell me you have something I can use to put a stop to all this madness."

Floyd Dorfman watched the story unfold, along with the rest of America, on television. He had been issued a restraining order, barring him from being within a mile of the elephants. It spelled the end of his career as an elephant caretaker. He spent his time, and his severance pay at a place called the Bar Bar Pub, complaining to anyone who would listen. After two weeks there weren't to many of those left, but he complained loud enough that everyone would hear anyway.

"It's not fair," shouted Dorfman, repeating his mantra over and over again, anytime the elephants appeared on screen. When the big news came, Dorfman was so out of control that he would have been thrown out of the bar, except that everyone's attention was transfixed on the television. The report was unbelievable.

"In an unprecedented development, both of the major parties, dissatisfied with their current respective representative, have extended offers to Anika Bator to be their presidential candidate. So, far, we haven't had a reaction from Bator." The attractive news anchor turned to her co-host. "Joe, has there ever been anything like this in U.S. history?"

Joe shrugged. "Well, during the Civil War, Lincoln did reach out to the War Democrats and they formed a 'National Union' ticket, but I don't think there's ever been anything like this. It's unprecedented, except for maybe George Washington."

Political correspondent Jim Hennings piped in. "I still don't see how he's eligible ..."

"Yeah, you got me on that one too, Jim," agreed Joe. "I've been asking that question for the last three months."

"Well, the constitution doesn't specifically disqualify him," offered Michelle.

"You know," Steve Harper, another guest on the show, began, "I kind of figured the excitement would die down eventually too, but it just keeps going."

Joe shrugged again, "Yeah, well look at the alternatives."

"Not only that," added Michelle, "Look at this guy. Bator's the perfect candidate, or he would be, if he wasn't an elephant. He looks like a Republican, but talks like a Democrat. Why wouldn't both parties want him?"

"And why wouldn't the public love him," concluded Jim.

"Because they're not real," spat Floyd Dorfman, but no one in the bar was paying any attention to him. They never did, decided Fred. He was less real than the elephants. Floyd resigned himself to the situation. His whole life was unfair. Why should this be any different?

J.A. Hunter wasn't having any of it. He looked at the stacks of files on his desk and threw up his hands. He had been spending the last six months, with considerable backing, running a campaign to delegitimize the elephants, and particularly their leader Bator. But not only wasn't it working, it may have propelled the pachyderm to the highest favorability ratings in recent history. He had to do something. He flipped through his files, and stopped on the picture of Floyd Dorfman, the now out of work elephant caretaker of Wade Park Zoo. He was the key. This had started with Dorfman, and it would have to end with him, too. Hunter searched through his desk. Where had he put that boy's number?

"Hello, may I help you?" the sales clerk sang.

Floyd Dorfman, looked like a deer caught in the headlights. He was surprised that anyone noticed him. He wasn't even sure if he was real, at least not most of the time. Did he imagine the sales clerk talking to him? He looked up at the sales clerk, saw that at least the clerk was real. He was looking at Floyd, with an expectant expression and a plastic smile on his face. Floyd recovered himself and answered, "Um, yes, I'd like to buy a gun, please."

"Of course, sir. Did you have anything in mind?"

"Well," said Floyd, as his eyes caught the large .585 Nyati rifle on display behind the counter. "That looks interesting."

"Hey, aren't you that guy from television?" asked the store clerk.

Floyd lit up. "Yeah, I was on tele..."

"Tell me what it's really like to be with those elephants. Are they as cool in private as they are on television?"

Floyd Dorfman left Brian's One Stop Gun Shop empty-handed. "I bet those damn elephants could get credit," he muttered. He turned and shouted at the storefront, "I had a job until those elephants you idolize got me fired!" Of course, that was only half true. Wade Park Zoo couldn't justify keeping an elephant caretaker in it's employ, when the elephants were quartering at the Ritz Carlton. Still, Floyd blamed the elephants. It was always the little guy that suffered, decided Floyd. "One day, the mice will have their day!" shouted Floyd. He startled when a small brown and white mouse scurried from under his feet, and darted into the gun shop.

Floyd blinked hard, staring at the place where the mouse disappeared. He could have sworn that the mouse shouted 'Watch it, buddy!' as he passed under Floyd's feet. He shook his head to clear the image, but couldn't escape the impression. Floyd needed a drink. He wondered if he still had credit at Bar Bar Pub.

As he stepped off the curb, a black SUV screeched to a halt inches from Floyd's face. Four men in dark suits and darker sunglasses jumped out. "Floyd Dorfman?" they asked in unison.

"I didn't do it," shouted Floyd trying to remember what it was he might have done.

"Come with us," the men said, rushing Floyd into the back of the SUV. The four men pressed in beside him and the SUV sped off.

"What? Where are we going?" Fred squeaked.

"Don't worry, Mr. Dorfman. No harm will come to you. Just do as you're told," advised the elderly occupant of the SUV sitting opposite Fred. "My name is Colonel Hunter and we need to talk about those elephants."

"It's not my fault," offered Floyd weakly.

"Oh yes, it is," countered J.A. Hunter. "It most certainly is. But you will help us fix it."

"I wish I could," sighed Floyd.

"Oh, you can," offered Hunter gently, "Only you can, and you will. People will take notice of you Floyd. You'll be a hero."

That made Floyd smile. Nobody ever took notice of him, and he'd always wanted to be a hero. He thought of the brown and white mouse, and his smile dipped.

"Cheer up Floyd," encouraged Hunter. "I have faith in you."

Floyd Dorfman watched the newsman talking to his millions of viewers, but Floyd wasn't one of them, he was standing to the side, on location. Fred thought is seemed more real when you watched it on television.

The newsman, Pete Anderson was as excited as the crowd. "In just a moment, we will witness history as, according to reports, Anika Bator, will accept the nomination from both the major political parties. The entire nation has longed for a candidate of his caliber for decades."

"With the exception of the birthers," noted the anchor from the studio.

Anderson dismissed them immediately. "Speciesists! A small fringe group, who question Mr. Bator's eligibility. I meant everyone in the nation who matters." Anderson returned to his point. "With his overwhelming popularity, the parties don't have much of a choice, but to offer him the nomination." Movement over his shoulder distracted Anderson's attention, and he pivoted. "Here he is now. Mr. Bator is about to speak."

The large amiable creature in the dark blue pinstripe suit and a red tie rolled towards the podium, lifted his trunk, and offered a smile. He looked to the crowd, to his mate Hattie, to his calf Tyke, before returning his gaze to the crowd. "It is an honor," Bator began. "A true honor ..."

Suddenly, a large commotion erupted at the edge of the crowd, and Secret Service swarmed in. They grabbed the man, but Floyd Dorfman wouldn't be stopped. He shouted above the crowd. "You're not real!" he yelled. "I created you! You're just a part of my imagination! I have proof!" Dorfman waved one of J.A. Hunter's Manila folders in the air over his head.

Bator quieted the crowd down with his trunk. Surprisingly, everyone complied. "Let him go," Bator instructed the agents. "He's harmless. Let him come up here." Bator gestured with his trunk. "Come on up here, Floyd."

Floyd was rushed to the stage by the crowd. He climbed the stairs and stood before Bator. "But I created you," he said. "How can they love you so much, when they hate me?"

Bator chuckled. He grabbed Floyd with his trunk and pulled him into an embrace. The crowd erupted with applause. "Don't you understand, Floyd," whispered Bator, "if they love me, then they love the part of you that is me."

"It's not enough," said Floyd, quietly. He shook his head. "It's not enough," he shouted, and pulled a round object out of the folder. Floyd dropped it on the ground in front of Bator. It was a small brown and white mouse.

"Watch it buddy!" shouted the mouse.

Bator panicked, and faltered back, tripped over himself and crashed into the podium, which disintegrated under his weight. Bator found his footing and he, Hattie and Tyke stampeded out of the park, stepping all over their supporters.

Floyd Dorfman picked himself out of the debris and brushed himself off. No one seemed to be paying him any attention. He decided, given the circumstances, that was a good thing. He would just go home. Floyd thought he saw the mouse scurrying through the rubble, and wondered if he should go after him. Then again, he was in no position to change his medical coverage, so he let it go.

The End

Choice is an Axiom

Author's Bio

Edmund Schluessel grew up reading his father's collection of Golden Age SF in a basement in Connecticut in the United States, and fell in love with short stories through reading anthologies much like this one. In 2011 he completed a PhD in the theory of gravitational waves & cosmology at Cardiff University, where he worked alongside the team that later made the first detection of gravitational waves. He was born in France and has lived in Wales and the Netherlands, and upon relocating to Finland he became involved in the Nordic science fiction fan scene and began writing science fiction in earnest. He also makes frequent appearances giving science & mathematics popularization talks at conventions across Europe. He is an avid let-wing activist and organized Finland's biggest demonstration against Donald Trump and Vladimir Putin. By day he teaches mathematics. "Choice is an Axiom" is his first professional sale as a fiction writer and was inspired by a course he took in axiomatic set theory as an undergraduate. He blogs at www.space-curves.org and can be found on Facebook at www.facebook.com/spacecurves.

Editor's Notes

As we conclude this volume of Mind Candy we are left with the universal truths that there are always choices, consequences . . .
. . . and no exceptions.

Choice is an Axiom
By
Edmund Schluessel

Babas and Stipnir had existed for an infinite amount of time.

In the mathematical space of possibility into which all universes were born, they two were beings of theorem and logic. Mathematics is without end, flourishing in forever-branching vines of certainty along every path of the undecideable. In a fertile and diverse thicket that sprouted mighty from a trunk of eight sturdy fundamental axioms, Babas's & Stipnir's consciousnesses had emerged.

Their thoughts were the lives of universes, and with every notion a new cosmos would explode into reality and die, as Babas's and Stipnir's beings grew further up the tree of postulates. They spent unbounded eons in meditation, contemplating the nature of being, and from time to time, they spoke to one another.

With an intellect beyond the vastest of material minds, in an act that expended the existence of ten trillion cosmoses, Babas asked her partner: "can you tell me the natural numbers again, Stipnir?"

"All right, Babas," the other being replied tenderly, and started to count. "One, two, three..." he recited until, after an infinite amount of time had passed, Stipnir had recited the largest number.

Babas's memory was an unending book, and between each page of every volume was interleaved a new parchment on which was scribed the cherished memory of a single number. She pondered each page for a moment.

But if one infinity is a moment, then two infinities or three infinities or a million are equally as long, so Babas's respite was fleeting.

"Where did we come from, Stipnir?" inquired Babas with languid, desperate curiosity.

"We've always been here, Babas. Time is for the bubbles we blow." To distract himself for an eye-blink, Stipnir idly called into existence a toy universe. This one was pink, and it lasted forever. Stipnir watched it until it died and a moment afterward returned to his ennui.

For her own part, Babas tried to distract herself by counting out all the negative numbers, then all the rational numbers, meditating on the uniqueness of each in turn. After two infinities had passed, the question still remained, and the way that thought lingered nagged at her as much as the question itself. To drive the demons from her head Babas counted again, aloud, starting from the smallest number she could imagine, a tiny fraction as close as could be to zero.

Annoyance was preferable to boredom, so Stipnir stirred. "You can't count the real numbers, Babas. You know you'll never finish. How are you even putting them in order?"

"It just seems to make sense," Babas retorted sharply, then returned to her reckoning. Babas herself didn't know where the order had come from. A lifetime ago Babas had tried to count the real numbers, then the complex rationals, then a host of others and found that some kinds of numbers simply did not seem to have a reasonable order from lowest to highest. Now Babas could recite them in order, though it was an endless task. Call it maturity, maybe?

After an epoch, Stipnir called out again, pleading. "I'm serious, Babas. Stop. It's making my soul ache."

"I'm sorry," growled Babas, without remorse. "I was just trying to relax."

Stipnir ruminated for an eon and started to count. "Epsilon, epsilon times two, but then there must be some number between those...this isn't working. How are you doing this, Babas?"

Babas felt a tingling dizziness. "Well," she considered, and began to recite her reasoning. The idea flowed from the axioms from which Babas grew but simply seemed true in and of itself, and after a trivial proof of a few hundred sentences Babas knew what she had said was right, and consistent. The real numbers could be put in order.

Stipnir paused in shock. He had understood Babas's argument, followed every line, and each step made sense, yet to him it felt wrong, not merely counterintuitive or startling but incompatible with his very being, like asserting there was a whole number between one and two that no one had ever noticed before. He lashed back at Babas, spitting lemmas. Just a few angry lines sufficed to show, beyond doubt, that counting as Babas had just done was nonsensical, impossible, a fool's errand.

Babas felt tremors of pain run through her. As children sometimes she and Stipnir had quarreled like this. With time, they learned to live with their differences--she would take a theorem and hold it true, Babas would take its opposite and hold it equally true, and so what? These were minor subjects the two of them could easily avoid talking about. This new disagreement felt different. Deeper.

Babas rolled her consciousness over and tried, panicked, to meditate. She looked inside herself and up and down the trunks of logic on which she and Stipnir grew. The eight basic axioms had joined a new branch: a new fundamental axiom, unprovable yet unfalsifiable, was now a part of Babas. Stipnir had instead, unconsciously, embraced that axiom's negation. A forest of new possibilities for growth existed for each of the two siblings, but it would have to be grown apart: what they each knew to be true would simply be too different.

After an era of worry and indecision Babas rallied as Stipnir called to her. "Babas? Babas? Don't go away!"

"I'm all right, Stipnir. It's just a new theorem but it's all right. We'll think around it like we always do."

Stipnir gave no reply. Babas sensed the absence of his attention. Stipnir was exploring the ropes of logic inside his own self. Surely he would learn just what Babas had learned. After a beat Stipnir re-emerged and, at last, spoke. "You're right, partner. A new theorem, that is all. We will think around it."

"We will." A pause. "I'm bored again, Stipnir," came the measured reply. "Tell me another story? Tell me all the kinds of knots again. I haven't heard it in a while."

Babas relaxed as Stipnir enumerated all the ways a torus could be tied in a knot, with supporting descriptions of the negatively-curved spaces complementing each one. There was an enticing familiarity in the knot complements: Babas had imagined universes shaped like each of them once, and watched them until they evaporated. The countably infinite enumeration came to an end and Babas's calm faded. The call of the new axiom still chirped in her mind.

Babas inflated another universe, a simple sphere, and toyed with it. She puzzled over it as Stipnir distracted himself with a contemplation of the polynomials. As Babas listened to the muttering incantation she gazed into herself and felt vertigo. Babas loved Stipnir, but was this all life could be, simply to count the infinite over and over with him? Maybe Stipnir could be convinced. The new axiom meant new distractions, and Babas could at least share the fruits, if not the full flower, of her discovery.

Babas prodded the toy universe, sifted through the points making up its spacetime, and saw a trick hidden inside its mathematics. Just like the pages of an endless book, space aplenty lay between each point in Babas's toy cosmos; but now that each point could be sorted, Babas could pull out every other point from the infinite set while destroying nothing...and with a twist and a snap, one universe, alive and evolving, had been duplicated and now existed side by side with an identical copy.

Identical? No--in the second universe, slightly different decisions had taken place, tossed coins had landed heads-up instead of heads-down, and the two universes grew apart, until when the time came for them to end their contents were completely different from one another.

This was nothing but a trick, a trivial amusement--universes were all basically alike to Babas, particles of thought bland in their diversity. The sleight of hand though, two identical universes becoming different, would be an ideal distraction for Stipnir. Thus Babas called to him and, at the same time, began to fashion the largest shiniest universe she could, thinking the most intricate thought she could. "Stipnir, look what I can do!" she called, as the new cosmos evolved and expanded.

Stipnir studied the new, glowing spacetime without enthusiasm. "It's very pretty--"

"Watch!"

With a flick of thought Babas's mind dove into the fractal points of her cosmos's fabric. The act of imagining was the same as the act of creating. Thus the tapestried universe was replicated and the two copies became distinct, this time with opposite fates: the original imploded, the second grew forever. The surviving cosmos was full of light and life beyond her imagining, and Babas was awed, so much so that she did not notice Stipnir's cowering from her creation. After the second universe had faded out into heat death, Stipnir spoke.

"I couldn't look at it. It was horrible. It made me feel pain all over. Just thinking about it now makes me feel like I'm vanishing into nothingness. It hurt, Babas. It hurts."

"I can't be part of this, Babas. Don't share it with me again," he commanded. Then Stipnir fell silent again, dormant apart for trembles and shudders. He had disappeared into himself. Stipnir's form was still there alongside Babas but she felt impossibly alone.

Frustration overwhelmed Babas. Ignoring the new axiom was impossible--these new ideas were part of Babas's identity as surely as one plus one equaling two. If Stipnir could never be a part of it, then what? There was no third being, nobody else to talk to, just Babas and Stipnir, and forest of logic, and the great void of contradiction that lay beyond it.

Where do we come from? In their youth Babas and Stipnir had examined each other, trying to find the answer--they knew each others' bodies intimately, to the point where now there was nothing more to learn, and in all that examination they had found themselves to be beings of pure thought. One consequence of this fact was that in order to experience time, Babas and Stipnir needed always to grow and take in new theorems. "We were always going to grow apart," Babas thought. But if a collection of thoughts was all they were, and thoughts were universes, and to duplicate a universe just took a flick of the mind... Babas had a new project. It was desperate and angry but it was perfectly logical. It would take effort but Babas had never had any choice but to be patient.

Stipnir meditated fitfully as Babas dove into herself and began the process of reproduction. To so minutely examine her own thoughts was, she found, a pleasant act of self-indulgence, and the time passed swiftly.

After a long time, Babas became sensed to a presence emanating from her handiwork. The companion was simple but already it quickened and Babas could feel tendrils of growth and independent thought reach into the vines around them all. The newcomer probed into Babas, and Babas felt a warming swell of emotion: from within herself accomplishment, and from her child, recognition. The newcomer probed its surroundings, matching the memories it had been given to the experience of the world around it. A curious paw touched Stipnir, pushed into him, and, with a jolt, Stipnir woke.

Stipnir peered out into the new world around him and locked his focus upon Babas. "Babas. What did you make? What did you make?" he thundered. He tried to shrink away from the new companion, but the companion's hand held tight.

Had Babas's plan been one of discovery, or of revenge? She didn't know anymore. The newcomer was growing fast with it absorbing ideas from Stipnir. Soon it would be as mature as either of them.

"Babas, tell me what this is! Did you make a new person? Did you make it without me?"

The newcomer shook at Stipnir's rage apprehensively. It held Babas's memories, and with an effort of thought, the youngling brought into being an iridescent bubble of a universe, shimmering and pink, and divided it with a deftness that exceeded Babas's own--Babas had learned by trial and error, but the new one was born to the task. As the arrival completed the duplication with a flourish, it prepared to announce its first word, its name.

It started with "Zer...Zer-me..." but it never finished.

With a lurch, Stipnir grasped outward, in a way which should have been impossible. He grabbed hold of a thick branch of logic: the axiom he had been denied, that Babas had taken. With electric rage behind his words, he intoned: "You don't need anyone else. I can be what you need." Fire flared in his body.

"You can't do this Stipnir. Let go! Forget about it! It's OK. I'll just meditate. I won't tell you about the new axiom ever again."

"It's part of me now, Babas. It's too late." Stipnir's voice echoed so loud the tree of logic shook. "I can see everything. I can see all the possibilities, all the ideas. I think I can do the impossible." Stipnir was shaking, breaking out in glowing patches, as the sparks of contradiction spread through him. "I understand what you wanted to show me now." His voice trembled too. "It's beautiful. I want you to keep doing it."

"Stipnir, you've got to let go. Doesn't it hurt?"

"If it means I can be with you, I'll live with the pain." Stipnir caught fire. His whole form was dissolving into nothingness—and the newborn, too, was ablaze. The cosmoses Stipnir spat out as thoughts were twisted dimensions of torture and mindless chittering.

The little one, joined to Stipnir, began to keen in terror. Babas' thoughts were racing--the idea that she herself, or Stipnir, might come to an end was something she had never considered except in the abstract. Did the little one, the one whose name began with Zerme, understand what was happening at all? Babas steeled herself, to pull the newborn away...

And then, in a ball of fire and a howl that rattled the tree of logic from its roots to its unending branches, the time to understand was over, and Babas existed alone.

What is time, what is consciousness, without a companion to mark them with? Babas had passed eons beyond infinity in exploration and meditation, but never without Stipnir's presence nearby. Babas had supposed that she could not exist, that her consciousness might be unable to *be*, without another mind standing in concordant opposition to her own.

Babas still existed but there was no way for Babas to measure how long she sat, unmoving and unthinking. She could only dive into herself, because Babas herself was all there was.

The act of counting was a kind of meditation, and Babas had half a mind to lose herself in a counting that could never be completed, in an annihilation of the self that would banish any troubling questions. She marked out all the rational numbers between zero and one, and dove into the spaces between them, into the cloud of irrationals, with no greater plan than to put them all in order. It was a project, something to think about that wasn't Stipnir, or the dead newcomer, or Babas' own purposelessness.

Deep in meditation, at the limits of her comprehension, Babas began to hear voices.

They spoke to no one, but shouted proclamations into the void: "I think, therefore I am!" and simply "I am!" and later "I was!" Babas nearly lost them the first time she looked for their origin, as she tentatively roused herself in preparation for a return to the cruel world. Instead it was deeper meditation that brought her to the place of the distant speakers: her thoughts were themselves alive.

Could they hear her? No, there was no way--every particle of thought was its own universe, and thinking about these universes simply created more thought.

Had she simply never heard the voices before? Babas had never meditated so deeply--before, there had always been Stipnir to come back to. She lamented at the prospect of all these voices so long vanishing unheard and unremembered, and then she watched her own thoughts in action, saw them bifurcate in the way she knew had been impossible until she had embraced the new axiom.

Babas had looked into the innards of her thoughts in the past and found little of interest. The thought-universes generally were built out of some kind of particles which moved in accordance with a short list of forces, in a handful of dimensions: little automata brought into being by a question and which in their deaths spat out an answer.

The new thoughts were made from a new kind of physics entirely, one of probability, where objects were at once waves and particles. A piece of matter might have a choice to jump right or jump left; rather than do one or the other, it would do both, one universe becoming two. A cosmos born from a question would explore every possible answer, and with the blossoming of this field of possibilities came a new kind of life, one that could think.

Even the greatest were microscopic, fleeting beings to Babas. Nonetheless, they were full of consciousness and beauty. Bound by physics as they were, they still built intricate civilizations.

Throughout their momentary lives, they were hardly ever alone. Yet so hungry were they for companionship and certainty, and so much vaster were their imaginations than their lives that they invented beings greater than themselves and believed in things they couldn't ever know.

An uncountable number of times over, they conceived of Babas, and Stipnir, and every being of every name that could possibly exist.

Babas lived in the space of logical possibility. In a flash, like noticing a direction she had never traveled in before, she saw all the other permutations of herself. She was one with them: part of an infinite sisterhood imagined by the conscious life dwelling in her own thoughts.

Stipnir was dead--but Stipnir was alive in the imaginations of the people in Babas's thoughts. She saw a world where Stipnir persisted. She saw an infinite number of such worlds, a number beyond counting.

In some of them Babas was still bored. In the others she was dead.

"I missed you," Babas felt she should to say to him--but it wasn't true the same way it had been. A long time had passed since Stipnir went away. Life before the axiom had been a dead end. Now instead, the whole space of possibility, uncountably infinite worlds and uncountably infinite selves to explore them with, beckoned her.

In infinity to the power of infinity Babas was finally complete. Worlds vaster than imagination were open to her, and she would never be alone, or bored, again. There could be no return to the status quo.

Babas released her grasp on the way things had been, and embraced the axiom of choice.

The End

Made in the USA
Middletown, DE
14 September 2018